Also by Jane Ashford

THE
DUKE
WHO LOVED ME

JANE
ASHFORD

sourcebooks
casablanca

Copyright © 2021 by Jane LeCompte
Cover and internal design © 2021 by Sourcebooks
Cover art by Aleta Rafton/Lott Reps

Sourcebooks and the colophon are registered trademarks of Sourcebooks.

Published by Sourcebooks Casablanca, an imprint of Sourcebooks
P.O. Box 4410, Naperville, Illinois 60567-4410
(630) 961-3900
sourcebooks.com

Printed and bound in the United States of America.
OPM 10 9 8 7 6 5 4 3 2 1

One

THREE DAYS AFTER HE INHERITED THE TITLE DUKE OF Tereford, James Cantrell set off to visit the ducal town house just off London's Berkeley Square. He walked from his rooms, as the distance was short and the April day pleasant. He hoped to make this first encounter cordially brief and be off riding before the sunlight faded.

He had just entered the square when a shouted greeting turned his head. Henry Deeping was approaching, an unknown young man beside him.

"Have you met my friend Cantrell?" Henry asked his companion when they reached James. "Sorry. Tereford, I should say. He's just become a duke. Stephan Kandler, meet the newest peer of the realm as well as the handsomest man in London."

As they exchanged bows James silently cursed whatever idiot had saddled him with that label. He'd inherited his powerful frame, black hair, and blue eyes from his father. It was nothing to do with him. "That's nonsense," he said.

"Yes, Your Grace." Henry's teasing tone had changed recently. It held the slightest trace of envy.

James had heard it from others since he'd come into his inheritance. His cronies were young men who shared his interest in sport, met while boxing or fencing, on the hunting field, or perhaps clipping a wafer at Manton's shooting gallery, where Henry Deeping had an uncanny ability. They were generally not plump in the pocket. Some lived on allowances from their fathers and would inherit as James had; others would have a moderate income all their lives. All of them preferred vigorous activity to smoky gaming hells or drunken revels.

They'd been more or less equals. But now circumstances had pulled James away, into the peerage and wealth, and he was feeling the distance. One old man's death, and his life was changed. Which was particularly hard with Henry. They'd known each since they were uneasy twelve-year-olds arriving at school.

"We're headed over to Manton's if you'd care to come," Henry said. He sounded repentant.

"I can't just now," James replied. He didn't want to mention that he was headed to Tereford House. It was just another measure of the distance from Henry. He saw that Henry noticed the vagueness of his reply.

"Another time perhaps," said Henry's companion in a Germanic accent.

James gave a noncommittal reply, wondering where Henry had met the fellow. His friend was considering the diplomatic corps as a means to make his way in the world. Perhaps this Kandler had something to do with that.

They separated. James walked across the square and into the narrow street containing Tereford House.

The massive stone building, of no particular architectural distinction, loomed over the cobbles. Its walls showed signs of neglect, and the windows on the upper floors were all shuttered. There was no funerary hatchment above the door. Owing to the eccentricities of his great-uncle, the recently deceased sixth duke, James had never been inside. His every approach had been rebuffed.

He walked up to the door and plied the tarnished knocker. When that brought no response, he rapped on the door with the knob of his cane. He had sent word ahead, of course, and expected a better reception than this. At last the door opened, and he strolled inside—to be immediately assailed by a wave of stale mustiness. The odor was heavy rather than sharp, but it insinuated itself into the nostrils like an unwanted guest. James suspected that it would swiftly permeate his clothes and hair. His dark brows drew together. The atmosphere in the dim entryway, with closed doors on each side and at the back next to a curving stair, was oppressive. It seemed almost threatening.

One older female servant stood before him. She dropped a curtsy. "Your Grace," she said, as if the phrase was unfamiliar.

"Where is the rest of the staff?" They really ought to have lined up to receive him. He had given them a time for his visit.

"There's only me. Your Grace."

"What?"

"Keys is there." She pointed to a small side table. A ring of old-fashioned keys lay on it.

James noticed a small portmanteau sitting at her feet.

She followed his eyes. "I'll be going then. Your Grace." Before James could reply, she picked up the case and marched through the still-open front door.

Her footsteps faded, leaving behind a dismal silence. The smell seemed to crowd closer, pressing on him. The light dimmed briefly as a carriage passed outside. James suppressed a desire to flee. He had a pleasant set of rooms in Hill Street where he had, for some years, been living a life that suited him quite well. He might own this house now, but that didn't mean he had to live here. Or perhaps he did. A duke had duties. It occurred to him that the servant might have walked off with some valuable items. He shrugged. Her bag had been too small to contain much.

He walked over to the closed door on the right and turned the knob. The door opened a few inches and then hit some sort of obstacle. He pushed harder. It remained stuck. James had to put his shoulder to the panels and shove with the strength developed in Gentleman Jackson's boxing saloon before it gave way, with a crash of some largish object falling inside. He forced his way through but managed only one step before he was brought up short, his jaw dropping. The chamber—a well-proportioned parlor with high ceilings and elaborate moldings—was stuffed to bursting with a mad jumble of objects. Furniture of varying eras teetered in haphazard stacks—sofas, chairs, tables, cabinets. Paintings and other ornaments were pushed into every available crevice. Folds and swathes of fabric that might have been draperies or bedclothes drooped over the mass, which towered far above his head. There was no room to move. "Good God!" The stale odor was much worse here, and a scurrying sound did not bode well.

James backed hastily out. He thought of the shuttered rooms on the upper floors. Were they all…? But perhaps only this one was a mare's nest. He walked across the entryway and tried the door on the left. It concealed a larger room in the same wretched condition. His heart, which had not been precisely singing, sank. He'd assumed that his new position would require a good deal of tedious effort, but he hadn't expected chaos.

The click of footsteps approached from outside. The front door was still open, and now a fashionably dressed young lady walked through it. She was accompanied by a maid and a footman. The latter started to shut the door behind them. "Don't," commanded James. The young servant shied like a nervous horse.

"What is that smell?" the lady inquired, putting a gloved hand to her nose.

"What are you doing here?" James asked the bane of his existence.

"You mentioned that you were going to look over the house today."

"And in what way is this your concern?"

"I was so curious. There are all sorts of rumors about this place. No one has been inside for years." She went over to one of the parlor doors and peered around it. "Oh!" She crossed to look into the other side. "Good heavens!"

"Indeed."

"Well, this is going to be a great deal of work." She smiled. "You won't like that."

"You have no idea what I…" James had to stop, because he knew that she had a very good idea.

"I know more about your affairs than you do," she added.

It was nearly true. Once, it certainly had been. That admission took him back thirteen years to his first meeting with Cecelia Vainsmede. He'd been just fifteen, recently orphaned, and in the midst of a blazing row with his new trustee. Blazing on his side, at any rate. Nigel Vainsmede had been pained and evasive and clearly just wishing James would go away. They'd fallen into one of their infuriating bouts of pushing in and fending off, insisting and eluding. James had understood by that time that his trustee might agree to a point simply to be rid of him, but he would never carry through with any action. Vainsmede would forget—willfully, it seemed to James. Insultingly.

And then a small blond girl had marched into her father's library and ordered them to stop at once. Even at nine years old, Cecelia had been a determined character with a glare far beyond her years. James had been surprised into silence. Vainsmede had actually looked grateful. And on that day they had established the routine that allowed them to function for the next ten years—speaking to each other only through Cecelia. James would approach her with "Please tell your father." And she would manage the matter, whatever it was. James didn't have to plead, which he hated, and Nigel Vainsmede didn't have to do anything at all, which was his main hope in life as far as James could tell.

James and Cecelia had worked together all through their youth. Cecelia was not a friend, and not family, but some indefinable other sort of close connection. And she did know a great deal about him. More than he knew about her. Although he had observed, along with the rest of the *haut ton*, that she had grown up to be a very pretty young lady. Today in a walking dress of sprig muslin and a straw bonnet decorated with matching blue ribbons, she was lithely lovely. Her hair was less golden than it had been at nine but far better cut. She had the face of a renaissance Madonna except for the rather too lush lips. And her luminous blue eyes missed very little, as he had cause to know. Not that any of this was relevant at the moment. "Your father has not been my trustee for three years," James pointed out.

"And you have done nothing much since then."

He would have denied it, but what did it matter? Instead he said, "I never could understand why my father appointed *your* father as my trustee."

"It was odd," she said.

"They were just barely friends, I would say."

"Hardly that," she replied. "Papa was astonished when he heard."

"As was I." James remembered the bewildered outrage of his fifteen-year-old self when told that he would be under the thumb of a stranger until he reached the age of twenty-five. "And, begging your pardon, but your father is hardly a pattern card of wisdom."

"No. He is indolent and self-centered. Almost as much as you are."

"Why, Miss Vainsmede!" He rarely called her that. They had dropped formalities and begun using first names when she was twelve. "I am not the least indolent."

She hid a smile. "Only if you count various forms of sport. Which I do not. I have thought about the trusteeship, however. From what I've learned of your father—I did not know him of course—I think he preferred to be in charge."

A crack of laughter escaped James. "Preferred! An extreme understatement. He had the soul of an autocrat and the temper of a frustrated tyrant."

She frowned at him. "Yes. Well. Having heard something of that, I came to the conclusion that your father chose mine because he was confident Papa would do nothing in particular."

"What?"

"I think that your father disliked the idea of not being… present to oversee your upbringing, and he couldn't bear the idea of anyone *doing* anything about that."

James frowned as he worked through this convoluted sentence.

"And so he chose my father because he was confident Papa wouldn't…bestir himself and try to make changes in the arrangements."

Surprise kept James silent for a long moment. "You know that is the best theory I have heard. It might even be right."

"You needn't sound so astonished," Cecelia replied. "I often have quite good ideas."

"What a crackbrained notion!"

"I beg your pardon?"

"My father's, not yours." James shook his head. "You think he drove me nearly to distraction just to fend off change?"

"If he had lived…" she began.

"Oh, that would have been far worse. A never-ending battle of wills."

"You don't know that. I was often annoyed with my father when I was younger, but we get along well now."

"Because he lets you be as scandalous as you please, Cecelia."

"Oh nonsense."

James raised one dark brow.

"I *wish* I could learn to do that," exclaimed his pretty visitor. "You are said to have the most killing sneer in the *ton*, you know."

He was not going to tell her that he had spent much of a summer before the mirror when he was sixteen perfecting the gesture.

"And it was *not* scandalous for me to attend one ball without a chaperone. I was surrounded by friends and acquaintances. What could happen to me in such a crowd?" She shook her head. "At any rate, I am quite on the shelf at twenty-two. So it doesn't matter."

"Don't be stupid." James knew, from the laments of young

gentleman acquaintances, that Cecelia had refused several offers. She was anything but "on the shelf."

"I am never stupid," she replied coldly.

He was about to make an acid retort when he recalled that Cecelia was a positive glutton for work. She'd also learned a great deal about estate management and business as her father pushed tasks off on her, his only offspring. She'd come to manage much of Vainsmede's affairs as well as the trust. Indeed, she'd taken to it as James never had. He thought of the challenge confronting him. Could he cajole her into taking some of it on?

She'd gone to open the door at the rear of the entryway. "There is just barely room to edge along the hall here," she said. "Why would anyone keep all these newspapers? There must be years of them. Do you suppose the whole house is like this?"

"I have a sinking feeling that it may be worse. The sole servant ran off as if she was conscious of her failure."

"One servant couldn't care for such a large house even if it hadn't been…"

"A rubbish collection? I think Uncle Percival must have actually been mad. People called him eccentric, but this is…" James peered down the cluttered hallway. "No wonder he refused all my visits."

"Did you try to visit him?" Cecelia asked.

"Of course."

"Huh."

"Is that so surprising?" asked James.

"Well, yes, because you don't care for anyone but yourself."

"Don't start up this old refrain."

"It's the truth."

"More a matter of opinion and definition," James replied.

She waved this aside. "You will have to do better now that you are the head of your family."

"A meaningless label. I shall have to bring some order." He grimaced at the stacks of newspapers. "But no more than that."

"A great deal more," said Cecelia. "You have a duty…"

"As Uncle Percival did?" James gestured at their surroundings.

"His failure is all the more reason for you to shoulder your responsibilities."

"I don't think so."

Cecelia put her hands on her hips, just as she had done at nine years old. "Under our system the bulk of the money and all of the property in the great families passes to one man, in this case you. You are obliged to manage it for the good of the whole." She looked doubtful suddenly. "If there is any money."

"There is," he replied. This had been a continual sore point during the years of the trust. And after, in fact. His father had not left a fortune. "Quite a bit of it seemingly. I had a visit from a rather sour banker. Uncle Percival was a miser as well as a…" James gestured at the mess. "A connoisseur of detritus. But if you think I will tolerate the whining of indigent relatives, you are deluded." He had made do when he was far from wealthy. Others could follow suit.

"You must take care of your people."

She was interrupted by a rustle of newsprint. "I daresay there are rats," James said.

"Do you think to frighten me? You never could."

This was true. And he had really tried a few times in his youth.

"I am consumed by morbid curiosity," Cecelia added as she slipped down the hall. James followed. Her attendants came straggling after, the maid looking uneasy at the thought of rodents.

They found other rooms as jumbled as the first two. Indeed, the muddle seemed to worsen toward the rear of the house. "Is that a spinning wheel?" Cecelia exclaimed at one point. "Why would a duke want such a thing?"

"It appears he was unable to resist acquiring any object that he came across," replied James.

"But where would he come across a spinning wheel?"

"In a tenant's cottage?"

"Do you suppose he bought it from them?"

"I have no idea." James pushed aside a hanging swag of cloth. Dust billowed out and set them all coughing. He stifled a curse.

At last they came into what might have been a library. James thought he could see bookshelves behind the piles of refuse. There was a desk, he realized, with a chair pulled up to it. He hadn't noticed at first because it was buried under mountains of documents. At one side sat a large wicker basket brimming with correspondence.

Cecelia picked up a sheaf of pages from the desk, glanced over it, and set it down again. She rummaged in the basket. "These are all letters," she said.

"Wonderful."

"May I?"

James gestured his permission, and she opened one from the top. "Oh, this is bad. Your cousin Elvira needs help."

"I have no knowledge of a cousin Elvira."

"Oh, I suppose she must have been your uncle Percival's cousin. She sounds rather desperate."

"Well, that is the point of a begging letter, is it not? The effect is diminished if one doesn't sound desperate."

"Yes, but James…"

"My God, do you suppose they're all like that?" The basket was as long as his arm and nearly as deep. It was mounded with correspondence.

Cecelia dug deeper. "They all seem to be personal letters. Just thrown in here. I suppose they go back for months."

"Years," James guessed. Dust lay over them, as it did everything here.

"You must read them."

"I don't think so. For once I approve of Uncle Percival's methods. I would say throw them in the fire, if lighting a fire in this place wasn't an act of madness."

"Have you no family feeling?"

"None. You read them if you're so interested."

She shuffled through the upper layer. "Here's one from your grandmother."

"Which one?"

"Lady Wilton."

"Oh no."

Cecelia opened the sheet and read. "She seems to have misplaced an earl."

"What?"

"A long-lost heir has gone missing."

"Who? No, never mind. I don't care." The enormity of the task facing him descended on James, looming like the piles of objects leaning over his head. He looked up. One wrong move, and all that would fall about his ears. He wanted none of it.

A flicker of movement diverted him. A rat had emerged from a crevice between a gilded chair leg and a hideous outsized vase. The creature stared down at him, insolent, seeming to know that it was well out of reach. "Wonderful," murmured James.

Cecelia looked up. "What?"

He started to point out the animal, to make her jump, then bit back the words as an idea recurred. He, and her father, had taken advantage of her energetic capabilities over the years. He knew it. He was fairly certain she knew it. Her father had probably never noticed. But Cecelia hadn't minded. She'd said once that the things she'd learned and done had given her a more interesting life than most young ladies were allowed. Might his current plight not intrigue her? So instead of mentioning the rodent, he offered his most charming smile. "Perhaps you would like to have that basket," he suggested. "It must be full of compelling stories."

Her blue eyes glinted as if she understood exactly what he was up to. "No, James. This mare's nest is all yours. I think, actually, that you deserve it."

"How can you say so?"

"It is like those old Greek stories, where the thing one tries hardest to avoid fatefully descends."

"Thing?" said James, gazing at the looming piles of *things*.

"You loathe organizational tasks. And this one is monumental."

"You have always been the most annoying girl," said James.

"Oh, I shall enjoy watching you dig out." Cecelia turned away. "My curiosity is satisfied. I'll be on my way."

"It isn't like you to avoid work."

She looked over her shoulder at him. "*Your* work. And as you've pointed out, our...collaboration ended three years ago. We will call this visit a final farewell to those days."

She edged her way out, leaving James in his wreck of an inheritance. He was conscious of a sharp pang of regret. He put it down to resentment over her refusal to help him.

∽

Thinking of James's plight as she sat in her drawing room later that day, Cecelia couldn't help smiling. James liked order, and he didn't care for hard work. That house really did seem like fate descending on him like a striking hawk. Was it what he deserved? It was certainly amusing.

She became conscious of an impulse, like a nagging itch, to set things in order. The letters, in particular, tugged at her. She couldn't help wondering about the people who had written and their troubles. But she resisted. Her long association with James was over. There were reasons to keep her distance. She'd given in to curiosity today, but that must be the end.

"Tereford will manage," she said, ostensibly to the other occupant of the drawing room, but mostly to herself.

"Mmm," replied her aunt, Miss Valeria Vainsmede.

Cecelia had told her the story of the jumbled town house, but as usual her supposed chaperone had scarcely listened. Like Cecelia's father, her Aunt Valeria cared for nothing outside her own chosen sphere. "I sometimes wonder about my grandparents," Cecelia murmured. These Vainsmede progenitors, who had died before she was born, had produced a pair of plump, blond offspring with almost no interest in other people.

"You wouldn't have liked them," replied Aunt Valeria. One never knew when she would pick up on a remark and respond, sometimes after hours of silence. It was disconcerting. She was bent over a small pasteboard box. It undoubtedly contained a bee, because nothing else would hold her attention so completely. A notebook, quill, and inkpot sat beside it.

"You think not?" asked Cecelia.

"No one did."

"Why?"

"They were not likable," said her aunt.

"In what way?"

"In the way of a parasitic wasp pushing into the hive."

Cecelia stared at her aunt, who had not looked up from whatever she was doing, and wondered how anyone could describe their parents in such a disparaging tone. Aunt Valeria might have been speaking of total strangers. Whom she despised.

She felt a sudden flash of pain. How she missed her mother! Mama had been the polar opposite of the Vainsmedes. Warm and affectionate and prone to joking, she'd even brought Papa out of his self-absorption now and then and made their family feel—familial. She'd made him laugh. And she'd filled Cecelia's days with love. Her absence was a great icy void that would never be filled.

Cecelia took a deep breath. And another. These grievous moments were rare now. They'd gradually lessened in the years since Mama died when she was twelve, leaving her in the care of her distracted father. She'd found ways to move on, of course. But she would never forget that day, and feeling so desperately alone.

Until James had come to see her. He'd stepped into this very drawing room so quietly that she knew nothing until he spoke her name. Her aunt had not yet arrived; her father was with his books. She was wildly startled when he said, "Cecelia."

She'd lashed out, expecting some heartless complaint about his financial affairs. But James had sat down beside her on the sofa and taken her hand and told her how sorry he was. That nineteen-year-old sprig of fashion and aspiring sportsman, who'd often taunted her, had praised her mother in the kindest way and acknowledged how much she would be missed. Most particularly by Cecelia, of course. After a moment of incredulity, she'd burst into tears, thrown herself upon him, and sobbed on his shoulder. He'd tolerated the outburst as her father would not. He'd tried, clumsily, to comfort her, and Cecelia had seen that there was more to him than she'd understood.

A footman came in and announced visitors. Cecelia put the past aside. Aunt Valeria responded with a martyred sigh.

Four young ladies filed into the room, and Cecelia stood to greet them. She'd been expecting only one, Miss Harriet Finch, whose mother had been a school friend of her mama. Mrs. Finch had written asking for advice and aid with her daughter's debut, and Cecelia had volunteered to help Miss Harriet acquire a bit of town polish. Now she seemed to be welcoming the whole upper level of a girls' school, judging from the outmoded wardrobes and dowdy haircuts. "Hello," she said.

The most conventionally pretty of the group, with red-blond hair, green eyes, a pointed chin beneath a broad forehead, and a beautiful figure, stepped forward. "How do you do?" she said. "I am Harriet Finch."

According to the gossips, she was a considerable heiress. Quite a spate of inheritances lately, Cecelia thought, though she supposed people were always dying.

"And these are Miss Ada Grandison, Miss Sarah Moran, and

Miss Charlotte Deeping," the girl went on. She pointed as she gave their names.

"I see," said Cecelia.

"They are my friends." Miss Finch spoke as if they were a set of china that mustn't on any account be broken up.

"May I present my aunt, Miss Vainsmede," said Cecelia.

Aunt Valeria pointed to one ear and spoke in a loud toneless voice. "Very deaf. Sorry." She returned to her box and notepad, putting her back to their visitors.

Cecelia hid a sigh. Her aunt could hear as well as anyone, but she insisted on telling society that she could not. It must have been an open secret, because the servants were well aware of her true state. But the ruse allowed Aunt Valeria to play her part as chaperone without making any effort to participate in society. Cecelia had once taxed her with feigning what others found a sad affliction. Her aunt had informed her that she actually did not hear people who nattered on about nothing. "My mind rejects their silly yapping," she'd declared. "It turns to a sort of humming in my brain, and then I begin to think of something interesting instead." Cecelia gestured toward a sofa. "Do sit down," she said to her guests.

The girls sat in a row facing her. They didn't fold their hands, but it felt as if they had. They looked hopeful and slightly apprehensive. Cecelia examined them, trying to remember which was which.

Miss Ada Grandison had heavy, authoritative eyebrows. They dominated smooth brown hair, brown eyes, a straight nose, and full lips.

Miss Sarah Moran, the shortest of the four, was a smiling round little person with sandy hair, a turned-up nose, and sparkling light blue eyes. It was too bad her pale brows and eyelashes washed her out.

The last, Miss Charlotte Deeping, was the tallest, with black hair, pale skin, and a sharp dark gaze. She looked spiky. "I thought you didn't have a chaperone," she said to Cecelia, confirming this impression.

"What made you think that?"

"We heard you went to a ball on your own."

"I met my party there," Cecelia replied, which was nearly true. She had attached herself to friends as soon as she arrived. That solitary venture had perhaps been a misjudgment. But it was a very minor scandal, more of an eccentricity, she told herself. She was impatient with the rules now that she was in her fourth season. "My aunt has lived with us since my mother died," she told her visitors.

"I thought it must be a hum," replied Miss Deeping. "It seems we are to be stifled to death here in London."

Cecelia could sympathize. Because her father paid no attention and her aunt did not care, her situation was unusual. She'd been the mistress of the house for nine years, and manager of the Vainsmede properties for even longer. Her father left everything to her, too lazy to be bothered. Indeed Cecelia sometimes wondered how she ever came to be in the first place, as Papa cared for nothing but rich meals and reading. She supposed her maternal grandmother had simply informed him that he was being married and then sent someone to drag him from his library to the church on the day. But no, he had cared for Mama. She must believe that.

"Every circumstance is different," said Miss Moran.

She was one who liked to smooth things over, Cecelia noted.

"And Miss Vainsmede is older than…" Miss Moran blushed and bit her lip as if afraid she'd given offense.

"Three years older than you," Cecelia acknowledged. "Do you all want my advice?"

"We must have new clothes and haircuts," said Miss Grandison. The others nodded.

"We're new to London and fashionable society, where you are

well established," said Miss Finch. "My mother says we would be wise to heed an expert."

"Which doesn't precisely answer my question," said Cecelia. "Do you wish to hear my opinions?"

They looked at each other, engaged in a brief silent communication, and then all nodded. The exchange demonstrated a solid friendship, which Cecelia envied. Many of her friends had married and did not come to town for the season. She missed them. "Very well," she began. "I think you, Miss Moran, would do well to darken your brows and lashes. It would draw attention to your lovely eyes."

The girl looked shocked. "Wouldn't that be dreadfully *fast*?"

"A little daring perhaps," said Cecelia. "But no one will know if you do it before your entry into society."

"Don't be missish, Sarah," said Miss Deeping.

Cecelia wondered if she was a bully. "You should wear ruffles," she said to her. She suspected that this suggestion would not be taken well, and it was not.

"Ruffles," repeated the dark girl in a tone of deep revulsion.

"To soften the lines of your frame."

"Disguise my lamentable lack of a figure you mean."

Cecelia did not contradict her. Nor did she evade the glare that came with these words. They either wanted her advice or they didn't. She didn't know them well enough to care which it was to be.

"You haven't mentioned my eyebrows," said Miss Grandison, frowning.

"You appear to use them to good effect."

Miss Grandison was surprised into a laugh.

"And I?" asked Miss Finch. There seemed to be an undertone of resentment or bitterness in her voice. Odd since she had the least to fear from society, considering her inheritance.

"New clothes and a haircut," Cecelia replied. "We could call on my modiste tomorrow if you like."

The appointment was agreed on.

"Oh, I hope this season goes well," said Miss Moran.

"There will be another next year," Cecelia said. She heard the trace of boredom in her voice and rejected it. She was not one of those languishing women who claimed to be overcome by ennui.

"I shan't be here. It was always to be only one season for me." Miss Moran clasped her hands together. "So I intend to enjoy it *immensely.*"

Two

"Thank you," said James to the club steward who brought his brandy. He sipped the mellow liquor and settled deeper into the plush armchair near the front window. Outside, it was growing dark, and rain sheeted over the pavement. Here within, all was comfort—warmth, color, paneled wood, and polished leather. The gentleman's club was a wonderful invention, James observed. For those who lived in a small set of rooms, as he did, it provided expansive spaces as well as fine dinners. The staff was impeccable. Friends passed through, offering conversation or a convivial game of cards without the effort of making arrangements. Or one could read the latest publications. Really a fine idea altogether. He took another sip.

"Tereford. Hullo."

James turned to find a stocky, older man standing by his chair. He couldn't immediately recall the man's name. He nodded a greeting.

"My wife hopes you will attend her evening party on Friday," the fellow said. "Be very pleased to see you there. M'daughter too. Most eager."

James stiffened. This was outrageous. The club was supposed to be a refuge, not another hunting ground for ambitious females. James focused the expression that Cecelia had called the most killing sneer in the *ton* on the man.

The look had the desired effect. The fellow flinched, muttered something inaudible, and walked away.

James remained, contemplating his unpleasant new state. Since inheriting the dukedom he'd been besieged by debs and their mothers. The attention he'd received as a mere heir was nothing compared to the hue and cry now that he actually possessed the title and a fortune to go with it. He thought this must be how the fox felt with the hounds in full voice—dogged by a predatory clamor. But he'd thought himself safe *here*. The club was meant to be an escape from all that.

Henry Deeping appeared in the doorway, tall, thin, pale skin offset by dark hair and eyes. He noticed James, and strolled over. "Hullo, Duke," he said.

"I thought we agreed that you would not call me that."

"Can't resist." Henry appropriated the chair opposite James and signaled the steward, pointing at James's brandy glass. "How does it feel to have paid off all your bills?"

"Oddly unsatisfying," said James. "Rather a feeling of game over."

"Poor old you." There was that trace of bitterness in Henry's voice again. "Happy for you, you know," he added, as if he had heard it as well.

James nodded. He knew it was true. Henry was a good-natured fellow, quick and convivial, which should serve him well among the diplomats. Had he needed some specific sum of money, James would have offered it. But that wasn't the issue. Circumstances were pulling them apart.

"I've been trotting Stephan Kandler about town," Henry went on, in a clear bid to change the subject.

"Who is he?" James asked, conceding the shift.

"Aide to a German princeling who's having a look around Europe."

"Some relative of the Regent?"

"No," Henry replied. "Nothing close anyhow. They come from one of those small countries south of Prussia. Not important enough for the government to pay attention. My uncle asked me to lend a hand." He shrugged, not needing to say more. Henry's uncle, well established in the Foreign Office, was important to his possible future there.

The second brandy arrived. They sipped together and talked of mutual friends and upcoming races, passing a pleasant hour before Henry said, "I must go. It's Lady Castlereagh's ball tonight. I'm ordered to support my sister's come-out."

James felt himself stiffen again.

Henry held up his hands, palms out. "Steady on, James. *Not* a hint. You wouldn't like her. She wouldn't like you."

"Are you certain? They all like me now." James heard the bitterness in his tone this time.

"Not Charlotte. She despises everyone. Almost everyone."

James laughed. "An unusual girl. Perhaps I'll come with you." He didn't want to become a recluse. The idea made him think of his great-uncle and shudder. *That* would never do. Besides, he liked many things about society, or he *had*. Surely if he kept appearing and fending off all advances the marriage mart would recognize the futility of pursuit?

"Oh, do. Think how it will add to my consequence to be seen with the new Duke of Tereford."

"Useless fribble, you have no consequence."

"Exactly why I need to ride your coattails," answered Henry with a grin.

Laughing, they went out together.

❧

The third set at Lady Castlereagh's grand ball was a waltz. Cecelia was about to accept an invitation to join it when James appeared and overawed the young man who had bowed before her. "You will dance with me," James said to her. The first gentleman faded back into the crowd without a word.

Cecelia was both piqued and amused. "Is that a command, *Your Grace*?"

"I will beg, if you like."

She gave him an inquiring glance, which also noted that he looked particularly handsome in his evening dress. The black hair and blue eyes were always a striking combination, and he had the face of an ancient statue. Apollo. Or perhaps Mercury. No, Mercury was too…willowy. Definitely Apollo with that body strengthened by all forms of sport. And why in the world was she thinking of that?

"If I am dancing with you, no ambitious mama can try to shove her hopeful offspring at me," he said.

"Your flattery puts me to the blush."

"Why should I flatter you?"

"Why indeed?"

He offered his arm. She took it, and they walked out to join the other couples. The music began. He set a hand at her waist, held the other in warm fingers, and they whirled away. Cecelia was aware that her gown of pale-rose gauze looked very fine. She also knew from past experience that their steps were well matched. She sank into the pleasure of waltzing with him. It was a delight, floating across the floor, guided by a sure hand, closer than they came in any other way. She felt her cheeks warm with more than exertion. Once again she was required to remind herself that she did *not* love James Cantrell. That would be an exceedingly foolish thing to do, and she was not a fool.

"I'm out of sorts," he said after a while.

"You don't say so?"

"I beg your pardon, but the…torrent of young ladies that has rushed in my direction since my great-uncle died is irritating. Two of them came to Jackson's boxing saloon yesterday."

"Surely not inside?"

"No, they were loitering by the door, waiting to pounce when I came out. One of them claimed to have hurt her ankle in order to beg for my assistance. This after they had not begged anything of the two men who preceded me out the door."

"They can't have been of the first stare." The Bond Street address was not a place where proper young ladies would linger.

"I'm sure you're right. But that did not prevent them from descending on me to titter and admire my 'physique.' It was scandalous."

"I've never known you to worry about scandal."

"I shall start if it is an excuse to evade that sort of simpering. I begin to understand Uncle Percival. Perhaps I'll retreat to the town house and refuse all visits."

"You'd do better to encourage them, insist even. And then decree that every visitor must take a bit of rubbish away with them."

He burst out laughing. "You are always a relief."

"Am I?"

"A breath of fresh air, at least. You have been obstinately honest since you were nine years old."

"Oh, before that, I think." Her voice was very dry, but then she didn't appreciate his patronizing tone. "Happy to be of service."

"Don't take one of your pets."

"One of my what?"

"Honesty is considered a virtue, is it not? I was paying you a compliment."

"In such a condescending tone." She did her best to match it.

"Nonsense."

This was one of his favorite words, and he always said it with complete conviction. He absolutely believed he was right. Well, if she was honest, he was infuriating. Cecelia started to tell him so, but he whirled her in a beautiful turn, and for a moment she felt as if she was flying. He held her so easily, his arm so steady and strong. It made her feel light as a feather.

"Also we have known each other so long, we need make no pretense to silly sentiment. I find that quite restful."

Cecelia plunked back down to earth.

"As well as being the same sort of person," he added.

"Sort?"

"You know what I mean."

"I don't think I do really, James."

"We have no ridiculous ideas about falling in love."

"Why do you say that?"

"Come, come, Cecelia. You have refused at least four offers that I know of."

"And if I have, is this not an argument for a belief in love? Perhaps I am waiting for it to come along."

"Good grief, are you?"

"For a while I was. But it...hasn't." He looked appalled at this slip of her tongue, which was lowering. Cecelia knew that James never thought of her and love in the same breath. The two were completely separate things in his mind. She ought to be the same. She *was*. She'd stifled her feelings about him years ago. They were gone! Or, if by any chance they weren't, they would never be allowed out, even though he'd begun talking of love. She would not have her feelings trampled by consternation, perhaps even revulsion. Horrifying. They were gone!

"And so you gave up that ridiculous illusion," James said, looking smug. "There, you see. We are the same."

Cecelia didn't try to deny it. That would be perilous and futile and other dangerous things she didn't care to contemplate. Instead, she would enjoy the fact that there was no one else she could talk to as openly as she did to James. "Love is an illusion?"

"The sort that the poets maunder on about, certainly. Look at me. I shall marry as a duty, to provide an heir for the dukedom. And a hostess I suppose." The latter idea seemed distasteful to him. "Another portrait for the long line of languishing females in the gallery." He grimaced. "Not that anyone can see them in the house's current state."

"That does sound rather dreary."

"Well, marriage is dreary, as far as I can see," said James.

Cecelia wondered if his parents had loved each other. She hadn't known them. Hers… They'd been affectionate, now and then. But she suspected that her mother had loved her daughter far more than her distracted husband. It was not an example she wished to emulate.

"I challenge you to name a happy one," James added.

"The Tuttles and the Burleighs and the Cranes," replied Cecelia promptly.

James shrugged as they danced. "They seem contented enough, I suppose. But what do we know of their private moments? Nothing."

"And so they may be as rhapsodic as the poets claim."

He made a contemptuous sound. And as if on cue the music ended, and they drew apart. As they always would, Cecelia acknowledged. He saw her as a fixture in his life, useful once, safe and familiar now. But nothing more. She must be reconciled to that.

James declared that he intended to take refuge in the card room and asked where she wished to be taken. Cecelia noticed her four new acquaintances sitting in gilt chairs on one side of the ballroom. They had not been waltzing because they were waiting to be approved by the patronesses at Almack's. She accepted James's escort over to them and his bow of farewell.

During their shopping expeditions Cecelia had discovered that these girls were intelligent, curious, and ambitious far beyond the next ball or the roster of eligible young men being brandished at them. They had moved to first names already and were on the way to becoming good friends.

"Did you enjoy your waltz with the new duke?" asked Sarah Moran. "They say Tereford is the handsomest man in England."

"They," repeated Charlotte Deeping contemptuously. "I am already sick to death of *them*, whoever they are. If indeed *they* exist."

Looking over her shoulder Cecelia watched James stroll through the doorway on the other side of the large room. Dozens of feminine gazes followed him.

"You must admit that he *is* handsome," said Sarah.

Charlotte rolled her dark eyes. "My brothers admire him." In the satirical tone she used to speak of her siblings, Charlotte began ticking off points on her fingers. "He is 'handy with his fives,' which apparently signifies an ability to knock people down whenever he pleases. He is 'up to every rig and row in town' and 'complete to a shade,' absolutely 'top of the trees.' I take this to mean that he sets fashions and possesses polished manners. Of course he has money and now a title, which boost people's opinions, I'm sure."

"And the coldest eyes," said Harriet Finch.

Cecelia wondered at this. James's blue eyes cold? She'd seen them blaze. Mostly with anger, admittedly.

"My mother considers him a very eligible *parti*," Harriet continued. "She tried to maneuver him into dancing with me. He refused as if I was a beetle to be crushed beneath his heel."

The eager mama would account for the coldness, Cecelia acknowledged. James hated having debs pushed on him. But this reference to insects must be an exaggeration. He had fine manners. She'd noticed that Harriet was eager to despise society.

"Lydia Pottington said he's the most selfish creature on earth. Is he really?" Ada Grandison asked. She turned to Cecelia. "You're quite well acquainted with him, aren't you?"

"Cecelia knows everyone," said Charlotte.

It wasn't a jab. By this time Cecelia understood Charlotte's sardonic manner. "I am," she answered.

"Well, then." Ada Grandison gazed at her. Cecelia had discovered that Ada was already engaged to a duke of her own, so her interest was clearly more abstract.

The others waited. Cecelia thought they were likely to accept her opinions about society and follow her lead, a heavy responsibility. What should she say to them about James? He *was* selfish. Didn't she often tell him so? He could be cold, and he saved his sympathies for his close friends. Indeed, he scarcely noticed other people. And when accused of these failings, he simply shrugged.

Yet Cecelia found herself reluctant to voice these familiar criticisms. It was one thing to throw them in his face, and quite another to share them with people who knew nothing of him or his history. "He can be a bit toplofty," she said. And was at once conscious of a desire to defend him. Better to change the subject. "Have all your new gowns arrived?"

They had begun a discussion of fashion when all four girls' eyes shifted, focusing on something behind Cecelia. What could be making them look so apprehensive? Cecelia turned her head, and was treated to the spectacle of Lady Wilton bearing down on them in full glare.

James's grandmother, a small, gnarled woman with snow-white hair and a nose designed for looking down on her inferiors—a wide and ever shifting group seemingly—wore a rich gown of deep-green velvet, magnificent emeralds, and a sour expression. She'd passed the venerable age of eighty without any sign of mellowing. Cecelia had sometimes wondered if she'd been such a bundle of prejudices and complaints when young—in the middle of the previous century—or had acquired them gradually along the way.

She stopped beside them. Sarah leapt up to offer her a chair, and Lady Wilton took it as a matter of course, with no thanks. She looked at Cecelia's companions one by one and visibly dismissed them. "I hear Tereford's town house is in a dreadful state," she said with her characteristic relish for the misfortunes of others.

Cecelia had known that her maid and footman would make a good tale of their visit. But gossip about the place was inevitable in any case. James would have to bring in workers to restore order. "There is quite a bit of clearing up to do," she replied.

"Percival always was a disgrace."

Lady Wilton and the deceased duke were of the same generation, Cecelia remembered. Indeed, she had been married to his younger brother, Wilton Cantrell.

"They threw him out of Eton for stealing, you know. Put it about that he was *unwell*. Odd sort of disease that made him cram his truck with other boys' treasures. Seems he never got over it." Lady Wilton loosed one of her disturbing cackles of laughter—loud and cruelly mocking. People nearby winced. Some moved farther away. Cecelia's four new friends faded back a few degrees.

"Not what I want to talk about," Lady Wilton continued. "Percival's dead." She clenched hands twisted with rheumatics in her lap. "Something must be done about Ferrington."

"I'm not sure I—" began Cecelia.

"Ferrington!" the old lady interrupted. "Surely you remember that my daughter married the Earl of Ferrington."

Cecelia didn't know why she should be expected to recall a wedding that must have taken place long before she was born.

"Not a bad match," Lady Wilton conceded. "I arranged it, of course. And Fanny did her duty. Two sons in two years. I thought all was well settled. Though she died not long after the second one."

She spoke without any sign of grief. Pity for this woman's daughter filled Cecelia. She saw the same emotion in the other young ladies' eyes.

"But then, Ralph turned out to be intractable," Lady Wilton went on. "Practically from the moment he could walk."

"Ralph?"

"The younger boy. Will you pay attention, Miss Vainsmede!"

Cecelia looked around for a means of escape. A new set was forming, but no gentlemen looked likely to approach them in the face of Lady Wilton's fierce glare. And James was out of reach, naturally. Despite the fact that this was *his* grandmother.

"Ralph fell prey to every vice imaginable," the old lady continued. "I had to pack him off to America before he was eighteen."

"*You* did?"

"His father was a drunkard. There was no one else to take charge."

Visions of a horrid childhood under this woman's thumb rose in Cecelia's mind. She could imagine acquiring a few vices herself under those circumstances.

"He was matching his father bottle for bottle at fourteen!"

"Ralph?"

"That is who we are speaking of. Can you not keep up?" Lady Wilton's frown grew more pronounced. "I had thought you a fairly intelligent girl. Do not tell me I was wrong."

This was too much. "It is just that I don't know why you are telling me this story, Lady Wilton."

"Because my idiot elder grandson broke his neck on the hunting field without producing an heir," the old woman replied. "And Ralph's son inherited the earldom."

"I see, but why…"

Lady Wilton bared her yellowed teeth. "This…American is the only one left," she said. "The estate's man of business had a dreadful time finding him, and he appears to be no better than Ralph. Gambling, of course, and who knows what else. Not to mention his moth…but none of that. We hauled him over here, though the fellow actually claimed he had no interest in being an earl!" She snorted her contempt at this idea. "Idiot. I informed him that I was capable of transforming even a graceless bumpkin into reasonable shape for his position. The next day, he was gone."

Thinking one could scarcely blame the man, Cecelia attempted a summary. And hopefully a conclusion to this strange conversation. "So one of your grandsons is the new Earl of Ferrington."

"Great-grandson," Lady Wilton interrupted. "My daughter married at seventeen. Did as she was told like a sensible girl. Tereford's father put it off until he was nearly twice that age. Always stubborn as an ox." She sniffed irritably.

"Great-grandson," Cecelia amended, suppressing her impatience. "And he is missing." She realized then that he was the subject of the letter she'd read in Tereford's chaotic library.

"Haven't I just been telling you?" Impatience was an inadequate word for Lady Wilton's expression.

"Yes, ma'am. You have. I still don't know why, however." Cecelia knew she sounded sharp, but she couldn't help it.

"So you will make Tereford do something, of course! He is head of the family now. He must bestir himself. Percival never would, but James hasn't the excuse of being half-mad." The old lady grimaced. "Or completely mad. Percival saw no one in recent years, but the signs were there."

Cecelia was puzzled by her odd command. "You should speak to Tereford about this matter," she replied. "Not to me. Indeed, I don't know why…"

"Because no one else has ever gotten James Cantrell to lift a finger."

This startled Cecelia into silence.

"Ha, you know I'm right about that," said Lady Wilton.

"I have not…"

"Don't play missish with me, Cecelia Vainsmede. Everyone knows that your father was never his *real* trustee. Tereford will listen to you. You must make him track Ferrington down and bring him back to London. I shall take over after that."

"I have no particular influence over…"

"Rubbish!"

"What does the new earl look like?" asked Charlotte Deeping.

Lady Wilton turned to glare at her. "He looks insolent, rather like you, young lady. I don't know why you are speaking to me as I do not believe we have been introduced."

"Lady Wilton, this is—" Cecelia began.

"I don't care," she interrupted. "I've no time for impertinent chits. You will do as I say, Miss Vainsmede. I expect to hear from you by tomorrow." She rose with no sign of difficulty despite her age. And then, just when Cecelia thought this ordeal was over, she snapped, "Did you come to this ball alone? Again."

"No, Lady Wilton, I am here with the Finch party."

"Good! Valeria is utterly useless, you know." With a final sniff, she swept away.

Cecelia's companions slowly drew closer again. Sarah reclaimed her chair. "I wonder if Lady Wilton is acquainted with your aunt Julia," she said to Ada.

"They certainly seem like sisters in spirit," the girl answered.

"Though Lady Wilton looks more like a buzzard," said Charlotte.

"Or an avenging harpy," said Sarah. "Her hands are rather like claws."

"She is a good deal older than Ada's aunt," said Harriet. "There is time."

Cecelia bit back a laugh, and then found she was facing four pairs of sharp, interested eyes.

"We are very good at solving mysteries," said Charlotte. "We could help you find the missing heir."

"I like the sound of *that*," said Sarah. "The search for the missing earl."

"I shan't be doing any such thing," Cecelia assured them. She didn't have to imagine James's response to such a request. She was certain he'd refuse. And she didn't see that it was any of her affair.

"But how can you resist?"

"It would be *much* more interesting than parties and balls," said Charlotte.

"Not more," protested Sarah. "But as."

"Ferrington," murmured Harriet. "I've heard that name. Mama was drilling me… I think there is a Ferrington Hall not too far from my grandfather's home."

"Drilling you?" Cecelia couldn't help asking.

"I've never been to Grandpapa's house. There were... difficulties in my family that have only recently been resolved. We are going for a visit after the season."

"We will come with you!" said Charlotte. "And unravel the mystery of the missing earl."

"I can't just invite..."

"You told us your grandfather encouraged you to bring friends along," Charlotte interrupted. "You should come too, Cecelia."

"I couldn't..." She realized that James had returned to the ballroom and was gazing at her from across the floor. Even at this distance she could tell that his eyes were dancing. He'd seen Lady Wilton haranguing her, and he was relishing the fact that it had been *her*, and not him. She wished there was some way to punish him for that glee. And then she thought—perhaps there was.

Three

JAMES PULLED A SMALL INLAID TABLE FROM A TOWERING PILE of furnishings in the left-hand parlor of his ruinous town house. He had to jump back as a cascade of furniture threatened to tumble down around his ears. A small, glittering object bounced twice and came to rest near his right foot. He bent and picked it up, turning it over in his hands. The silver sugar bowl was tarnished but richly embellished; it looked antique as well. This had to be worth a good deal, and it was one of the reasons that his first impulse—just to have everything cleared out and taken away—was impossible. The mess was seeded with valuable items, and he'd noticed documents stuffed into some crevices, too. His great-uncle had had no system whatsoever, meaning that James couldn't leave this task to just anyone. Someone needed to evaluate each item and make a decision about its fate.

"The devil!" he said, pushing the sugar bowl back into the pile. This task was colossal and unbearable. He'd tried to begin several times over the last week, and he could not tolerate the teetering chaos. Today, once again, he retreated, locking up the house to continue moldering, for now.

A household was a woman's job, he thought as he walked down the street and away. A chatelaine was the person to separate the wheat from the vast pile of chaff the previous duke had left behind. James felt certain of this even though he'd never experienced such a regime himself. His mother had died when he was three. He didn't remember her. His father had remarried a year later and then lost his second wife in childbirth, along with James's infant half brother. After that, they'd made do with a housekeeper. But she'd been a woman. Perhaps he could hire a supremely competent housekeeper? Where did one find such people? James employed a valet, but he had no other servants, and he'd found Hobbs through a friend's recommendation.

James shook his head. No, for this incredible labor he needed someone like Cecelia, an expert at organization and managing and an intelligent judge of what should be kept and what discarded. *She* would not be daunted by Uncle Percival's detritus. She was tenacious as a bulldog. However, she'd made it clear that she did not intend to help him. He knew her; she would not be cajoled into it.

The conversation from their waltz came back to him. It *had* been a relief. There was no other female he could talk to like Cecelia, no other that he knew so well. And with that observation came a startling idea. What if he married Cecelia? As his duchess, she would be obliged to set his house to rights. Ha!

Immediately, he rejected the thought. He didn't wish to be married! Oh, he would tie the knot someday to provide an heir for the title, but there was plenty of time for that. Years. Also he'd known Cecelia since she was a child. He'd never thought of her in that way. True at twenty-eight and twenty-two the disparity in their ages was effectively gone. But she was…Cecelia.

And yet. Marriage to her would solve so many of his current problems. It would end the pursuit of the ambitious mamas. It would put a person of supreme competence in charge of his chaotic town house. And other properties. There were quite a few of them. James stopped walking, suddenly filled with horror. What if all the ducal estates were like the London house? A picture of decrepit, refuse-filled houses dotted over England rose in his mind. Clearly, Uncle Percival had done nothing for many years. It was all too likely that he had left such a nightmare behind. But Cecelia would plunge into managing them. She reveled in that sort of tedium. If experience was a guide, she would put all in order so quickly it made one's head spin.

Moreover, Cecelia knew his habits, and they had already

established a way of dealing together during the years of his trust. A somewhat acrimonious method, but still… It was almost as if their youth had prepared them for this partnership. And finally, perhaps most of all, she wouldn't expect him to make sickly protestations or constantly dance attendance on her. Had they not agreed as they waltzed that love was a silly illusion? Another— eventual—bride might look for all sorts of wearisome declarations and services. There was a dismal prospect.

James walked on, nearly decided on offering for Cecelia. But, no. Marriage was such an irrevocable step. He wasn't ready. He would think of some other solution. He turned to his club and the prospect of sporting talk or a game of cards instead.

The following day, James received a formal letter from his great-uncle's man of business resigning his position. The fellow claimed that he was retiring from active service, but James suspected that he simply didn't wish to deal with the tangle Uncle Percival had left behind. Which he had *allowed* Uncle Percival to leave behind! Admittedly, James had shouted at him at their first meeting. And the second. But that was no reason to shirk his responsibilities.

"Where shall I put the boxes?" asked his valet as James crumpled the letter in his fist.

"What boxes?"

"Seven large boxes were delivered along with the letter," the man replied. "Containing documents, according to the carter." Hobbs's expression was neutral, but it was obvious he knew this was unwelcome news. The valet had worked for James for two years and was well acquainted with his moods.

"Damn the fellow," said James. "He's running like a coward."

Hobbs said nothing.

"Have them sent over to the town house." James remembered there was no one there to receive them. Stifling a curse, he got the key and handed it to Hobbs. "Hire a carrier. Ride along and have the boxes put in the entryway."

The valet took the key without enthusiasm, but he did not go so far as to protest. However, James was aware that at some point, he probably would. Hobbs was not the sort of valet who gladly accepted tasks outside his area of expertise. He took superb care of James's clothing, achieved an enviable shine on his boots, and dressed his hair in the latest mode. His skills had attracted attention, and more than one friend had tried to lure him away from James. Hobbs was not above hinting at this when asked to do more than he thought right. He would not be a help with Tereford House.

James sighed as the valet departed. He needed a staff. He needed a new man of business. He needed help. This couldn't go on. He must face the fact that drastic measures were required. And sacrifices. One had to make sacrifices for one's heritage. James fetched his hat and set off to call on Cecelia. He knew he would find her alone at this hour. Her aunt would not be pulled from the garden for anything less than torrential rain in the afternoons.

Cecelia received him in the drawing room of her father's house, solitary as expected, a book open on her lap. James noticed that she looked exceedingly pretty in a blue cambric gown with a deep flounce at the hem. Her hair gleamed golden in the sunlight from the front windows, and her luminous blue eyes were soft when she greeted him. James realized that he hadn't really been paying attention. Cecelia was lovely. He'd known that, and yet he hadn't *known* it. He hadn't fully appreciated the curves of the body beneath that smooth cambric. She was delectable. Marriage to her would hardly be a penance.

He took the seat she indicated and accepted the offer of a glass of wine. There was a soothing sense of peace and order in the room, the sort of atmosphere a man wanted in his own home when he returned to it.

"How is work going at the town house?" she asked him.

"It is not."

"Have you come looking for sympathy then?"

Seeing no reason to delay, James said, "I have come to ask you to marry me."

"What?"

"I would like you to be my duchess," he said.

It was one of the few times in their long association that he'd managed to render her speechless. Indeed, she was gaping at him.

"I think it a sensible plan," he explained. "Offering advantages for both of us."

She still seemed unready to speak.

Recognizing that he had surprised her, James went on. "You would be established with a respected position in society. That must be an important consideration for you. When your father is gone, your circumstances will be much reduced."

"Papa is quite healthy," she replied in an odd tone.

"For now. He is prone to overindulgence."

Cecelia bent her head so that he couldn't see her face.

James acknowledged that his last remark had been tactless. Yes, it was true. But a proposal should probably not dwell on a father's death. Certainly it should not. What was wrong with him? He turned to another tack. "You enjoy having estates to run."

She raised her head and gazed at him, her eyes wide and unreadable. "Would you really go this far to have me do your work for you?"

"You are practically trained to be a duchess already."

"Trained! Like a performing animal?"

"What? Nothing of the sort. You are speaking as if I've insulted you."

"I'm astounded, rather." She looked down again. "I—I had no notion you were contemplating marriage at this time."

"Well, I wasn't, but this would thwart the ambitious mamas. And, you know, the dukedom requires an heir and so on." James faltered as his mind was suddenly full of the process of gaining said heir. How had he failed to appreciate Cecelia's lithe, lovely curves? They were right *there*, an arm's length away.

"So on," repeated Cecelia with parted lips.

They were quite enticing lips. Was she too thinking of marital embraces? The idea sent a flush of heat over his skin.

She blinked and sat straighter. "But chiefly I would set the estate in order for you," she said. "That is why you are here."

"I know you like to be useful."

"Is that what you know about me?"

He couldn't understand why she was being so prickly. "One thing. Do you deny it?"

"No, but…"

"There! I am offering a task you enjoy. And we are familiar with each other's ideas and habits."

"Do you mean that I am accustomed to dealing with a vain, indolent man?" Cecelia asked. "Two of them actually."

"That is not the way I would put it," James replied, nettled.

"No, of course you would not."

"You are being tiresome."

"Am I? Perhaps it's fortunate then that I am not going to marry you."

"What?" Taken up with his own doubts about this momentous step, James hadn't considered that she might refuse. The possibility hadn't occurred to him. "Why not?"

"You've treated me like an annoyance nearly all my life, James. Why would I shackle myself to you?"

"Nonsense."

She shook her head. "The very way you say that word. So certain. And condescending. Allowing no possibility of another view."

"Non—" James bit off the word. "Nothing of the sort."

"And now you come and say you want me to be your drudge."

"Drudge! Are you out of your senses? I am proposing to make you my duchess."

"So that I will be under your thumb. You've always delighted in tormenting me."

"Tormenting?" James didn't know whether he was more angry or incredulous. "That is the most ridiculous thing I've ever heard."

"When I was ten, you hid my essay on Shakespeare and told my governess that I'd been shirking. *And* that I'd said she was a fubsy-faced prune."

"How do you remember…?" James shook his head. "I was a sulky stripling. I meant it as a joke."

"I didn't find it amusing. When I was sixteen, you told Reginald Quentin that I was mad about him."

James laughed. "That spotty toadeater!"

"He followed me about for weeks trying to steal a kiss. I had to be quite cruel to make him stop. Which I do not like to be!"

"Did he? I'm sorry. I apologize for all my youthful follies. But I can't believe you've been holding grudges all this time."

"They are not grudges, James. They are…evidence that we would not suit." Cecelia frowned. "Though I never did find my essay." She looked around the drawing room. "I don't suppose you remember where you hid it?"

"Of course not."

"Of course you don't," she echoed.

"What is the matter with you? You are always such a sensible creature."

"Am I?"

"Yes, Cecelia, you are. You argue for curtailed expenditures and considered decisions. You are an excellent manager and a master of accounts."

In the face of these compliments, she looked chagrined. Perhaps even distressed? But why should that be? Thinking he must be mistaken, James pressed on. "As we have both decided that we are not going to fall in love…"

"That is not precisely true."

"You said that love never came along," James pointed out.

"Yet," Cecelia said, seeming to bite off the word.

"And declared that you are on the shelf, so you must not be expecting it any longer."

"It is very irritating to have my words thrown back in my face in this way."

"I know," said James. "You've done the same to me on many occasions."

"There you have it. We don't get along. Haven't you often called me the bane of your existence?"

"That was another joke. I thought you had a better sense of humor."

Her blue eyes blazed at him. "And so you discover that you are wrong. Again."

James had never seen her so animated, or so beautiful. Cecelia had been a fixture in his life for years, useful or frustrating, tolerable or irrelevant. But in this moment he realized that she was a woman of passion as well as intelligence. The fire in her gaze, the taut challenge of her body, made his senses flare with desire. "I am not wrong," he said. He hadn't seen it until now.

"You never think so." The flame in Cecelia's eyes died. She turned her head away. "You should go now, James. We have no more to say to each other."

"I'll show you," he said.

She sighed. "You know you're persisting just because you've been refused. We've spoken of this before. You don't need to fight every time you're thwarted. Some matters are best forgotten. I wager you'll be very glad, in an hour or so, that I rejected your offer. It will be an immense relief." Her voice trembled slightly on the last word.

James brushed this irrelevance aside. He would convince her. He knew how to frame pretty compliments and send bouquets and play the suitor, even if he'd never bothered before. He would show her that she was mistaken and have her for his duchess. And then she would see... *He* would see that fire in her eyes again. For him. James found he wanted that very much indeed. And he was accustomed to getting what he wanted.

There was no more to be done here today, however. This step of the campaign had not gone well. It was time to withdraw and prepare for the next. He stood, offered a polite bow, and walked out.

Cecelia sat on when he'd gone, stunned and shaken. She never would have imagined... But that wasn't true. A year or so ago, she *had* imagined him on one knee, his heart in his eyes, asking for her hand. She'd simply never thought that dream would come true.

As it had not, commented a ruthless part of her brain. He hadn't shown the slightest sign of kneeling. And hearts had not been mentioned. Still less love. With a sinking sensation, she heard his description of her again: "You argue for curtailed expenditures and considered decisions. You are an excellent manager and a master of accounts." What a cold and distant picture. He might have been describing a competent estate agent he wished to engage. He didn't think of her with love. She'd known that.

And she'd known that she must be the same—indifferent.

She'd tried, in the last few years. Whenever he was heedless or infuriating, she'd consigned her feelings to perdition. But before they could wither away, James would do something that belied his careless surface. He'd once spent two days searching the streets for her lost dog, and found him, too, after others had given up. He'd taught her to play cutthroat whist when she asked—partly as an amusement, she knew, but he'd seemed to take real pleasure in it. How they'd laughed when she demonstrated her new skills at a card party.

He'd stayed by her side at her court presentation, a polished, devastatingly handsome young man of twenty-four. His attentiveness had eased her nerves and increased her consequence among the *ton*. Last year, when her father had taken ill, James had actually called every day to ask about his health and showered Papa with fruit and the confections he particularly liked.

Whenever they attended the same gatherings, which was often, James talked with her and danced with her. No occasion passed without some interplay. He'd even defended her after she'd gone to that ball alone, despite his private criticism. She'd heard as much.

"But none of those are love," Cecelia said to the empty drawing room. She'd concluded that James viewed her as a sort of possession, a connection who was not to be condemned, except by himself. But not as a woman he might truly care for. She'd accepted the disappointment, hidden her affections so thoroughly that she was certain no one suspected, and resigned herself to distance. She was no languishing miss to sigh over an unrequited passion. She got on with life.

And then he'd come here and asked her to marry him as a convenience, to…hire her in effect to take his work off his shoulders. It was like one of those fairy tales where granted wishes come in a form that makes them horrid. The fates had fulfilled her dream in a way that she could not want it. Cecelia laughed. When the laugh threatened to turn into something else, she ruthlessly cut it off.

She was certain James would come to his senses and be glad she'd refused. In fact, she would be surprised if he hadn't already, now that he was well away. How sorry he would be if they'd become engaged! That would have added the final unbearable straw to this fiasco—to see him regretting his impulsive proposal even as he stood by his word. No, James would get over his pique and move on. He never lacked female company when he wanted it. Cecelia had become aware of that when she passed out of her first youth. There would be some awkwardness between them perhaps, and then this episode would be forgotten. Or, not forgotten. That was too much to ask. Unmentioned, rather. Receding with time until it began to seem fictional.

Her aunt Valeria strode into the room, bringing with her the sweet scent of honey. "Are you sitting here doing nothing?" she asked.

Nothing but shoring up the shattered fragments of my heart, Cecelia thought, and scoffed at her inner dramatics. "I suppose I am," she answered.

"You might have come and helped me put the caps on the hives then."

"We agreed that the bees and I do not get on, Aunt."

"They don't sting if you're not afraid of them."

"That is why you wear long gloves and a coat and a veil whenever you go near?"

Her aunt snorted a laugh. "Insolent girl. I do have extras of all those things."

"Thank you, Aunt Valeria, but I shall leave the bees to you."

Taking her customary chair at the table by the front window, her aunt said, "Very well, but you ought to develop some interests of your own." She opened her notebook and reached for a quill.

Did she mean that Cecelia was on the road to spinsterhood? With a future resembling her aunt's? The idea was unnerving. She did not have her aunt's intellectual rigor or her lack of interest in people. But if she could not accept James's chilly offer—of course not!—and she could not care so much for any other man, what was to become of her?

One of the footmen entered. "Several young ladies have called to see you, miss," he said to Cecelia.

"Oh good," said Cecelia, glad to have her thoughts interrupted.

"Oh blast," said Aunt Valeria at the same moment.

Inured to the older lady's manner, the footman did not even blink.

Cecelia had been expecting her new friends. It was fortunate that their visit hadn't coincided with James's. "Send them up," she said to the footman. "And fetch tea and cakes."

"Honey cakes?" asked her aunt.

"Of course."

"Well, I will stay a little while. But I shan't speak."

"You never do, Aunt." The words came out sharp after their previous exchange, but her aunt didn't seem to notice.

Sarah Moran, Charlotte Deeping, Harriet Finch, and Ada Grandison entered in a chattering mass. It appeared that they had taken advantage of numbers to dispense with duennas. Cecelia welcomed them as a happy diversion until their first words to her. "We passed the handsome duke in the street as we were coming here," said Ada.

"He looked out of sorts," said Sarah.

"He was glowering," said Charlotte. "I was so pleased to see it."

"Why would you say that?" asked Harriet.

"I like knowing that very handsome people have troubles. Men in particular."

"Oh, Charlotte, everyone has trials and tribulations," said Sarah.

"Tribulations? What a word. He was scowling. There was no plague of frogs raining from the sky. He'd probably mussed his neckcloth or scuffed his boot."

Cecelia didn't wish to discuss the causes of James's frown. She turned to Harriet. "Your note said you had something particular to talk about."

"We've received some invitations," Harriet replied.

"Harriet had the most, of course," put in Charlotte. "As she is so grand now." She and Harriet made faces at each other. "Ada is next because of her ducal fiancé."

"My charming personality," argued Ada.

"Or your frightening eyebrows," Charlotte teased. "Sarah and I are neck and neck in last place with only a few."

"There seem to be so many different kinds of parties," said Sarah. "We wanted to ask you how to choose."

"And how to go on at each sort," said Ada.

"I have begun a chart." Charlotte took a sheet of paper from her reticule, unfolded it, and held it up. A grid had been drawn on it.

This attracted the attention of Cecelia's aunt, who peered over at the page.

"I've put the types of events across the top," Charlotte continued. "Then there is a space for each of us down the side with our strengths and weaknesses. Well, not Ada. She is finished with all this nonsense."

"What nonsense?" asked Cecelia.

"Husband hunting," replied Charlotte with distaste. "Or at least seeing if we wish to acquire a husband."

"What other choice do we have?" asked Sarah.

"That is the trouble." Charlotte's scowl deepened.

"You will meet someone and fall in love," said Ada. "All of you."

"Because you did? Not convincing evidence," replied Charlotte.

"The bees have a much better system," said Aunt Valeria.

The girls all turned to look at her.

"The queen manages reproduction, and the rest of the hive has important work to do. Very fulfilling, I would think. They are all female, you know."

"I thought you could not…" began Charlotte.

"Except for the drones. But they are thrown out after they do their job. They are useless otherwise. They don't even have stingers." She noticed the stares. "There is no need to gape at me like a school of goldfish."

"We thought you said… That is, indicated that you could not hear us," said Sarah.

Aunt Valeria made a dismissive gesture. "If I am deaf, I don't have to take part in empty chatter."

The four visitors looked at Cecelia, then back at her aunt.

"But you hear perfectly well?" asked Harriet.

"I would hardly call it a perfection," scoffed the older lady.

"Aren't you afraid people will find out?" wondered Sarah.

"I think a good many people suspect," said Cecelia. She had mentioned this to Aunt Valeria in the past.

Her aunt's response was the same this time, an indifferent shrug. "What if they do? I don't care what the vast majority of people think. But you seem like sensible girls. I don't mind speaking to you. A chart is an efficient tool." She held out an imperious hand.

Charlotte hesitated, then passed her grid over.

"Balls are obvious, of course," said Aunt Valeria, reading. "Dancing. I like this." She set a finger on one corner of the page. "Opportunities for a scant bit of private conversation to judge a man's character. Well put." Her finger moved to the right. "Ah, rout parties."

"Isn't a rout a great defeat?" asked Sarah.

"The name makes one think of hordes of people running away in panic," said Ada.

"If only they would," said Aunt Valeria dryly. "That might be somewhat entertaining. Unlike the reality."

"Routs are large gatherings," Cecelia said in a bid to regain control of this visit. "The hostess hopes so, at any rate. And they do include a good deal of…milling about. People attend to pay their respects to the lady of the house and perhaps talk to friends. One stands, or walks from room to room."

"Showing off one's fine clothes," said Ada.

"Yes, and observing others. There is no particular centerpiece, as at a concert. Many only stay a little while and then go on to another party."

"That sounds quite tedious," said Harriet.

"Exactly," replied Aunt Valeria. "Which one are you?"

"Harriet Finch, ma'am."

"Ah yes, the daughter of the old school friend."

"Such an occasion might be pleasant if one sees friends," said Sarah, returning to the ostensible subject.

"Much of the interest comes afterward," said Cecelia. "In the gossip about who fainted from the heat or was snubbed in the crowd and so on."

"So on," mocked her aunt. "That would include the intrigues carried on in the crush. As if they would not be noticed. People in general are so very stupid." She returned to the chart. "What next? Ah, *conversaziones*."

"I've heard there are salons where serious topics are discussed," said Sarah hopefully.

"Those are smaller," said Cecelia. "With a much more limited guest list. Some are confined to established literary circles, along with people of rank and fortune who wish to patronize literature."

"I don't suppose they would invite us then," said Charlotte.

Sarah sighed.

Cecelia started to mention a friend of her father who held select evenings devoted to spritely talk. Lady Tate's soirees were known for interesting guests and competitive wit, as well as exquisite suppers. Then she hesitated. Perhaps it would be best to wait and see if the noble widow was willing to invite her young friends. Lady Tate might require some convincing. She wouldn't want to disappoint them.

"Venetian breakfasts," said Aunt Valeria in a contemptuous tone. "Such a ridiculous label."

"An afternoon party that may last well into evening," explained Cecelia.

"What is Venetian about that?" asked Harriet.

"Well, I don't…" began Cecelia.

"Nothing whatsoever," declared her aunt.

"I thought they might be on the water, with gondolas," said Ada.

"That would entail logic," said Aunt Valeria. "A trait that society lacks."

"Perhaps Venetians prefer afternoon gatherings," said Sarah. "I will…"

"Look for a book that explains the matter," finished Charlotte.

"Well, I will."

"Good for you," said Cecelia's aunt. "Research is never wasted." She ran her finger along the chart. "Musicales. That is rather obvious."

"Hostesses vie for well-known singers or musicians to entertain their guests," said Cecelia.

"I'd like that," said Harriet.

"Not I," said Charlotte.

"Card parties," read Aunt Valeria from the chart.

"Papa enjoys those," offered Ada.

"Young ladies aren't often invited," said Cecelia.

"Because they require some skill?" asked Charlotte sarcastically. "And we are meant to stand about looking vapidly pretty. Well, as pretty as possible, which is easier for some than others."

"You have a sharp tongue," said Aunt Valeria. "I like you. What is your name again?"

"Charlotte Deeping. Ma'am."

"I believe it's more the gambling," said Cecelia. "Some card parties set high stakes."

"Young men gamble, young ladies amble," said Charlotte.

Aunt Valeria gave a crack of laughter.

"Young men drink, young ladies shrink," said Harriet.

Ada snorted. "Young men roister, young ladies cloister."

Sarah thought for a moment. "Young men are educated, young ladies are rusticated."

"Ha," said Aunt Valeria. "I was right. Sensible young ladies indeed."

The four visitors looked at Cecelia. "Your turn, Cecelia," said Charlotte.

She surveyed their lively faces. "Young men roam, young ladies stay home." Though she felt her contribution weak, she received a chorus of approving laughter.

"Or so they would have us believe," said Charlotte when it died away. "I don't care much for shrinking myself."

Neither did she, Cecelia acknowledged. And she was happy to have found friends who felt the same way.

Four

JAMES'S CAMPAIGN TO WIN A BRIDE WAS DELAYED BY AN invitation to view a race between two of his friends in their new high-perch phaetons. The event ended at a country inn with a good many rounds of rack punch to congratulate the winner and some sore heads the following day. But he took up the issue when he returned to town.

James was quite confident of success. He had, after all, been acquainted with Cecelia for many years. He'd had ample opportunity to observe her, and he felt he must know her better than he realized. It was simply a matter of concentration and exertion. Clearly he outshone the fellows who had previously offered for her—those he knew about at any rate. And, without undue vanity, he couldn't think of any other gentleman of the *haut ton* who was a better match. Didn't the hordes of matchmaking mamas show as much?

He'd merely been too hasty. Women liked a bit of wooing. Cecelia was intelligent and impressively competent, but she was still a woman. He'd startled her with a stark question. He was sure she would see the sense of his plan, and fall in with it, once her pride was soothed. For that, he must be seen to have made an effort. He'd learned over the years that there were ways to get around her, if one bothered. And so he set about doing so.

Cecelia's father seldom went out, even during the height of the season. But he did attend gatherings given by his friend Lady Tate, a widow with literary aspirations, and Cecelia always accompanied him. These evening parties were not particularly fashionable. Indeed, James suspected they were a dead bore, but his appearance at one of them would impress Cecelia. She would see that he was serious. And so he'd gone to some lengths to procure an invitation. It had been more difficult than he'd expected. Lady Tate appeared unmoved by his new title despite her own noble lineage. She'd practically interrogated him about why he wished to come. He'd had to hint at his interest in Cecelia before she begrudgingly allowed that he might attend if he promised to behave himself. Without having any idea what that was supposed to mean, he had vowed to do so. He had rather resented her tone.

On the night, he dressed with care. Having been told that formal evening dress was not required, and suspecting that this was some sort of test, he decided on buff pantaloons and a long-tailed coat of dark blue crafted for him by Weston. Standing before a long mirror, he arranged his neckcloth in austere folds and added a single sapphire pin. Hobbs had achieved his customary shine on his boots, and altogether James looked what he was, a Corinthian complete to a shade. James had been told often enough that he was handsome. He didn't set a great deal of store by it, but women did. Cecelia would notice that he'd taken pains.

He found Lady Tate greeting her guests in the doorway of her large, comfortable drawing room. The widow of an earl, she had pale eyes, nearer gray than blue, and what appeared to be a permanently satirical expression. Her white hair was piled up on her head under an elaborate cap, and her purple gown was richly simple. Now about sixty, she'd been left well provided for at her husband's death and had famously stated that she intended to do as she pleased now that the "nonsense" of marriage and procreation was finished.

"Tereford," she said when James made his bow. "You did come. Not your sort of party, I would have thought. We discuss ideas, you know."

Did she suggest that he had no ideas? It certainly seemed so. "Most interesting ones, I'm sure," he replied.

"Are you?"

What was he to say to this? "So I have heard."

"Indeed? Well, your request for an invitation made me curious, and I always indulge my curiosity. Once."

Apparently she indulged in rudeness as well. James imagined that she thought of it as plain speaking. Such people usually did. He was saved from replying by the arrival of another guest, a bearded man in a turban who was clearly a friend of the hostess.

James moved forward into the room and joined a small but varied crowd. There were a number of dark-skinned individuals and several with Asian features. People's dress showed no concession to current fashions and yet was opulent and colorful. One woman had on the flowing wrapped dress of India. The turbaned man who had entered after him wore a brocaded tunic of cerulean blue over narrow trousers. An aged gentleman seated by the fireplace sported the powdered wig and skirted coat of a previous generation; jewels winked in the lace at his throat. Altogether an interesting grouping.

James was accustomed to encountering acquaintances at an evening party, if not good friends. But here he saw none other than Cecelia's father, gesturing emphatically in a far corner. In fact, he had never seen Vainsmede so animated. For a moment he feared that Cecelia had chosen not to come tonight, and his effort was wasted. Then he saw her, talking with a group of four young ladies who didn't seem to fit with this older crowd. They stood like a cluster of commonplace flowers in a bed of exotics.

He made sure that Cecelia saw him. Her look of surprise was gratifying. James gave her a nod and smile, but he didn't approach her at once. He intended to be more subtle than that. Instead, he went to speak to her father. As he crossed the room, he noticed the fellow Henry Deeping had introduced in another conversational group. The name came back to him—Stephan Kandler. No sign of Henry, however.

Nigel Vainsmede started when James joined his group. He did

not smile. Over the whole course of their association James couldn't recall a single instance when Vainsmede had been glad to see him. At fifteen, this had bewildered and wounded him. It no longer did.

They were about the same height, but Vainsmede was a soft man, not fat but well padded by indulgence, which had also blurred his features. His hair was more golden than his daughter's and his blue eyes less acute. Or perhaps they only seemed that way because he habitually evaded James's gaze. "I wouldn't have expected to see you here, Tereford," he said.

"Broadening my experience," James replied.

"Really?" Vainsmede actually looked interested.

A part of James wanted to say, "Of course not. Don't be ridiculous." Just to see the older man squashed. But that wouldn't suit his purposes, so he simply nodded.

Vainsmede glanced at his companions. "Tereford, you know."

The two men clearly didn't know. They looked at each other, at James, and then at each other again.

Vainsmede murmured their names, but the sound was lost as Lady Tate called for everyone's attention and began to urge them to chairs and sofas. Only then did James discover that the evening's entertainment was a reading from a new work on philosophy, followed by a discussion of the ideas presented. He strove to keep the chagrin from his expression as Lady Tate herded him to a seat.

James found he had made a tactical error. He was being placed far from Cecelia. He tried a lunge toward her, but he was trapped by the hostess before he took three steps and plumped down between two strangers—the man in the turban and one of Vainsmede's group. He might have rebelled and shifted his position, but Cecelia was settled among her bevy of young ladies by then, with no space nearby.

He fumed through the introduction of the writer and Lady Tate's retreat. The author—stocky, pale, and earnest—stared out at his audience. James resigned himself to a stretch of boredom.

The man began. "My topic tonight is Kant's statement: 'A categorical imperative would be one which represented an action as objectively necessary in itself, without reference to any other purpose.'" He looked down at a sheaf of pages in his hand and started to read.

Within five minutes, James was completely at a loss. Each of the words the fellow used was familiar to him, but they made no sense in the order presented. They were strung together—or rather woven into vast webs—that tangled in his brain and made him frantic to claw his way out. Now and then a concept wavered toward clarity, he thought, but it was at once overwhelmed by another spate of words, like a deer pulled down by a pack of dogs.

Around him, people nodded and murmured as if they understood and approved. James thought of himself as reasonably intelligent, but he couldn't make head nor tail of this argument. He became conscious of a longing to rise, flee the room, and run home at a pace that would sweep the confusion from his mind.

After a seeming eternity, the reading ended. There was a smattering of elevated applause. Lady Tate indicated that refreshments were available even as the discussion opened.

James made a restrained leap from his seat and strode across the room to Cecelia. Two of the young ladies in her party had risen, presumably to seek sustenance. He captured a vacated chair and resolved to defend his place against all comers.

"Tereford," said Cecelia. They did not use first names in public.

"Miss Vainsmede."

"May I introduce my friends?" She reeled off a set of names that James immediately forgot. There were far too many eager young ladies to keep track of in London. He wished they would all go away.

"Charmed," he muttered.

The two who had stood departed for the buffet tables. The others gazed at James with bright interest, showing no sign of taking themselves off. James became more certain that he'd chosen the wrong place for his initial bout of wooing. But he'd had no way of predicting the horrors of philosophical discourse.

"I must say I'm surprised to see you here," said Cecelia.

"Your presence was an irresistible attraction," James replied.

She blinked, startled.

It had not been a first-rate compliment. The interminable prosing had thrown him off. He could do better. He had to adjust. He never spoke to her this way.

"Not the philosophy?" asked one of the young ladies. Dark-haired and sharp-featured, she reminded James of someone.

He shook his head.

"I wouldn't have thought so," she went on. "Not your sort of thing at all."

How would she know this?

James's expression must have conveyed the question, because she added, "You are acquainted with my brother Henry."

Was he?

"Henry Deeping."

"Oh, you are the girl who despises everyone." He'd forgotten her first name. Henry had mentioned it. Charlotte, that was it.

"I beg your pardon?" Her dark eyes skewered him.

The remark had slipped out. But it wasn't his fault. "Henry said so."

"To you?"

"Yes."

"I shall kill him when I get home."

He should not have repeated it, of course. But James didn't think saying so would help. Best just to drop the subject.

"I do *not* despise everyone," the girl—Charlotte Deeping—added. "Only those who deserve it." Her fierce gaze indicated that James might well be numbered among them.

He needed to separate Cecelia from the feminine herd. But

as James was concocting schemes to do so, the two young ladies returned with laden plates. He admired the red-haired one's ability to juggle three at once. He didn't rise, however. He was not going to give up his spot beside Cecelia, no matter how gauche this made him appear. There was no other place in the room he wanted to be.

Plates were handed round. James endured a barrage of expectant and then annoyed looks. He pretended not to notice. Finally, the red-haired girl found another chair and dragged it over.

The ladies began to eat. James kept his eyes off the delicacies, though he was rather hungry.

"Would you like a lobster patty?" asked the one with fearsome eyebrows. She speared it with a fork and held it out to him.

He was *quite* hungry, actually. He took it.

After that, all four of Cecelia's friends began to offer him food, as if he was a zoo animal or a pet dog. Cecelia refrained. She was suppressing laughter though. James could tell. It *was* ridiculous. This was why he never sat in the midst of a group of young ladies.

Lady Tate approached with a tall, muscular young man in tow, clearly intending introductions, and they were all obliged to stand. "Prince Karl von Osterberg, may I present to you…" And she reeled off all their names with an ease that left James in awe. But she was the hostess, after all. She would know who she'd invited.

The man clicked his heels and bowed. "You have the best place to sit," he said to James. His appreciative gaze took in all the ladies.

Blond, with pale skin, jutting cheekbones, and hazel eyes, he had a deep voice and spoke with a slight Teutonic accent.

"Prince Karl is visiting London as part of his tour of Europe," said Lady Tate. "And he was kind enough to join us this evening."

"A pleasure," said the newcomer. He gazed at Cecelia. "You are the daughter of Nigel Vainsmede?" he asked her.

Cecelia nodded. She was still bemused by James's appearance at this gathering, when he certainly had no interest in this evening's discussion. And to see him sitting in a cluster of debutantes and accepting tidbits from their plates! He never did such things. He never offered her silly compliments. And yet here he was, and so he had. Did he actually intend to pursue the idea of marriage? She would not have believed it. But she could see no other reason for his presence.

"I was most impressed by your father's commentary on *Grund und Erfahrung*," said Prince Karl.

He was ruddy, muscular, and confident. If the prince had been English, Cecelia would have put him down as one of the hunting, shooting, hard-drinking fellows who infested the countryside. But his hazel eyes were sharply observant. There was compelling intelligence in them. And Lady Tate chose her company for mind not rank, though she did not mind the latter, of course.

Prince Karl certainly looked much more like a prince than the aging Regent, whom Cecelia had met when she was presented at court. The foreigner had the face and frame for a fairy tale, craggy and resolute. He was nearly as handsome as James in quite a different style.

"Perhaps I may sit with you?" the prince added, including all of them with a gesture.

Lady Tate signaled a servant, and another chair was brought. Once the prince was installed on Cecelia's right, their hostess drifted away. James shifted his seat a bit closer on her other side.

"Your father told me that you help with his work, Miss Vainsmede. You are a German scholar?"

"Papa was being overly kind. I merely do fair copies for him when he has finished his essays."

"You are too modest, I am sure."

She was not, actually. Cecelia was no kind of scholar. But she was rather enjoying his appreciative gaze. And even more, the sense that James was practically…simmering on her other side. The combination was exhilarating. "Are you also a student of Kant, like tonight's speaker?" she asked the prince.

"Indeed I am," he replied.

"Who is Kant?" asked Sarah.

"Perhaps the greatest philosopher of our time," the prince replied, only slightly pompously. "He sought to determine what we can and cannot know through the use of reason."

"And what did he decide?" asked Charlotte with her customary touch of irony.

"That our knowledge is constrained by the limited terms in which the mind can think. We can never know the world from the 'standpoint of nowhere,' and therefore we cannot conceive its entirety, neither via reason nor experience."

"Pure gibberish," James murmured.

For a moment Cecelia was concerned that the prince had heard. But he gave no sign.

"Standpoint of nowhere?" Sarah looked confused.

"I think it means we are constrained by our personal points of view," Cecelia told her. "We cannot get outside them." She had learned this much from her father.

"Bravo," said the prince. "You are interested in philosophy."

"I'm not really."

"Not?" Prince Karl's thick blond brows went up.

"I can work my way through the text," Cecelia replied. "With difficulty. But I don't find the…result worth the effort."

James made an approving noise, as if she'd taken his side somehow when she'd only told the truth.

"Wonderful," said Prince Karl. He leaned a little closer to her. "I am most happy to hear it."

"You are?"

"I have many other interests myself." His tone was almost caressing.

A sound rather like a low growl came from Cecelia's other side. It could not be James. He would never do such a thing.

"My…companions on this journey have arranged many serious

meetings and lectures, such as tonight." Prince Karl indicated the room with a small gesture. "They are of course interesting. I enjoy debating ideas. But I also wish to see more of the world before settling into a round of duties in my country. And thus I am so very glad to meet you lovely ladies." He bowed to them all from his chair.

"Really," said James.

He was piqued, Cecelia realized. He was accustomed to being the center of attention, even fawned over, at evening parties. But for the moment all the feminine attention was focused on the prince.

Prince Karl continued to ignore him, though Cecelia now thought he was very much aware of James in a sly, contentious way. "Perhaps you and your friends would show me about London, Miss Vainsmede? I cannot conceive more charming guides."

"Do you want to see the museums and the Parliament?" asked Sarah.

"I wish to do all that is proper," Prince Karl replied without marked enthusiasm. "I am very fond of dancing. Do you like the waltz, Miss Vainsmede?"

Cecelia nodded. Did he expect her to procure invitations for him? That would be awkward.

"The Regent not trotting you around?" asked James. "I'd've thought he would. Being German and all." His tone skirted the edge of rudeness.

"I have been presented to him of course," replied Prince Karl with the tact of a diplomat. "Our families are not closely connected. And we are, of course, of different generations." He turned back to Cecelia. "I have received a great many invitations. Perhaps you would help me choose among them? Particularly those events you mean to attend."

His interest was obvious. He was clearly singling her out.

"Cecelia is very good at that," said Sarah. "She knows everyone."

"Ah, then I may benefit from your advice?" The prince smiled at her winningly.

Cecelia could only agree.

"I'd be glad to take you to Gentleman Jackson's for a round," said James. "If you box?" His voice held an edge of challenge.

Prince Karl shook his head. "I don't care for fisticuffs." He managed to make the pursuit sound faintly déclassé. "Fencing now. You have a well-known school here, yes? Angelo's, it is called?"

"Yes."

"I should like to visit there." He touched a small scar at the corner of his square jaw.

James's lips turned down. He gave the prince a curt nod.

"I am at the Carleton Hotel for now." Prince Karl stood. He bowed over Cecelia's hand, not quite kissing it as he met her eyes. "I shall call on you. And your father naturally. If I may?"

She nodded. He was a bit brash, but she was intrigued by this addition to English society.

"Until then." He smiled at them all and walked away. Lady Tate intercepted him at once and steered him to the center of the discussion on Kant.

"An actual prince," said Sarah.

"Of some tiny country, probably smaller than Yorkshire," said James. "With a toy-soldier monarch."

The whole group turned to look at him. Cecelia met his blue eyes and felt a shivery thrill. James was obviously jealous.

"So many of them are," he added defensively. He leaned toward Cecelia. "Would you care to take a turn about the room?"

"To join the debate over *Grund und Erfahrung*?" she asked him.

"I don't believe you know what that means. Anymore than I do."

"Well, it translates as reason and experience, but that is all I know," Cecelia admitted. "Perhaps you wish to meet some of the other guests? Who are better informed?"

"I do not. I came to see you." James stood. He held out his arm.

Very aware of the interested gazes of her four friends, Cecelia rose and took it. He led her toward the least populated corner of the large room. "You don't think it's rude not to join the discussion?" she asked.

"I'd be more likely to offend if I did," James answered. "Because I should tell them they are speaking utter drivel."

"And they would observe that you reject what you don't begin to comprehend."

"It isn't worth comprehending. The 'standpoint of nowhere' indeed!"

Cecelia shrugged. If she had wanted to argue ideas, she would be on the other side of the drawing room. Seeing James sputter was far more enjoyable.

"You are not usually surrounded by chattering chits." He still sounded annoyed.

Had he forgotten the girls who had come out with her and supported each other through a first season? Those now married and gone? Yes, no doubt he had. "Should I not make new friends?"

"Like this prince? You are not really going to take him about town, I hope?"

"Do you?"

"What?"

"Hope that?"

"Are you *trying* to annoy me?"

"I never have to try very hard."

"Cecelia!"

"Yes, what is it? You have been strange and prickly since you arrived tonight. I don't know why you came." The proposal lay between them, but surely he would not mention that here before all these people. She trusted that he would not. And at the same time she longed to know what he felt now that he'd had time to reflect on his impulsive offer.

"I came to—" He bit off the words. He was silent for a moment, then said, "I made a mistake."

Cecelia blinked at this unusual admission. James rarely admitted to being wrong about anything. Ah. Her spirits sank. He *had* come to regret his proposal. Had he altered his habits just to come and tell her that? Surely he could see that was unnecessary?

"Do you attend the Yelverton party on Thursday?"

"I mean to," she answered, bewildered. "Along with my new friends."

James sighed. "It promises to be a pleasant occasion."

Platitudes now, Cecelia marveled. What was he up to? "Music rather than philosophy," she said.

"Precisely."

"And you are so fond of music."

"I like it."

"You endure it, James. With varying degrees of… One can't really call it patience. Grim toleration rather."

"That is not true. I appreciate a fine performance. But so often at these occasions we are subjected to a troop of amateur warblers. Or females pounding the pianoforte like half-trained apes."

"You are a font of complaints," Cecelia replied. "I would add 'tonight,' but your grumbling is habitual."

"What? No, it is not."

"Really? Make a statement of unalloyed praise. About anything you wish."

"I…" The most curious expression came over his face. "I am fond of a good claret."

"Oh dear, is that the best you can manage? Fi, James. Paltry. Not praise at all, in fact." Cecelia wanted to laugh at him, but the bewilderment in his blue eyes stopped her. And then she remembered that he had offered no warmth for her when he proposed, and levity dissolved.

"I should be going," he said.

And he went, leaving Cecelia thoroughly unsettled.

Five

James could see that Mrs. Yelverton was surprised when he arrived in good time at her musical evening. He'd been invited, of course. He was invited everywhere. But it was not the sort of party he usually attended. "How very good to see you, Your Grace," she said.

As he made his bow, he remembered that she had a hopeful daughter.

"I do hope you will enjoy Beatrice's performance," she added, confirming his recollection.

He couldn't call the girl to mind. Which suggested that he probably would not. But as he moved on into the drawing room, he murmured, "A pleasure." And wished Cecelia might have heard. He'd been brooding over her accusation since he'd left her at the philosophical evening. She was quite wrong. He did not complain. The very word was distasteful; it smacked of whining brats or fussy old women. He discriminated. He appreciated wit and cleverness. But that was entirely different. And he was full of praise for many things. He'd thought of a whole list. Too late. But tonight he would show her.

James scanned the crowd, searching for her golden hair. He spotted her at the far side of the room in a group that included her four new friends and Prince Karl. James set his jaw. The fellow was leaning over Cecelia as if she belonged to him, or at least as if she was his for the taking. And she was smiling up at him and laughing. A startling surge of anger ran through James. He'd seen men flirt with Cecelia, of course, and he knew she'd had offers of marriage. But none of those had seemed serious, and none had occurred after he'd made up his mind to marry her. The playing field had altered. He *would* triumph.

"Of course the best music is Teutonic," the prince was saying when James joined the group. "There is no one to match us in that area—Bach, Handel, Telemann, Beethoven, Mozart."

"Wasn't Mozart Austrian?" James asked.

"A similar sensibility," replied the other man smoothly.

"It is good that you think so, since Austria is the head of your German Confederation."

The prince stiffened. He started to speak, paused, then said, "I do not care to discuss politics. My tour is a pleasure trip only." He looked at Cecelia, smiled. "And it is becoming a greater pleasure each day."

James refrained from gritting his teeth, barely. "Didn't Handel spend most of his life in London?" he said. "He was practically an Englishman."

"But actually from Saxony," replied the prince. His hazel eyes were those of a wily fencer. With word or blade, James concluded.

"We English have Purcell," said one of the young ladies—the smallest one, with the sandy hair.

"Indeed," said James, though he'd never heard the name. He held Prince Karl's gaze, putting a wealth of resolve into the look. Silently, a challenge was proffered and accepted.

"Oh, there's Henry," said another of the young ladies. She waved.

Henry Deeping came to join them. He shot James a quizzical look when he made his bow, as if to ask what he was doing here. The greeting he exchanged with the prince showed they'd already met.

"Miss Vainsmede," said Prince Karl. "May I ask you a favor? Would you present me to Miss Yelverton? I should like to ask what she means to play. I am most interested."

"Oh. Certainly."

The prince offered his arm and walked off with Cecelia.

James was violently irritated. He didn't believe the man cared one whit about the music. He'd simply wanted to snatch Cecelia from under James's nose. At that moment, Prince Karl looked back over his shoulder, caught James's angry look, and smiled—a provocative display of strong white teeth that confirmed every suspicion.

James saw red. Cecelia belonged to him! That is, she didn't yet. He hadn't had the chance to persuade her. But he would! They'd worked side by side for years. They'd talked of intimate, private matters. They'd struggled to solve problems together. Obviously she would never prefer some foreigner to him.

But this foreigner was a prince, commented a dry inner voice. Romantic tales were full of princes. Rescuing damsels, breaking curses, vanquishing monsters. They were the heroes of all the stories. Where were the dukes? He recalled several who played rather ambiguous roles in Shakespeare. Had Bluebeard been a duke? No! What the deuce was he thinking? Cecelia was too sensible to be swayed by a title from some insignificant little country, held by a sneaking, self-satisfied…buffoon.

Princess, whispered that inner voice. Could any woman spurn that title?

James watched her, standing beside Prince Karl, talking to a younger lady near the pianoforte. Cecelia was smiling, animated, lovely in her rose-colored gown. James had never seen her look more desirable. Had she done something new with her hair or style of dress recently? Perhaps. Very likely. Something had certainly drawn his notice.

The prince glanced over at him with another brief, sly grin. The wretch was enjoying himself at James's expense. Apparently, he was one of those men who had to contend, to win. And he obviously thought that he was.

This meant war.

James turned and found that Cecelia's four young friends, and Henry Deeping, were all gazing at him. For an instant, he felt exposed. Which was silly. They couldn't know his thoughts. He might have frowned, but they didn't know why. He returned their looks, appraising now. A war went better with allies. Might these be his?

Henry would be on his side, should it come to...anything. The young ladies' loyalties were less certain. Cecelia liked them; she'd said so. That meant they must have some redeeming qualities. She didn't befriend just anyone. It also meant that she would care about their opinions. He should enlist them to his cause. If only he could remember their names.

James had never bothered to learn how to converse with debutantes. His chief aim in life up to now had been to avoid doing so, to discourage any false hopes. Was it possible to make friends with quite young ladies while not rousing wrongheaded expectations? How would one go about that?

"What do you make of Prince Karl?" asked the dark, spiky one.

Henry's sister, James knew her last name at least. And he'd been assured that she was not romantically interested in him. Her satirical tone seemed to confirm this. "Make of him, Miss Deeping?"

"Think, judge, evaluate."

"Charlotte," said the one with the ferocious eyebrows. She really was a fierce-looking girl. But she'd provided one name, which James appreciated.

"Well, it wasn't a difficult question," replied Miss Charlotte Deeping. "There is no arcane philosophy involved tonight." The glance she shot James suggested that she remembered his remarks at Lady Tate's.

"You'll never attract a beau if you snap at people, Char," said Henry Deeping.

Precisely what James had been thinking.

"Isn't it fortunate, then, that I had no such intention? There is no one here I wish to attract."

The red-haired girl choked on a laugh. Her name was lost to James.

Henry's sister frowned. "It is just...if he is to be pursuing Cecelia, I think we should investigate him."

Pursuing—the word vibrated in James's brain, making him think of hares and hounds, deer and thundering hooves. He had never disliked a word before. Now suddenly he despised one.

"He does seem to be," said the short, sandy-haired one. "Don't you think so, my lord duke?"

These were unlike any young ladies James had encountered in society up to now. He threw Henry Deeping an imperative look. Clearly amused, his friend said, "Is that your view, *Miss Moran*?"

"I just said it was," she replied, puzzled.

"We shouldn't talk about such things in present company," said the redhead.

"Oh, don't mind us, Miss Finch," said Henry. "I am only a brother, and Tereford has been acquainted with Miss Vainsmede for half his life."

"Half his life," repeated the girl with the fearsome eyebrows.

"Yes indeed, Miss Grandison," replied Henry.

His sister wrinkled her nose at him. James suspected that she knew Henry had been identifying the ladies for him. This time, he committed their names to memory.

"I wish Peter had come tonight," said Miss Grandison.

"Peter is Miss Grandison's intended, the Duke of Compton," Henry explained to James.

"They are to be married in May," said his sister, speaking to James as if he had no brains at all.

James had never heard of this fellow duke. He tried to imagine the man who had chosen to live with those eyebrows for the rest of his life. And then forgot all about him as Cecelia returned. Without Prince Karl, thankfully. "The music is about to begin," she said.

"May I find you a chair?" James answered. He offered his arm.

"We should all sit tog—" began Miss Moran. But James pulled

Cecelia away before she could finish her sentence. He looked for the prince and saw that he had been accorded a place in the front ranks of the gilt chairs set out for the audience. Triumphantly, he led Cecelia to a pair of seats near the very back.

"I had intended to remain with my friends," she said.

"Surely you see enough of them? They seem to be constantly about these days."

Cecelia sighed. "Will you complain about them now?"

"I do not complain! That was, and is, an unfair accusation."

"I don't want another argument, James. Let us listen to the music."

"There is no music."

"When it begins, in a moment," said Cecelia, exasperated.

He started to reply, stopped, started again, stopped.

Cecelia waited through this uncharacteristic wavering, puzzled.

"You are right," he said.

"I beg your pardon? Did you actually say…?" She gave him a wide-eyed stare. "Could you repeat that? I cannot have heard you correctly."

He brushed aside her teasing. "You are right that we shouldn't argue. I don't wish to do so. I came tonight only to spend time with you. I am determined to show you that we are an ideal match."

"James, you must abandon this idea of marriage. I have told you…"

"Because of Prince Karl?"

"Ah," said Cecelia. Much suddenly became clear.

"Is it?" he demanded. If she said yes, he didn't know what he would do. Something extreme.

"I see now," she said.

"See? What is that supposed to mean?"

She knew him so well. She had watched him grow from fifteen to manhood. She knew he had taken to sport because he was an instinctive fighter. Perhaps due to his dictatorial father, he saw life as a series of battles to be waged, opponents to be vanquished. "It means, I understand," she said. "You had this silly notion of marrying me. I'm sure you would have dropped it quite soon, even though my refusal goaded you. But now another man has shown some slight interest. And so you've turned this into a contest. As you are so prone to do. And you will not give up until you 'win.' But this is no boxing match, James."

"Of course not. The prince prefers swords."

"I'm not joking." In fact, Cecelia was experiencing a sinking sensation. She'd thought James was jealous, but he didn't care for *her*. Only for victory. She did *not* wish to made a prize in some sort of male game. Indeed, she would not be!

"Neither am I. You get nothing in life unless you fight for it."

His blue eyes seemed to burn. Perhaps with more than pugnacity? Cecelia didn't know. It was certainly not the soft light of love. She turned away and watched Beatrice Yelverton sit down at the pianoforte. Miss Yelverton took her time arranging her skirts and placing her hands. Clearly, she had a sense of drama, which Cecelia rather admired. "I don't agree," she began.

Miss Yelverton let her hands fall. A crashing chord startled the room.

"Good lord," James said.

It was followed by a ripple of quieter notes.

"I wonder," Cecelia said.

Once again a chord crashed through the room, vibrating with both volume and emotion. Softer notes chimed in behind.

"We are not to hear the usual insipid ballads, it seems," James said.

"Is that Beethoven?"

"I have no idea," he replied. "It is certainly—"

Another dramatic chord cut him off.

"Striking," James finished. He mimed pounding on a keyboard. A woman nearby frowned at them.

"We shouldn't talk while she's playing," said Cecelia.

"She is making it impossible to do so," he answered over another raging trill of music. "My luck seems to be quite out."

Feeling something similar, Cecelia set herself to listen. The alternation of crashing sounds and softer trills continued. It was the signature of the first piece, it seemed. Cecelia tried to accustom herself, but the loud bits kept making her start. Perhaps that was the idea. Or perhaps Miss Yelverton simply enjoyed rattling her audience.

She played for an hour, a series of pieces all at a high pitch of feeling. Oddly though, her passion seemed to reside only in her hands. Her expression remained distant, her body stiff, throughout the performance. When she finished, she rose and dropped a perfunctory curtsy in response to the applause, which was enthusiastic in some parts of the room and merely polite in others. Then she stepped away from the instrument.

"Beatrice Yelverton is a talented musician," said Cecelia. Her ears were ringing. The music had been better suited to a large concert hall than a private drawing room.

"Indeed," replied James.

"You cannot complain…criticize her skill."

"Did I make a peep of complaint? On the contrary, I commend her…ferocity."

The word was actually quite apt. The girl had played as if the music was an enemy she must subdue. "I can see why some people speak of attacking a piece," Cecelia said.

"Exactly."

"You would admire that."

"I do. I approve of people who seize what they want." He bent closer to her with a suddenly searing gaze.

Cecelia blinked, startled. She'd never seen him look that way before. Not at her. Demanding, possessive. As if he wanted to sweep her up and carry her off, right now. And damn the consequences. A sharp response leapt in her, ran through her like a flame. She wanted...*had* wanted so much. She'd resigned herself to a narrower life, but his gaze promised all she'd imagined and more. It made her reel. She was leaning toward James, she realized. His lips were mere inches away.

Cecelia became aware of the murmur of conversations around them. Guests had begun to move about, seek refreshments. They had become an island in a sea of empty chairs, subject to interested glances. She felt bared before them, perilously exposed. This was James. How often had she seen his selfishness, his disregard for others? Years of it. She could not take such a risk. She stood. "Uh, perhaps a glass of lemonade," she managed.

He rose to stand beside her, so very handsome, so...riveting. "Oh, are you warm?" he said.

She was. And she knew that her cheeks had flushed bright red. "You look...warm."

His voice caressed. James, who could be so cold, had set her afire.

He leaned closer. "We must..."

"What did you think, Miss Vainsmede?" boomed a deep voice on her other side. Prince Karl came up to join them.

Cecelia was caught wondering what it was that she and James must do. What he *thought* it was. What she could dream it might be.

"I was most favorably impressed," the prince continued. "I did not expect to hear Beethoven's *Sonata Pathétique* here among the English. And quite affectingly played. I have complimented Miss Yelverton."

"Wouldn't you rather talk to her?" James asked him.

"I have. I believe I just said so."

"Surely you must have more to say. About the, er, pathetic sonata, was it?"

"You have very little knowledge of music, I see," responded the prince.

"I prefer more…active pursuits." James's tone managed to imply that his interests were more manly.

"Beating other men with your fists?" Prince Karl's voice suggested this was a barbarous practice.

"On occasion," said James with a breath of threat.

The two tall, differently handsome men squared up in front of Cecelia, frowning, jaws clenched. James's fists were clenched as well, as if he might actually hit something. Their rivalry was ridiculous, and…quite stimulating. She had to admit the latter, though it seemed a base impulse. But she couldn't let them go on. "Lemonade," said Cecelia. "I should like some lemonade."

Prince Karl's head swiveled in her direction. He came to attention, not quite clicking his heels, but seeming as if he had. "Of course. At once, Miss Vainsmede. Come with me." He stuck out his arm.

James stepped forward to block him. "I was just about to escort Ce…Miss Vainsmede to the buffet."

"Yet you did not," replied the prince. "You allowed her to wait here, thirsty, while you postured and boasted."

"Boasted!"

James lurched, bumping the prince's shoulder in what could have seemed like an accident from a little distance. Prince Karl bared his teeth and jostled James in return. They actually strained against each other for a moment.

"Stop it," said Cecelia. The snap in her voice seemed to recall them to some semblance of manners. "You are creating a spectacle!"

She walked away from their shocking—and, yes, all right, thrilling—display. As she moved toward her friends, she was conscious of whispers from the crowd and speculative glances. Cecelia had to admit that having two very attractive men vying for her attention was…interesting. She'd been a creditable success in society up to now, never lacking partners at a ball or moderate male approval. But she'd never inspired open contention like that. The tussle had been…outrageous, of course. Improper, offensive. Not to be repeated. Would they come after her? Did she want them to?

On the whole, no. Not just now. She wasn't accustomed to mediating. There were women who kept strings of suitors vying with each other. She'd never been one of them.

She reached her friends and turned to glance back at the pugnacious gentlemen. Prince Karl had been snagged by their hostess. She obviously meant to make the most of her august guest. And James… Ha! He was about to be accosted by his grandmother, Lady Wilton. He wouldn't like that.

"Tereford!"

James recognized the harsh voice before he turned. He tried not to grit his teeth as he faced the small, gnarled woman who'd spoken. "Grandmamma," he replied. "I was just going—"

"You are *going* to talk to me." Lady Wilton grasped his arm with surprising strength and practically hauled him to a sofa against the wall, small but quite irresistible. Her snow-white hair was adorned with feathers tonight, and she wore a rich gown of cerise silk. Her scowl was all too familiar. "You cannot ignore me here, as you have my *several* notes."

"I have been much occupied."

"No, that is just what you have *not* been! Nothing has been done at the town house, as far as I can learn, and you haven't lifted a finger to find Ferrington."

"Who?"

"The heir to the earldom. I wrote to you about it. And Miss Vainsmede must have given you my message."

"I don't believe she did." James looked across the room. Cecelia had rejoined her four inconvenient friends, and they seemed to be having a lively conversation. Did he dare to hope that she was talking about him? Or would he rather she did not just now? She was even lovelier when animated. As for the fire he'd seen in her a few minutes ago—ravishing.

"More likely you forgot," his grandmother accused.

"True." It *was* more likely, though he didn't think that Cecelia had mentioned anyone called Ferrington.

His grandmother literally growled at him. "You are worse than Percival."

James began to be a little amused. "Really, Grandmamma! I am not so bad as that. My great-uncle was touched in his upper works, I think."

"Do not employ your ridiculous slang with me."

"I beg your pardon." He tried a smile.

It did not work on Lady Wilton. "Peacocking about town," the old lady muttered. "The handsomest man in the *ton* indeed. *Pfft.* A prancing coxcomb."

"Never that!"

"It is your *duty* to find Ferrington, now that you are duke!"

James had never much cared for that word. His father had been fond of it, and applied it to all the most distasteful orders he gave. Now he resisted whenever he heard it. "Why? Who the dev… Who is this Ferrington fellow?"

His grandmother heaved a long-suffering sigh. "The new Earl of Ferrington is the son of my scapegrace grandson," she said as if repeating a tale he should know. "We hauled him over here from America, and I assured him that I would train him up for his new position. Even though he was mannerless and ignorant. The next day, he'd disappeared."

"Had he?" James thought he might like the fellow, even as he envied his ability to flee Lady Wilton. "Well, I'm sure he'll return in his own time."

"You must *bring* him back!"

"I don't think I will do that, Grandmamma."

She glared at him. "Our family is cursed with useless, selfish men," she said.

But James was no longer listening. Prince Karl had escaped their hostess and joined the group around Cecelia. Once again, he was bending over her possessively. James ground his teeth.

"Prince Karl von Osterberg is making quite a splash in society," said Lady Wilton.

James glanced at her. She'd followed the direction of his gaze.

"He seems to be very taken with Cecelia Vainsmede, does he not? Everyone is noticing."

Damn them all, and the prince with them. James considered telling his grandmother that he had decided to marry Cecelia. Perhaps he could enlist her help? He tried to imagine what that might entail. So many people were afraid of Lady Wilton. What if she simply *ordered* Cecelia to marry him? The idea made him smile even as he recognized that Cecelia would not be commanded.

"Does that amuse you?" asked the object of his reflections.

He'd forgotten what she was talking about.

"Tereford?"

No, Grandmamma was more of a petty tyrant than an ally. She would want to manage him, and the choice of his duchess. Better to leave it. And her. "I must go," he said.

"Where?"

"What?"

"Where must you go?"

He wasn't prepared to explain the necessity of squelching Prince Karl. But just then a flurry of movement indicated that Cecelia and her friends were preparing to depart. James decided to cut his losses. He had to find a better way to court Cecelia than these wretched evening parties. He needed to get her alone. He *longed* to get her alone and show her how very much she would enjoy being his duchess. "Home," he said, rising to offer his grandmother a bow. "Good night, Grandmamma." He walked off before she could try to stop him.

Six

BUT JAMES FOUND THAT HE COULD SCARCELY GET NEAR Cecelia, and certainly not for any satisfying length of time. He was plagued by interruptions from a host of annoying other people. In past years, when it had been necessary to communicate about the trust, he'd often seen her in private. Too often, it had sometimes seemed, when they disagreed or her father was being particularly lethargic. After the trust was wound up, he'd thought he would be glad *not* to see her. And yet he'd always been drawn to conversing or dancing with her when they were at the same gathering, he realized now. She'd been a bright spot in otherwise tedious events, a constant in his life. Now suddenly she was too busy to see him, with her talkative new friends and the appearance of this thrice-damned prince. He began to miss her. He had not expected that.

It was the most frustrating situation imaginable. Prince Karl's attentions had caused other members of the *ton* to take more notice of Cecelia. She'd never been unpopular. She'd had an established place in society. But now she was, seemingly, inundated with invitations and attentions. If James saw her at a ball, she was besieged by eager partners. He could scarcely snag one dance. He was very nearly jostled to the floor during a rush to secure her hand for a waltz. And he'd lost out in that contest. How he'd wanted to flatten the wretched fellow who carried her off to dance!

If he sought her at a rout party, she was surrounded by annoying chatterers. His newly elevated status made no difference. They did not yield to him. Some seemed to make a point of cutting him out, in fact.

In the park, when Cecelia walked or rode, saunterers continually paused to have a word. One couldn't speak two sentences without interruption. James invited her for a drive, thinking to have her to himself in a phaeton at least, and was told she had not a minute to spare for the next week.

Maddeningly, everywhere he went to find her, there was the prince. Pushing himself forward, insinuating himself into conversations where he wasn't wanted. Prince Karl seemed to have an uncanny instinct for buttonholing Cecelia. James began to wonder if the German had spies roaming society drawing rooms, gathering intelligence about her movements. He certainly reveled in circumventing James. He turned Cecelia aside, stepped between them, diverted her attention. James was heartily sick of the man's gloating smile.

As he was disgusted with the host of young gentlemen intrigued by their rivalry. James had heard the idiots talking. What two great matrimonial prizes wanted must be worth winning—such a feather in one's cap! Dolts!

And if it wasn't the men, it was the women. They flocked to be seen with Cecelia and partake in the luster of her success. Along with her four new friends, who were always hanging about, she had acquired a constant entourage. The thought occurred to James that it was worthy of an actual princess. The idea was worrying.

Worst of all, Cecelia seemed to be enjoying her new status. He hadn't thought it of her. She flirted. She laughed. She glittered. She was newly entrancing. In a flash of time, she'd gone from being a fixture in his life, a steady, available presence to be counted upon, to a dazzling star in society's firmament. How unfair that this should happen just when he'd decided to marry her. And how unsettling to admit that the more others chased her, the more fiercely he wanted her.

James racked his brain for an occasion that would throw them together, allow them to be alone. He wanted to arrange a special outing, something she would particularly like. He ought to know what that would be. She must have mentioned things over the years. But he pondered alternatives without success. Surely she *had* expressed preferences. She must have. Had he somehow failed to notice? He had an uneasy feeling that this was not a good omen.

But he pushed this worry aside. He was engaged in an all-out battle. Look at the words people used about courtship. One laid siege to a celebrated beauty. One fended off rivals, cutting them out by whatever means necessary. Actual duels were even fought—or had been in less civilized times. He dismissed an attractive, fleeting vision of shooting Prince Karl. Out of the question, obviously.

One persisted in a romantic campaign until victory was declared by the announcement of an engagement. And he would prevail! He was accustomed to winning. He would get what he wanted.

He needed tactics, strategy. He couldn't remember the difference between these two things, but thought he probably required them both. In whatever order was appropriate.

James returned to the idea of allies. Wellington had assembled allies to defeat Napoleon. He still thought that the four young ladies who trailed everywhere after Cecelia would be useful recruits to his cause. The question was: how to enlist them? They hadn't shown any signs of taking his side so far. On the contrary, Miss Deeping and Miss Finch seemed inclined to mild mockery.

Remembering a quote he'd heard attributed to Wellington, "Time spent on reconnaissance is seldom wasted," James invited Henry Deeping to dinner at their club.

"I have decided to marry Cecelia Vainsmede," he said when they were settled with their meal.

"She has accepted you? Congratulations, James." Henry raised his glass for a toast. "I wish you very happy."

Leaving his glass where it stood, James said, "She hasn't yet." He surveyed his friend's expression. "You don't seem surprised by my news."

"Well, it's been rather obvious you were after her."

"It has?"

Henry raised his dark eyebrows. "After the way you and Prince Karl square up like gamecocks in front of her? Yes, James, it has."

"That fellow has shown up at just the wrong moment."

"To reach for what you thought was your own?" asked Henry.

"What?"

His old friend surveyed him with a wry smile. "You've been closely acquainted with Miss Vainsmede for years and never mentioned marriage. Not to me, at any rate. But now there's a rival on the scene. Suddenly you want her."

This was unfair. "I had decided to offer for Cec…Miss Vainsmede before this blasted prince arrived." James almost told Henry that he *had* proposed. But then he would have to admit he'd been refused. He decided to keep this defeat to himself.

"Indeed?" Henry sipped his wine. "I would have thought… You know how ferociously you respond to competition."

"Why do people say such things about me?" asked James, remembering Cecelia's similar remark.

"Because they're true?"

"Nonsense! I'm no more competitive than the next man."

"That would be the fellow you leave lying prostrate at your feet in the boxing ring?" suggested Henry.

"Will you stop joking?"

Henry held up his hands, signifying surrender.

James accepted it with a nod. "I have been developing my strategy. That is the overall plan of a campaign, you know. Tactics are the means used to carry it out." He'd looked this up and was rather pleased with his new knowledge.

"Campaign?"

"To win Miss Vainsmede."

"Ah." Henry's tone was still dry.

James ignored it. "I have concluded I need allies," he said. "Your support I take for granted, of course."

"Of course you do," replied Henry.

"Why do you use that phrase so slyly? Cec…Miss Vainsmede does the same."

"As if it was a truth universally acknowledged?" Henry's dark eyes laughed at him.

James began to feel insulted. If they meant to imply that he was some silly, transparent creature, they were wrong.

"I beg your pardon," said Henry. "Pay no attention. You were speaking of allies."

"I was." He was half-minded to drop the subject. But it was important to his cause. "I wish to enlist your sister and her friends on my side. By subtle means."

Henry burst out laughing. "You are never subtle, James."

"I am perfectly capable of—"

"Beating a point into submission," interrupted Henry through his laughter. "Flattening with a sneer."

"Happy to be such a source of such amusement," said James, feeling wounded by Henry's mockery. "I had thought you might wish to help me, as a friend."

"Are you asking me for advice?"

"I…suppose I am."

"You've never done that before. Not in seventeen years."

"Of course I have." James tried to think of an example.

"No, James, you haven't."

He actually couldn't remember having done so. Which seemed a bit odd. He'd *given* advice often enough.

"I suppose the first thing would be to make friends with Charlotte and her cohort." Henry smiled wryly. "My sister will be rather a challenge."

"I have no friends who are young ladies," James replied. Except Cecelia, who was both more and less than that. "Can one really be friends with them?"

"Them?" repeated Henry.

James frowned at him.

"You say the word as if young ladies were an alien species," Henry added.

"Nonsense."

Henry gazed at him briefly, then shrugged. "I've found that the best way to become better acquainted is to ask people about themselves."

"Ah. That would also make it easier to tell them apart."

"Yes, James, it should do that as well." Henry picked up his wineglass and sipped. Fleetingly, James thought he had the air of an audience member at a play. Then he turned back to his own concerns.

❧

Cecelia entered Mrs. Landry's evening party with a heightened sense of anticipation. This London season was unfolding so differently from the ones that had preceded it. She felt as if anything might happen. She'd never had a group of friends as close as the four young ladies whose company she now enjoyed. She'd never been the object of rivalrous attention by two sought-after beaus, along with a string of other young men who followed their lead. And most of all, she'd never received such marked attentions from James. Many nights found him eyeing her from some little distance, his stance positively Byronic, his mouth set, his gaze hot. She knew that the unfolding contest with the prince goaded him more than her surely familiar charms, but it was still a delicious thrill. The intensity of his look filled her with a heat that made her glow. She felt it elevate her to heights of animation she'd never attained before.

The excitement had led her to expand her wardrobe. The new gown she wore tonight was the height of fashion—a scooped neck and puffed sleeves on an underdress of aquamarine satin with an overlay of floating pearly gauze. Her mirror had told her it became her very well. She had a spray of creamy blossoms in her hair, and she could almost feel the sparkle in her eyes.

And there was James across the room, looking at her. In the past he'd come late to parties. Those he bothered to attend. She couldn't recall one where she'd arrived after him. Now the tables were turned.

He was gazing at her, single-minded, demanding. And so very handsome in his austere evening clothes—his broad shoulders filling out the dark coat, his face a classical perfection, his dark hair an artfully tousled Brutus. Things had changed so quickly between them. She didn't truly believe in it. She continually expected everything to fall back like Cinderella's coach reverting to a pumpkin. And yet the reversal was delectable. She nearly laughed aloud with delight.

He began moving toward her—a slow process in the crowded room. He was stopped repeatedly to speak with acquaintances. She wouldn't stand here like a mooncalf watching him. Cecelia turned away and joined her friends' conversation. But she felt it when James came to her side a bit later, even before he said, "Miss Vainsmede." The thread of connection that had long been established between them had shifted to a higher vibration recently.

His bow included them all. "Ladies."

A chorus of murmured greetings answered him.

"We were talking of tonight's tableaux," said Charlotte.

"Tableaux?" He frowned over the word.

"Mrs. Landry's daughters will be recreating famous scenes from ancient history," said Sarah.

Briefly, James looked appalled. Cecelia saw it. She wasn't certain whether the others did. She bit back her smile.

"You can see why they might choose to," said Harriet. "Clio, Euterpe, Melpomene, and Calliope." She ticked the names off on her fingers as she spoke.

Cecelia had rarely seen James at a loss. Even when much younger he'd been good at hiding ignorance. Now, he'd gone blank. She took pity on him. "Mrs. Landry's daughters have classical Greek names," she said.

"From the Muses," said Sarah. "Some of them."

"She took care to avoid the racier ones, like Erato," added Charlotte.

"And I would have chosen Thalia over Melpomene," said Sarah. Seeming to notice James's confusion, she added, "Comedy over tragedy, you know."

"It is also far easier to pronounce," said Harriet dryly.

"No doubt you studied all nine muses at Eton," Cecelia couldn't help but add.

"Studied?" replied James. His tone implied that she'd mentioned some alien activity. "I don't recall doing anything like that."

"How very aristocratic of you," said Harriet with dry disapproval.

She'd nonplussed him. James was not accustomed to being criticized. Cecelia nearly pitied him. But not quite. It should be a salutary process.

He turned to Sarah. "What part of England do you come from?" he asked her.

Cecelia blinked, surprised. This was not James's sort of question. Nor was he prone to such sudden, awkward shifts of subject.

"I grew up in Cornwall," replied Sarah. "Padstow. It's very near Tintagel."

"Tin…?"

"Where King Arthur's mother lived and Uther Pendragon visited her disguised as her husband."

Once again, James was clearly bewildered. He'd never been much of a reader. This was nearly as good as a play, Cecelia thought. What would he say? She had no intention of helping him.

"Disguised?" was the response he chose.

"Well, magically altered," said Sarah. "By Merlin. So Igraine would think it was Gorlois. And, er...ah, welcome him. Uther, that is. Because their union was fated and..."

Ada cleared her throat audibly.

Sarah grimaced in response. "Once I begin on King Arthur, I talk too much," she said.

James glanced at Cecelia. She gave him a sweet smile that said, no, she wouldn't rescue him. Why should she? It was too amusing to watch him extricate himself. Or not. She rather hoped he would not.

"Are you enjoying the season, Miss Moran?" he asked.

He was going to fall back on platitudes. Probably wise. But Cecelia gave him full marks for recalling Sarah's name. That was quite unlike him as well.

"Oh yes!" replied Sarah. "And as it is to be my only one, I intend to savor it to the *full*."

"It happens every year," James said.

"My family cannot afford another," replied Sarah.

It seemed James was not accustomed to such frankness. He said nothing.

"I will invite you to visit whenever we come," said Ada.

"You'll be restoring your castle for years. You won't be back in town."

"Have you a castle, Miss Grandison?" James asked. He seemed to be trying to avoid looking at Ada's eyebrows.

Cecelia was overtaken by a sense of unreality. James seldom bothered about other people, particularly unknown young ladies. He didn't care about their lives. That is, he never *had*. Was this a real change? Doubt intruded. More likely it was a ploy in the game he was playing.

"My future husband does," answered Ada.

"We told you about him," Cecelia said. This would be a test. The old James would never have remembered her fiancé's name or their situation.

"Ah, yes." James waited. No one elaborated. "I dined with your brother recently," he said to Charlotte.

An acceptable save, Cecelia decided. He *had* forgotten. But he'd recovered and lobbed the conversation ball in another direction. People didn't expect gentlemen to be interested in engagements and weddings in any case. Aside from their own. And sometimes not even then.

"I suppose he has to eat," said Charlotte. Sarah gasped at her rudeness.

James looked amused. Indeed, this seemed to be the first remark he'd enjoyed in the entire conversation. "As do we all, Miss Deeping."

A low exclamation escaped Harriet. It sounded involuntary and distressed.

"What is it?" Ada asked her. "Oh, your grandfather is here."

They all looked. James followed their collective gaze to the fat, choleric-looking man standing in the entry. "You mean Winstead?" he asked.

"Yes," said Cecelia, conscious of Harriet's unease.

"Winstead the nabob?"

Harriet scowled at James. "Yes. He became very rich and now he has decided to leave his money to me, so we must never mention the fact that he allowed us to scrimp and scrape all my life and said some despicable things about my father when he died. Before that, too. *And* I must not mind his 'abrupt' manners or ever lose my temper in his presence. He is to be catered to like a veritable monarch." She put her hands to her flaming cheeks. "Oh, I–I shouldn't have. I'm sorry. Please don't repeat..." The others moved to shield her from curious eyes, a ruffled phalanx. Harriet took a deep breath.

Cecelia threw James a speaking look. She knew he was no gossip, but he might inadvertently expose Harriet if he described this scene. Should she just say so? She tried to convey the idea with her expression first.

James held her gaze. For a moment, it seemed as if they were alone in a silent, intimate conversation. They *had* come to understand each other over the years. When it really mattered. He turned to Harriet and said, "My father was just such a petty tyrant. It is terribly burdensome, is it not?"

Harriet gaped at him, mouth and eyes wide. Then she recovered, blinked, and nodded.

Cecelia was equally stunned. Indeed, the whole group seemed to be. James was not known for sensitive confidences.

"But at some point they no longer have power over you," he added.

"When they're dead?" asked Harriet, then clapped a hand over her mouth. "What is wrong with me?"

"Mostly," James agreed, as if she'd said nothing unusual. "I don't suppose his health was weakened by incessant working?"

Harriet choked on a scandalized laugh. Charlotte looked at James with the first sign of approval she'd shown him. Sarah and Ada exchanged astonished glances.

James met Cecelia's eyes again. He raised one brow as if to ask how he'd done. She bowed her head in grateful acknowledgment.

"Oh, there's Prince Karl," said Sarah.

Cecelia watched James's expression turn sour. She didn't enjoy it quite as much as she might have earlier.

"His country is small and mostly mountainous," Sarah added, with the air of one who felt obliged to change the subject, whatever awkwardness that required.

"Not overly prosperous," Ada chimed in.

"His father is a grand duke, not a king," said Sarah. "Even though he is a prince. Which I don't precisely understand."

"How do you know all that?" asked Cecelia.

"We've been investigating." Charlotte was eyeing the prince. "Perhaps I'll ask him about the titles."

"Please don't," muttered Harriet, her voice still strained.

"Investigating?" asked James. He seemed torn between curiosity and puzzlement, with an underlying hint of admiration.

"My aunt Julia knows Countess Esterhazy," said Ada. "A little. And the countess knows all the Germans."

The wife of the ambassador from Austria-Hungary would be well informed about that part of the world, Cecelia thought. She hadn't realized that her friends had been making inquiries.

The prince had seen them and was striding over, the crowd parting at his martial stride.

"Good evening," he said, bowing and clicking his heels. He wore a blue coat with frogged closings and epaulettes tonight, more florid than the English style. "Such a garland of lovely ladies," he continued. "Like a bouquet of flowers—Miss Moran a daisy, Miss Deeping a slender pale lily, Miss Grandison a primrose, Miss Finch a ruddy tulip, and Miss Vainsmede of course a rose."

This sounded like a prepared speech, and Cecelia didn't think the blooms really matched their individual personalities. Prince Karl offered James a bare nod. It was returned in kind. They might have been two tomcats meeting in a narrow alley ready to contest the territory.

"What are these tableaux they speak of?" the prince asked Cecelia. "I have not seen such things before."

"It's all beer and sausages where you come from then?" said James.

"More likely a fine Riesling and *intelligent* conversation." The bluff blond prince stood in contrast to James's dark hair and blue eyes.

"You speak English so well, Prince Karl," said Sarah.

If there was smoothing over to be done, Sarah always stepped forward. Cecelia liked her for it, though she doubted it would do much good in this case.

"I am well educated. It is thought important *where I come from.*" The prince's deep voice held just a brush of menace.

"Tableaux," said Cecelia, feeling this had gone far enough. "The daughters of the household will be re-creating scenes from ancient history this evening."

"Like a play?" asked the prince.

"No, it is a static presentation. A curtain is drawn back and we all…appreciate the picture."

"I see. How authentic are they to be, I wonder? The ancients wore some scanty draperies." His gaze drifted over the crowd in speculation.

"You are offensive," said James.

"*Ja*? Perhaps my English is not so perfect after all." Prince Karl bowed to Cecelia. "I beg pardon if I said something wrong."

His hazel eyes gleamed with something. Cecelia didn't think it was remorse. Was he teasing them? She hadn't expected that.

The prince turned to James. "We had spoken of fencing. But we have made no arrangements. Perhaps you are reluctant?"

"I will meet you at Angelo's whenever you like," James snapped.

"That is the famous fencing school, isn't it?" asked Sarah. "I wish I might see inside. I've always wanted to observe real swordplay. It is so historical."

"Females aren't admitted," said James.

"I know." Sarah sighed.

"Because we can have no interests beyond embroidery and tea cakes," said Charlotte sourly.

"Perhaps we should hold a public bout," suggested Prince Karl. "So that the ladies might be…edified."

"A vulgar display, you mean?" asked James, his tone a drawling setdown.

"A demonstration of skill."

"I don't think so."

"Ah. Well, I suppose it would be humiliating to lose in front of everyone." Prince Karl gave Cecelia a sidelong look and a smug smile.

James clearly saw it. "I am not concerned about losing," he answered.

"Yet you have found so many excuses for avoiding me." The prince shook his head. "It seems like…timidity, shall we say." He cocked his head at Cecelia. "This is an English word, yes? Timidity? Like a *Maus*?"

"I will meet you where and when you like," said James through clenched teeth.

"Ah, good. Let us set a day and time."

Cecelia thought of speaking, but it was obvious that nothing anyone said would stop the two men now. She could at least signal her dislike of the plan, however. Gathering her friends with a glance, she left the gentlemen to their wrangling over details.

The tableaux began soon after this. The household had gone to a great deal of effort to show off the beauties of the four Landry daughters, creating elaborate scenes with pillars, vases, antique weapons, and draperies. The costumes the girls wore were not scanty, but they did show them to best advantage, and they looked terribly proud of their achievement. Which made it really too bad, Cecelia thought, that the effect was lessened by word of the proposed fencing match, which threatened to overwhelm their presentation. She caught murmurs about the contest running through the crowd, bouncing from one side of the room to the other. Inevitable since the two men *would* discuss it in public. Eyeing them, she decided that Prince Karl was very pleased with himself. James exhibited a mild glower. In other circumstances she would have put it down to boredom with the party. And perhaps it was, for he left before the tableaux were finished.

The evening lost some of its sparkle with his departure. Cecelia did her part in congratulating the performers. She talked with her friends and accepted the attentions of Prince Karl and gentlemen who were following the current fashion of admiring her. It was still novel to *be* a fashion and a little amusing to watch fellows try to top each other's empty flattery. But she was ready when the festivities ended and her group headed for their carriage.

Back home, passing the drawing room doorway on her way to bed, Cecelia was surprised to hear a voice calling her name. She stepped inside. "Aunt Valeria, you are awake."

"I am," said her aunt, who sat in her accustomed chair still dressed for the day.

"Why?" Aunt Valeria never waited up for her.

"Because of an irritating visit from Mrs. Mikkelson," she replied. "Who wished to be sure I was aware of the excessive attentions you are receiving this season. As I 'do not go out.'"

"Mrs. Mikkelson is a notorious gossip and generally gets her stories wrong," Cecelia pointed out.

"Undoubtedly." Cecelia's aunt snorted. "She had written out her whole case, in deference to my deafness." She held up some handwritten pages. "I was never more glad of that ruse as she soon tired of shouting at me and took herself off."

"I don't know what she could mean by *excessive*," Cecelia said, still absorbing this unexpected annoyance.

"More than you deserve, apparently. Though how such a thing is to be calibrated I do not know."

"Nor do I, Aunt."

"She particularly mentions that you attended a ball by yourself." Aunt Valeria shook the pages she held.

Cecelia sighed. "That was some time ago, before all this… And it is a mistake that I have not repeated."

"I know. But she suggested that this loose behavior had led to the increased male attention."

"Loose! The evil cat!"

Aunt Valeria sighed. "She is. And her type is one reason I don't care to take part in the doings of the *ton*. That and the crushing tedium. But I cannot entirely ignore my duties as your chaperone." She looked at Cecelia, waiting.

"The 'excessive' attention has been stirred up by the...interest shown by Prince Karl von Osterberg, who is visiting London. And by James. Tereford." Cecelia felt a degree of awkwardness. She and her aunt never discussed such things.

"Tereford. Ha. I often wondered if you and he would make a match."

"Us?" replied Cecelia inelegantly. Had her aunt guessed at the feelings she'd thought so thoroughly hidden?

Aunt Valeria nodded. "You are better acquainted than many young people ever get the chance to become and have been through much together."

"Much disagreement and contention," said Cecelia.

"Disputes are a sign of emotion, are they not? They do not occur where there is no..." She gestured as if searching for a phrase. "Buzzing," she finished.

"We are not bees, Aunt." Yet Cecelia was struck by her aunt's suggestion. Was there emotion behind James's prickly manner? What sort precisely? What if he loved her as she did him? No, that was impossible.

"If only you were," replied the older woman. "We would have none of this fussing. You would take flight, and the drones—in this case a prince and duke, ha!—would race after you, vying for the right to be your mate. The queen flies as high and far as she can to test her suitors, you know. Only the strongest can be allowed to catch her."

"Human females don't have that power," said Cecelia. "They must sit and wait to be asked."

"That is the convention," said Aunt Valeria. "But not how it works oftentimes. Look at your mother."

"My... What do you mean?"

"She decided she wanted Nigel. Lord knows why, but she liked him. Loved him, I suppose. Hard to imagine, but there it is."

Cecelia pressed her lips together to keep from speaking. It was exceedingly difficult to stay silent. But she didn't want to interrupt, and perhaps cut off, this unprecedented flow of information. She'd never heard even this much about her family before.

"Of course Nigel has always been the most indolent creature on earth. Getting him 'up to scratch' as they say was not likely. So Eloisa took matters into her own hands."

"Do you mean that Mama proposed to Papa?" Cecelia couldn't stop the question from popping out.

Her aunt waved a hand. "I was not privy to the details. I didn't know Eloisa at the time. And I never pay attention to such stuff. But from remarks that Nigel has let drop, it seems that she presented a list of the advantages of marriage, and he conceded."

"Conceded," said Cecelia. It didn't sound tender or passionate.

Her aunt, unusually, seemed to notice her concern. "It is rather a significant thing, for Nigel to concede."

Cecelia considered. It was true, in the world of ideas her father was a different creature—tenacious, immovable. If he'd agreed with her mother, he must have wanted her as well.

Aunt Valeria stood. "This is all very tiring. I must get to bed. You will take care with your flying, Cecelia, and not go too high?"

Though not certain what that might mean, she agreed. They walked upstairs together, Cecelia's mind full of new thoughts and wild speculations.

Seven

THIS WAS NOT A DUEL, JAMES TOLD HIMSELF AS HE MADE READY for the public fencing bout. Much as he resented his opponent and wished to teach him a lesson, duels were private matters. Secret even. This was more like…a boxing match. He'd attended many mills in fields or country barns with crowds of observers. But those were not fought by gentlemen or observed by ladies. No, this… performance that Prince Karl had engineered had no precedent.

James knew he'd been goaded into the match. The prince had chosen words that would enflame him—or any man, he judged. James didn't care. It might be a vulgar display, but he looked forward to trouncing the German blusterer in front of Cecelia. He enjoyed picturing the admiration that would show in her eyes, her disdain for the loser. She would see who was the better of them. Perhaps he would even go down on one knee and offer for her at that moment. It would be a dramatic finish to this battle. All of society would see him claim his prize.

The betting books in the clubs were running about even. James was known to be a skilled fencer. Prince Karl had boasted of his prowess, and Germans had a reputation with blades. Some of them saw dueling scars as a badge of honor. James looked forward to administering a sharp setdown to this one.

He hadn't expected the event to become quite such a sensation in polite society, though upon consideration he could see why. Novelty always attracted. People were vying for invitations with fierce intensity, guaranteeing that there would be a crowd on hand to see them fight. Prince Karl had persuaded an acquaintance to lend his extensive back garden for the occasion, and James had heard that the man's wife was in transports of delight.

Her invitations to all the leading lights of society would at last be accepted. James wondered what she would have done if the weather had turned rainy? Set up a marquee for this raree-show? Fortunately the day was fine.

James's valet ushered in Henry Deeping, who said, "Why do I feel like a second in an affair of honor?"

"Perhaps you are."

"I was joking, James."

"I am not."

"You don't think you're taking this too seriously?"

James simply shook his head.

The place was not far away. They chose to walk. James's valet followed with the case containing his fencing gear.

They found the garden crammed with gossiping spectators— some seated but most standing—surrounding a square marked out with chalk on the lawn. James looked for Cecelia and found her with her friends on the far side. She met his gaze. He could read nothing in her expression. She might have offered an encouraging smile.

"You have come," said the prince from behind him.

He made it sound as if there had been some doubt, but James refused to react. How often had Angelo the fencing master pointed out that anger did not win matches? In fact, it often lost them.

James removed his coat and tied on a wire mask often used in bouts at Angelo's school.

"Ah, you wish to protect your face," said Prince Karl. "I am not accustomed to that." He made it sound like a form of cowardice.

With a heroic effort, James kept his temper in check. They drew their swords and squared up for the salute.

Prince Karl was a hair taller, James realized, and he had a slightly longer reach. His arrogant confidence might be partly feigned, but it was convincing.

And unfortunately, it turned out to be justified. Three

minutes into the bout, James knew that he was outmatched. Prince Karl was a superb fencer, and obviously trained by a master. He was faster than James and had a wider repertoire of moves. James might be one of the best at Angelo's school. Prince Karl was better.

The points on their weapons were blunted. No one would die here today. But James realized that his winning reputation was in serious danger.

He fought grimly on, barely evading hit after hit. He grew winded while his opponent showed no signs of flagging. James tried a desperate flurry of strokes. All were parried without visible effort. His lesser ability must be visible to all by this time.

James waded in again. Prince Karl beat him off and then made a clever twisting motion with his weapon. The flat of it slapped against James's wrist so hard that the arm went numb for a moment, and he dropped his blade. The prince kicked it away, gave James an odiously triumphant smile that seemed to last for an eternity, and then bowed to the audience, receiving their applause with smug enjoyment.

James shook his arm to restore feeling.

"Hurts, does it?" asked Prince Karl, smirking as he straightened.

The stares of the crowd felt like lashes. His opponent's smile was insupportable. Cecelia was right there, witness to his humiliation. Shame and fury filled James's brain, sweeping away every other consideration. He stepped forward, swung, and landed a crushing left to the prince's midsection.

Prince Karl dropped his sword and folded over, clutching his stomach and gasping for breath.

There was a blank silence. The cream of society gasped, gaped, began to murmur, and then to chatter. The sound rose to a din that filled the garden.

James stood frozen. This was not done. The prince had not been ready for a blow. James had flouted the rules of sport. He'd been a poor loser, dishonored himself before everyone. His eyes found Cecelia. She looked shocked.

Abandoning his sword, James pushed his way through the thinnest part of the crowd. He ignored the stares—avid, gratified, sympathetic. Some people even looked frightened, as if he was going to start raining blows on bystanders as well. Did he seem berserk? Ought he to say something?

But he could not. Even now, the thought of an apology choked him. He fled. He didn't even remember to remove his fencing mask until he reached his rooms, explaining the puzzled looks that followed him down the street.

Once home he threw it aside, shut himself in his bedchamber, and contemplated disaster. He'd lost the fight. Decidedly, definitively. The least knowledgeable observer could have seen that. Prince Karl von Osterberg had shown the polite world not only that he was a better fencer, but also that he was more sporting. Why had he hit the fellow? He might have bowed to a superior athlete, graciously admired his prowess. He was capable of magnanimity.

Only in victory, a sly inner voice murmured. But it wasn't true. He had conceded others' skills. Hadn't he? He tried to remember an occasion, and could not. Had his hatred of losing driven him mad, James wondered. He'd behaved disgracefully. In the very arena that he had always claimed as his own.

James put his head in his hands. He didn't do things he was no good at, he realized. He was wholly unaccustomed to losing. Still less to making a fool of himself before the *ton*. Worse than a fool. What was he to do now?

There was a knock on the door. "James?" called Henry Deeping's voice.

"Go away!" replied James.

A brief silence followed.

"Wouldn't you like to talk?" Henry asked.

"No!"

"I really think…"

"No!" James repeated, shouting this time.

"I'll come back later," said Henry.

Listening to his friend's retreating footsteps, James decided to run.

⁂

Cecelia watched James stride away from the fencing debacle. He was moving fast; clearly, to her eyes, running away. He disappeared into the house at the front of the garden and was gone.

The crowd erupted like one of her aunt's beehives overturned. Exclamations flew back and forth. Eyes gleamed with scandalized delight at this unprecedented happening. Prince Karl stood at the center of a commiserating group, taking full advantage of their sympathy and outrage. He'd recovered from James's blow quite quickly, but he preened under the attention. A man brought his coat and helped him into it as if it was a privilege.

Cecelia knew that society was plagued by boredom. The progression of the season tended to be the same, year after year. Any unusual occurrence was avidly welcomed and talked over until every ounce of novelty had been extracted. This public contest had provided such an outlet, and now the outcome was even more thrilling. People would be chattering for weeks. Those who'd seen it would lord it over those who hadn't. The latter would languish under their pity.

The prince came toward her, his new entourage trailing after him. He moved like a victor coming for his prize. He was the former, she supposed. But she was *not* the latter.

"That was too bad," he said, claiming a place beside Cecelia as if by right and forcing her friends to step back. "He saw that he could not match my skill, of course. But that is no excuse for dishonorable behavior." His tone was complacent. He was enjoying this very much.

"Dishonorable," said Cecelia. She hadn't meant to speak, but the word popped out. Because it seemed unfair. Gentlemen were always hitting each other at their boxing club. James and the prince had been exchanging blows with actual weapons, though blunted. Should one punch make such a difference? The prince had hurt James, too. She'd seen the blow to his wrist and his flinch. No one seemed to be mentioning that.

"We had set rules for this encounter," Prince Karl replied, speaking as if to a simpleton. "He broke them."

It was true. Cecelia understood rules. She also understood how much James hated losing. Loathed it, despised it.

"He should have conceded defeat like a gentleman," said the prince.

Cecelia wasn't sure James knew how. He was so accustomed to winning. She looked around at the chattering crowd. They were used to seeing James best his rivals at everything he tried. James was a nonpareil. But now, all at once, he'd been beaten and *then* exposed, his humiliation made obvious when he'd snapped and hit the prince. A number of people here were delighted at his fall from grace. She could see them. Certainly James knew that, and she could imagine his chagrin. The terrible depth of it made her cringe.

That didn't mean James was right. It was only a sporting contest. He should have been gracious. Winning was not everything. Except that it had been, to a youngster who had no other power.

She saw Henry Deeping depart and hoped he might be going to James. A male friend was probably what he needed now.

"I require refreshment after my efforts. Shall we explore the buffet?" Prince Karl's tone was lofty. He offered his arm as if there could be no question that she would take it.

Cecelia felt a spark of anger. She wasn't a bauble to be acquired in some mock battle—not by him or anyone else. "I'm not used to witnessing violence. I think I shall go." Let him think her missish. She didn't care.

"Go? You cannot go."

"I beg your pardon?"

"You must help me celebrate my victory."

"Must?" He could not miss the edge in her voice. Cecelia did not understand why it made him smile, however. The prince's hazel eyes positively sparkled. "You *must* excuse me," she said. He bowed. She turned and walked away. Many eyes followed her. She didn't care.

"That was unusual," said Charlotte Deeping.

Cecelia realized that her four friends were with her. They'd moved up to help her make a way through the crowd. It was rather like being a small vessel cresting the waves. People gave way slowly, with stares and whispers. The company was a comfort.

"The prince is an outstanding swordsman," said Sarah.

"He did make it look rather easy," replied Ada.

"One can see why the duke wished to hit him," said Harriet quietly.

"Harriet!" exclaimed the others.

"I didn't say he was right to do it," Harriet replied. "Of course he was not. I simply said I understood. Prince Karl was so very smug about his victory."

They reached the house and traversed the hallway toward the front door.

"The prince comes here, a foreigner, and makes him look foolish before his friends and acquaintances," Harriet continued. "Anyone would resent that." She had been more sympathetic toward James since the conversation about her grandfather.

"Did you think he looked foolish?" Cecelia asked. A footman held the door for them. Cecelia was conscious of sidelong looks from her friends as they went out.

"Overmatched certainly," said Ada.

"Henry said that Tereford always wins his fights," added Charlotte.

"Yes." A surge of impatience mixed with the sympathy running through Cecelia. "Well, perhaps it will be good for him not to, for once."

The next day it seemed that society could talk of nothing but the fencing match. During a walk in the park with Sarah and Harriet, Cecelia heard the story recounted over and over, with wildly varying degrees of accuracy. She grew heartily sick of the tale, but the sly questions and sidelong looks that went with it were worse. "Do people actually imagine that a few minutes of flailing about with swords decided something about my future?" she asked.

"It is silly," replied Sarah. "Did you see Mrs. Landry's expression when she asked when we could 'anticipate an interesting announcement'? I thought she was going to slaver like a bloodhound."

"'Slaver,' what a word!" exclaimed Harriet.

"Well, I did."

Cecelia nodded. This was the other side of the attention she'd been receiving this season. Now the eyes on her were sharper. "Why should they think it has anything to do with me?"

"Don't you understand how they see us?" asked Harriet in an oddly distant tone. "We young women are commodities. Set out on display—as attractively as possible, of course—to be picked over before being acquired by an attractive prospect. We must take great care about the picking over—showing enough but never becoming shopworn. A fate worse than death! Look at a girl whose engagement has been broken off for some reason. Acquisition rejected! Where is the flaw? Sometimes, when we are all five together at a party, I can almost hear how they are ranking us. Pedigree, fortune, manner, physical attributes. Like goods on a shelf. Or horses in a race, to mix my metaphors."

"I think that's a bit harsh," said Cecelia. She was surprised, and a little impressed, by her friend's long speech.

Harriet nodded. "No doubt. But you've never experienced

a radical change in your 'value,' Cecelia. I have gone from being worthless to a prize in the course of a year, through no actions of my own."

"You were *never* worthless!" exclaimed Sarah.

Harriet's expression relaxed. "Not to my friends. And I am grateful. But to society, yes. I was. And the alteration has been… unsettling."

"You've changed since we've come to London." Sarah sounded distressed.

"Isn't that what I just said?" Harriet replied.

"Not precisely," said Cecelia. "There is something in what you say, Harriet. But young women have the opportunity to choose." She remembered her aunt's description of the queen bee's flight. That would be more satisfying.

"A few do. The ones at the top of the heap."

Sarah looked even more uneasy.

"There's Prince Karl." Harriet nodded toward the park gate where a group of riders was just entering. "He's gathered quite a following since the match."

Cecelia turned and walked swiftly toward a line of shrubbery. "I don't want to speak to him today." She particularly didn't want to be the target of all eyes while she did so. She stepped around a bush and out of sight of the gate.

Sarah and Harriet followed smoothly, but their successful evasion of one peril led them slap into another.

"Miss Vainsmede," called an imperious voice from a side path. Lady Wilton, leaning on a cane and the arm of a maid, stumped up to them. She stopped very close to Cecelia and peered up into her face. "Where has he gone?" she demanded.

"I beg your pardon?"

"Tereford. Where has he gone? He is not at his rooms. His man seems to have no idea where he is."

"What?" Feeling crowded, Cecelia backed up a step.

"Is there something wrong with your hearing, girl? He has not been seen since that idiotic sword fight. Where is he?"

"I don't know." Surely Lady Wilton must be mistaken.

"Well, you ought to know. You have let this matter get out of hand."

"I? What has it to do…"

"You know very well what I mean."

Cecelia stood straighter, resenting the old woman's dismissive tone. "I assure you that I do not, Lady Wilton."

"A woman can always maneuver a man if she makes the effort."

"Indeed? Can you give me lessons?"

"Don't be insolent with me, girl!"

"I was quite sincere. Wasn't I, Harriet?"

Harriet started, surprised to be brought into the conversation. Then she bit back a smile.

Lady Wilton scowled at all of them. "This is an outrage! Tereford has important matters to attend to. He shouldn't be playing with swords, and he certainly can't go off sulking like a spoiled child." She fixed her intimidating gaze on Cecelia. "I expect you to do something about this."

"Then I fear you will be disappointed, ma'am."

"Miss Impertinence! How dare you speak to me so?"

"I did not mean to be rude. Simply clear. Tereford is not my responsibility."

"You've decided to take the prince then?" asked the old woman. She shrugged. "I'm not certain that is wise. He comes from a small, insignificant country. Nothing to compare with an English duke."

Cecelia had to struggle with a flood of anger. "There has been no occasion for a *decision*. Nor do I have any expectation of making one. Of *any* kind."

"He hasn't offered? After the way he hovers over you? I know foreign manners can be different, but that is outside of enough." Lady Wilton appeared quite indignant on her behalf.

"Like a gourmand debating his choice in a chocolate box," said Harriet.

"What?" James's grandmother swiveled to frown at her.

Harriet looked as if she wished she'd kept silent.

Lady Wilton examined her from head to toe. "Improved expectations do *not* give you a license to say whatever you please," she said. "Still less to be offensive."

"She wasn't," said Sarah.

This brought Lady Wilton's glare over to her. "In my day, girls did not speak unless spoken to. And often not even then!"

"So you were silent and demure?" asked Cecelia. "I beg your pardon, but it is difficult to picture, ma'am."

Lady Wilton gave a snort of laughter. "That is neither here nor there. We were speaking about James. You must find him and bring him to me, Miss Vainsmede. I insist!"

"I cannot promise that," replied Cecelia. She sketched a curtsy. "We must not keep you from your walk any longer, ma'am." She moved away quickly and managed to ignore Lady Wilton's burst of indignation.

That did not end the matter, however. Cecelia was asked about James over and over through the remainder of their outing, as if she was some sort of authority on his movements. And his absence was the talk of the party she attended that evening.

By the end of the following day word had spread everywhere that the new Duke of Tereford had disappeared from London society.

The gossips went wild.

Eight

JAMES CANTRELL, AT THE END OF HIS FIRST MONTH AS ONE OF the highest-ranking peers in the realm, sat in a house crammed with broken-down furnishings and decided that his life had become a rather similar mare's nest. Somehow, steps that had seemed reasonable one by one had led him to that blow at the end of the fencing match. And its consequences, which he must of course face. Just not now.

He'd discovered one functional bedchamber on the first floor of his great-uncle's town house. It contained the customary furnishings, not an insane, dusty tangle of discarded items. The single servant had clearly cleaned and aired it out before she departed. The sheets on the bed were fresh, and whatever clutter Uncle Percival had left was tidied away. The previous duke's clothes remained in the wardrobe, however, and his shaving gear on the washstand. James hadn't brought himself to use either. He still wore the shirt, coat, and breeches in which he'd fought the disastrous bout. His cheeks rasped with whiskers. His hair had been left to its own devices.

James was aware of the irony, and that he was sulking. But awareness seemed to make no difference to his mood. He couldn't bear to see anyone after that shameful public loss. It was all too easy to envision the stares, the titters, the sly enjoyment of men he'd bested in the past. The pity! He would not endure it. His distinguished place in society was based on his athletic prowess, his enviable style, his unflappable manner. Now, with one foolish impulse, he'd destroyed the identity he'd been shaping since he was fifteen years old. He couldn't see, at this point, what he was to put in its place.

So he stayed quiet in the large, eerie house. He didn't use lights where they could be seen from the street. He lit no fire in the bedchamber. When twilight fell, he sneaked out a side door with his hat pulled low, swathed in a scarf from his great-uncle's wardrobe, to buy pies from a nearby shop. The greasy pastry barely sufficed to keep body and soul together. He was increasingly hungry, and the poor diet was upsetting his innards as well. Fortunately, his great-uncle hadn't interfered with the wine cellar. James had made good use of the dusty bottles there and was not reduced to the water pump in the kitchen.

Perhaps too good a use, he decided as he stared into the mirror on a gray rainy morning. He barely recognized the image staring back at him. There were smudges of dirt on his clothes despite all his care. This place was rife with dust. His scruff of whiskers shadowed his face. His hair stood up in lamentable spikes, and he hadn't even put on his neckcloth today. The open collar below his stubbled chin demonstrated an utter abandonment of standards. He'd lost the person he had been. He was no longer the Corinthian who'd led society before the prince defeated him.

James turned away from the mirror. He knew this was unacceptable. He had to return to his rooms and take up his life. But he wasn't ready to do so until he could see what it would be after this.

He left the bedchamber and edged along a corridor nearly filled with detritus. This house made one feel like a serpent, slithering through narrow spaces, bending and twisting around a dusty maze. He navigated the obstacles to the room he'd chosen to begin the work of clearing away. It was the smallest he could find on the ground floor, which had been his sole criteria. A place to begin when isolation and boredom had goaded him into action.

He wedged into the space he'd dealt with so far. He'd found a few things he wanted to keep and taken those to his bedchamber. When he had this space emptied, he would store them here, lest it also fill up around him. Items he wished to be rid of went out a window that opened onto a walled garden. He'd forced a path to the window and thrown it open first thing in a bid to disperse the musty smell.

James confronted the jumbled pile of *things*. What had been in Uncle Percival's mind as he accumulated all this? How had he not seen the madness?

James reached into the mass and pulled out a large hourglass in a carved wooden frame. Rubbing at the dust covering it, he found that the glass was cracked in several places. The sand had run out. "How very apt," he told the air. "But I find it difficult to appreciate the humor." He carried the hourglass to the window and tossed it onto the pile of moth-eaten tapestries he'd thrown down to muffle any noise from his discards.

As he turned back, a thumping sound intruded. Someone was knocking on the front door. He stood still until the rhythm stopped, and then for a few minutes afterward. This had happened once before. Whoever it was could go away.

When he felt certain they had departed, he went back to work, pulling out a burnished case that looked as if it might hold dueling pistols. Those would come in handy if he decided to shoot himself. "Not amusing," he said aloud to whatever aberrant part of his brain had produced this thought. "Not in the least."

Opening the case he discovered a set of flint blades that looked very ancient. They were beautifully crafted—a spearhead and several knives. He couldn't imagine how anyone had made such exquisite leaf-like shapes with primitive tools. He picked one up and sliced a tiny cut in the ball of his thumb. They were incredibly sharp, as effective now as when they were created centuries ago. Carefully, he set the blade back in the case. He would keep these, he decided, though he had no use for them. They were too lovely to discard.

He set the case aside and went to haul out a massive wooden chair. Various small items rained on his head as he pulled. Narrow and probably nine feet tall, the seat had an ornately carved canopy that towered over him. This looked like something a Tudor king would sit in while he ate his way through your stores on a royal visit. It was also riddled with woodworm. Powdery residue darkened his hands. When he yanked again, one arm came loose and fell off, eaten through by the pests. Which made it much easier to chuck the chair out the window onto the pile of fabric.

With the chair gone, the mound of rubbish in the room groaned, tilted, and resettled, fortunately without burying him in a painful avalanche. A skitter of tiny feet told James that the local residents were not pleased by his incursion. "Your days are numbered," he declared.

"And now you are speaking to mice," he added. "Splendid." He reached for the next bit of ducal inheritance.

≪≫

Cecelia felt certain that James was in the town house. She didn't know why, but she was sure he'd gone there. And whatever she'd told Lady Wilton, she couldn't resist checking her intuition. She'd come to Tereford House alone, however, in a plain dress and bonnet to avoid servants' gossip.

She'd pounded on the front door and called out to him, with no result. Unsurprised, she walked around the corner to the mews behind the house. She did not sneak, but she did check to see that no one was watching before she slipped into the narrow cobbled lane.

The house wall turned the corner and extended along it. Cecelia soon came to the stables that served the town house. They were closed up, naturally. She tried the door beside the larger carriage portals, expecting it to be locked, and found that it opened easily under her hand. She stepped inside and came face-to-face with a very thin, worn-looking woman in a threadbare stuff gown.

For a moment, they were equally startled. Cecelia nearly dropped the basket she held over her arm. Then the woman scowled and said, "What do you mean, walking in here without so much as a by-your-leave?"

"I didn't realize anyone was here," replied Cecelia.

"Well, we are."

There was a quiver in the woman's voice. Several ragged, skinny children peered from behind her skirts. "Did you work for the old duke?" Cecelia asked.

A flash of fear in the woman's pale-blue eyes told Cecelia that matters were not that simple. "The old man's dead," the woman said. "And we ain't leaving."

She looked desperately tired. Examining the group more closely, Cecelia concluded that this poor family had somehow discovered the unusual situation and taken advantage of it to move into the empty building. So, despite her bravado, the woman must know that they could be ejected at any time. But it wasn't Cecelia's place to do so, even had she wished to. "I don't care about that," she said. "I just want to get inside the house."

"There's a little door in back," said one of the children, a boy who looked about ten. "Mostly they forget to lock it."

"Ned!" exclaimed his mother. She evaded Cecelia's eyes, making Cecelia wonder if they slipped inside now and then to steal small bits they could sell. No one would ever discover the losses from the old duke's hoard. In fact, she thought this might be a worthy use for some of it.

"I ain't gone in since the new fellow come," said Ned with an air of wounded virtue.

"New fellow?" asked Cecelia.

"Been here a day or so. Came through the front real quiet like. We was thinking he might be…"

"Ned," repeated his mother.

The boy fell silent.

He must be referring to James. She'd been right then. "Will you show me this door, please?"

Ned glanced at his mother for permission, received a defeated shrug, and led Cecelia through the dim, neglected stables and out into a cobbled yard behind the house. In better light she could see that the boy's clothing consisted of layers of tattered garments. Beneath them he was even thinner than he'd first appeared. The family was obviously destitute with no home to go to.

He took her over to a low door at the back of the house. As he'd promised it opened without difficulty. Cecelia dug in her reticule for a coin and handed it to the lad, then shut the door on his incredulous delight. Not wishing to be followed, she shot the bolt.

She was in a small, dark space facing a stair leading down to the cellar. Light came through a half-open door on the right. She went through it into the kitchen, large and echoing. She saw no sign that the room had been used recently. The hearth was cold. But at least it was not crammed with things like the other rooms she'd seen here.

She made her way quietly across it and down the cluttered corridor to the front entry. There she stood still, listening. At first there was nothing, just the vacancy of a cold, empty house. Then something—a quick, sharp exclamation came from the hallway she'd just traversed.

She followed continuing sounds to a cross corridor and then to a small chamber at the back corner of the house. There she found James maneuvering a battered footstool out of the ceiling-high pile.

Cecelia stopped in the doorway, shocked by his appearance. He looked like a vagabond—dusty, unshaven, disheveled. She'd never seen James in such a state in all the years of their acquaintance. A small sound escaped her.

James whirled, dropping the footstool. He stared as if she was an apparition. "What are you doing here? How did you get in?"

"I was looking for you," she answered. "Of course. Everyone is wondering where you are."

His dark brows came together in a scowl, and his fists clenched. "It's no business of theirs." He glared at her. "I suppose you told *everyone* you were coming here to look for me."

"No, James, I did not."

His features relaxed a bit.

Cecelia breathed the stale mustiness that permeated the house. The air was full of dust. "How can you stay in this place?"

He grimaced. "Uncle Percival's bedchamber is…not insupportable." He put a hand to his chin as if suddenly conscious of its unshaven state. "So now you know where I am. You can go."

"You won't even offer me a cup of tea?"

"I have none."

"There must be some tea left in the kitchen."

It seemed he had not thought of this. "I have no idea." There was a spark of longing in his blue eyes.

"Also, I brought you scones."

The longing ignited into burning avarice.

"As well as some other things," Cecelia continued. "Bread and cheese and apples. Because I couldn't imagine, if you had come here, what you'd been eating."

"Pies," he said hollowly. "Horrible, greasy pies. With ominously unidentifiable fillings."

"Oh, poor James."

"May I have an apple?"

She took one from her basket and tossed it to him. He caught it and bit in as if he was starving. "I will even make the tea if we can find some," she added.

James devoured the apple as they navigated past the piles of hoarding to the kitchen. Cecelia found a nearly empty box of tea in a cupboard and began to fill a kettle at the pump. "Will you make a fire? Can you?"

"Of course. May I have a scone first?" James reached toward the basket she'd set on the table and seemed to notice the dirt under his fingernails. He drew back. Cecelia set the kettle aside, took the cloth from the basket, and gave him a scone.

He took a bite. "Ah." He gobbled it up in seconds.

He started a small fire in the hearth, then ate a second scone as they sat on a wooden bench and waited for the kettle to boil.

"You must be quite uncomfortable here," Cecelia said.

He looked away, annoyed or ashamed. She couldn't tell.

"You cannot stay on. You should go home, James."

His jaw tightened. "I suppose everyone is talking about the fencing match."

She could not deny it.

"That never would have happened if you'd simply accepted my offer."

"What?" She couldn't believe she'd heard him correctly.

"Or if I hadn't ever thought of marrying you," he added as if conceding a point. "But I have."

Cecelia simply stared.

James's petulant expression slowly shifted, as if an idea was unfolding in his brain. He gazed at her. "You know, if we were to announce our engagement now, everyone would see that Prince Karl hadn't really won anything."

"I beg your pardon?"

"You may have it and welcome if you do as I ask. Finally."

The kettle boiled, sending a plume of steam into the chilly air. There was a fireplace poker standing right next to it. Very tempting. Resisting its silent blandishment, Cecelia rose to go. She considered taking the basket of food away with her, but she couldn't quite leave him to starve.

"Where are you going?" he asked as she walked toward the back door.

"Home."

"You're not going to make the tea?"

She turned to glare at him. "You expect me to make tea for you after what you've said?"

"What?" He gazed at her blankly.

"Did you not *hear* yourself try to blame me for your foolishness?"

"But you—"

"*I* did not behave like a childish rudesby or throw a punch at Prince Karl after losing a fencing match!"

He winced.

Cecelia turned back toward the exit.

"Wait. You aren't going to leave me here?"

She felt like the kettle, steaming with exasperation. "No, James, you are 'leaving' yourself here. It has nothing to do with me."

"I thought you came to help."

"Did you?" Why had she come? Curiosity chiefly, she supposed. Though she had brought food. She had been worried.

"But you have always helped me."

His tone stopped her. He sounded so much younger suddenly.

"I've gotten myself into a tangle that I have no idea how to escape," he added.

The timbre of his voice took Cecelia back to a moment not long after they'd first met. He'd been fifteen, and even though she was years younger, a lifetime of dealing with her wayward father had sharpened her emotional "ear." She'd understood that behind his sulky ill temper, he was lost and in pain and near tears. And that he would rather die than let her see him cry. Her heart had responded. She'd had to help him then. And so many times after.

She sighed. They were adults now, and this tangle was entirely of his own making. It wasn't a serious matter. Only humiliating. Everyone had to deal with humiliations now and then in life, if they grew up. And to speak again of marriage as if it was simply another chore she could perform for him, upending her life for his convenience, expecting no tender sentiment… She shoved aside the hurt and the longing and any idiotic slivers of hope that tried to creep in. "I have helped," she answered. "I came to check on you. I brought you food. I have been a friend. You must find your own way out of the tangle *you* created."

"You are choosing the prince then?" he asked in a hard voice.

Cecelia felt an almost irresistible desire to throttle him. "*Why* do people ask me this? Does no one understand that your ridiculous posturing had nothing to do with me? *I* did not ask you to jostle each other like vulgar children. Or to bash each other with swords."

"Foils," he said.

Her hands rose of their own accord, crooked into claws. She struggled with the impulse and won, lowering them again. "This is not a case of me choosing anything," she said through clenched teeth. "Except that right now I am choosing to go."

"Will you come to visit again?"

"Do you ever listen to me, James? Even the least little bit?"

"If I apologize?"

She blinked. He never apologized.

"And admit you are right," he added in a cajoling tone.

"Let us see if you can," answered Cecelia too curious to resist.

"I…" He looked around as if an apology might be lurking in a corner of the kitchen. He seemed to notice the jet of steam for the first time and moved the kettle off the fire. "I am sorry."

"For?"

"Making you angry."

This was so typical of him. "And for not persuading me to do as you wish."

"Well, of course that." He smiled. Even in his current disreputable state, the smile was charming.

Cecelia ignored it. "And I am right that…"

His perplexed expression was almost comical. Or it would have been if Cecelia had not allowed herself a foolish instant of optimism. She abandoned it. "You can't think of anything, can you?"

"What if I simply say that you are right about everything?"

"And so, admitting this, you will go back to your rooms and stop behaving like a spoilt child?"

He frowned, shook his head.

She sighed, wondering why she kept on, and turned toward the door.

"Cecelia."

She stopped. It was so difficult to resist the appeal in that voice. Even when she knew it was the only sensible course of action. She couldn't quite abandon him. "The poor family in the stables would probably do errands for you if you paid them," she said.

"There are servants here?"

"Well, I don't think they've ever been servants. They are more...opportunists."

"In the stables?"

"Yes."

"Living there without leave? Like gypsies?"

Cecelia turned to stare at him. She looked around the abandoned room, and then back at him.

"Ah." He shrugged, acknowledging the similarity. "But you think they would be willing to do tasks for money?"

"Just about anything, I would imagine." She considered the family's plight. "They certainly need it." Perhaps James could aid them while helping himself.

"I have very little money with me." He looked mournful.

"Oh, James." She took all the funds from her reticule and put them onto the kitchen table.

"Splendid. If you come back, I will be in better trim."

"I shall not come back."

"I've found some very interesting objects in the muddle here. I'm setting to work, you see."

He knew how to lure her. But she would not be enticed. She couldn't afford to be. She'd let James coax her into supporting his schemes too many times. And this time was different. She couldn't wager her life's happiness on his caprices. No matter how tempting he still managed to be.

Cecelia reached home without encountering anyone she knew, but Aunt Valeria emerged from the drawing room as she was passing up the stairs. "I thought you had given away that old gown," she said.

Tugging at the ribbons of her bonnet, Cecelia once again sighed over her aunt's penchant for noticing things just when you wanted her to be oblivious. It was some sort of annoying instinct, she decided. Her aunt missed all manner of obvious cues, just not the ones you wished her to.

"You said it was hopelessly outmoded," Aunt Valeria added. "You can't have been making morning calls in it?"

"I had an errand," Cecelia replied.

"Alone, carrying off a basket, which now appears to be missing."

An infuriating instinct, Cecelia decided, and a sharp eye when she exerted herself. She tried to control her temper. "You don't care in the least about a basket," she pointed out.

Her aunt acknowledged the truth of this with a gesture. "Cook was complaining that the kitchen maid had lost it."

"I'll speak to her." Cecelia started to walk on to her bedchamber.

"Lady Wilton has written to me about you," said her aunt. "She seems to think I should do something about your marital prospects."

"It's too bad you can't pretend to be illiterate as well as deaf," said Cecelia.

This earned her a frown.

"I beg your pardon. That was impolite."

"It was." Aunt Valeria examined her. "You are out of sorts."

Cecelia could not deny it.

"That isn't like you."

"No, I'm always good humored and gracious and accommodating, aren't I?" And where had it gotten her?

Her aunt startled her by laughing. "You have been. In the main. If you are giving that up, I congratulate you."

Cecelia gazed into her aunt's clear blue eyes. She meant it. She was encouraging Cecelia to be as acerbic as she pleased. Cecelia had to smile at her. "Please don't do anything about my marital prospects."

"Of course not. You must know I have no such intention."

She did. One could trust Aunt Valeria not to interfere in any matter that was not related to bees. Cecelia gave her a nod of thanks and went on up the stairs.

But she did not escape to her bedchamber unscathed. She found her father turning away from its door, a petulant expression on his round face.

"Oh there you are," he said, as if she usually lurked up here in the daytime. Cecelia noticed that he had an ink-stained wad of papers in his hand and immediately knew what he would say next. "I brought this to be copied out."

He extended the pages. No one but Cecelia could read his scrawled handwriting or decipher the maze of circled text, arrows, and emphatic cross-outs he created when penning an essay.

"Tomorrow would be sufficient," he added. He shook the paper a little.

He never asked if she was busy or when it might be convenient for her to produce a fair copy of his work. In Papa's mind, she was at his disposal. It sometimes seemed to Cecelia that he didn't quite see her until he had need of her services. She had tried to discuss this with him, but the incisive brain that grappled with the intricacies of German philosophy seemed incapable of absorbing her concerns. He really did not appear to understand what she meant. Just doing his copying had come to seem simpler. She took the pages from his hand.

"Splendid," said her father. He turned and walked away, his attention already elsewhere. Certainly not on any expression of gratitude.

"Splendid," repeated Cecelia in quite a different tone and went to remove her bonnet.

Nine

THE BACK DOOR CLOSED BEHIND CECELIA WITH A DECIDED snap. James sat for a while in the dingy kitchen, which suddenly felt emptier than it had yesterday. Seeing Cecelia had been a comfort, he realized. She'd always been that, even when they disagreed. Particularly when they disagreed—somehow. Mysteriously. He hadn't quite seen it before. Not the depth of it. He looked at the basket she'd brought. That apple had tasted ambrosial and like… kindness. Even affection?

He'd made her angry today. No doubt about that. He hadn't meant to blame her for his situation. Sometimes he said things that sounded right at the time and wrong later, when he was alone and heard their echo. This was one of those times. His apology hadn't come out right either. The humor had fallen woefully flat. And now she was gone.

He rose and made the tea. It didn't taste quite right, and there was no milk. But it was better than none. Why hadn't he thought of it himself? He had it with another scone. Proper food was so much more satisfying than the stuff he'd been eating.

Surely Cecelia would visit him again? She was curious as a cat. She wouldn't be able to resist. This was assuming he was actually going to stay in Uncle Percival's wretched house. James looked around the empty kitchen, the antithesis of the cozy, bustling, aromatic place it should be.

He thought of going home, ordering Hobbs to fill a bath, sharpen his razor, lay out fresh clothing. The idea was tempting. Hobbs, at least, wouldn't criticize. He rarely said much of anything. He would do as he was told, and James would soon look like himself again.

And then what? He would have to face society as the man who'd lost control and behaved dishonorably. There would be whispers and impertinent questions, and of course Prince Karl's smug triumph. There was no doubt that man would gloat. He seemed to have a distinct talent for it.

James could brush through the gossip. Now that some time had passed, he could see the possibility. It wasn't as if he'd never made a mistake. His reputation would withstand the errant punch. Eventually. He could turn the whispers back on themselves. A few hotheads would even admire him for exploding. After a time— tedious and annoying—all would go back as it had been.

But the odd thing was, he wasn't sure he wanted that.

James looked around the ill-kept kitchen again. Cluttered, forlorn. And yet this ruined household was part of his new responsibilities as duke. There were others as well. Tasks more important than any he'd been required to do before. His established routine began to look stale, a bit small, from this new vantage point. Changes were called for. But what kind? And how?

He'd proposed to Cecelia; she'd refused him. James felt a stab of resentment and regret at the memory. She ought to have taken him. Each time he thought of it, the idea made more sense and held more attractions.

He gazed at the basket she'd brought, the money she'd left on the table. He'd counted on Cecelia so many times. He'd turned to her, trusted in her. Could she say the same of him? He had a sinking feeling that the answer was no. Worse, he hadn't cared about the disparity. Not until he was about to lose her to some fool of a prince.

Every sentiment rose up in James to protest this. His competitive streak might be uppermost, but other less familiar urges jostled behind it. That could not be! He had to get her away from that smug blusterer. He would return to his rooms, repair the ravages to his appearance, and find her. He would convince her!

In the midst of a crowd of yammering gossips and inconvenient friends, another part of him noted. He remembered how impossible it was to see her alone now. And with his recent behavior, it would be even worse. Society would be wild to corner him, question him, twit him about his loss of control. Cecelia would be pulled even further away.

His gaze caught on the basket once again. In this house, there were no distractions. Just the two of them, face-to-face. They would not be stared at and interrupted. Most importantly, there was no Prince Karl to stick his nose in where he was so emphatically not wanted. James would have time to find the right words, to show her...whatever it was that she needed to see.

James nodded. He had no doubt he could lure her back. His uncle Percival's epic level of untidiness would eat at Cecelia Vainsmede, offending all her instincts. Knowing he was here, dealing with the chaos, she would return, and he would win her over. He felt a smile spread over his face at the idea. The conquest of Cecelia offered so many delectable possibilities. They filled his mind and roused his body.

But none of that could happen while he was living in squalor. James looked down at his dust-smudged hands, pushed the teacup away, and stood. Something had to be done about that. And she had given him a clue.

James went out the back door and across the cobbled yard behind the house. He entered the stables without knocking. They were his, after all. The creak of the hinges set off a flurry of motion in one of the loose boxes. Four figures leapt up from a pile of musty hay and faced him, at bay in the dim light.

The tallest, a woman, pushed three children behind her. Very thin, dressed in layers of ragged clothing, she was visibly trembling. The smallest child whimpered. James had intimidated people in his time, but he had never knowingly terrified anyone. It was an unpleasant sensation. "Hello," he said. "I am Tereford."

Immediately he wondered if his name would mean anything to them.

Apparently it did. "We didn't mean no harm, milord," said the woman. Her voice shook. "It was just so cold in the night, and we didn't have nowhere…" She broke off, swallowed. "If we could stay one more day. Then we'll move on." The tallest child, a boy, stepped up beside her, his expression belligerent.

"Where would you go?" James asked. He'd never had dealings with people in their situation. One passed them in the street now and then, dropped a coin, and thought no more about it.

The woman slumped. Clearly she had no answer. She looked beaten.

"These stables was empty," said the boy. "Nobody using them. Why shouldn't we get out of the rain? No harm done, eh?"

"Ned," said the woman.

"That is your name?" James asked. "Ned what?"

"Ned Gardener."

"How old are you?"

"Eleven." At a glare from his mother, the boy added, "Sir. Milord."

James would have thought him younger from his meager frame. All three children had hollow cheeks and wrists that showed every bone. That wasn't right. "And so you are Mrs. Gardener?" he asked the woman.

"Yes, milord." She stood straighter. "I was married in a church and all." As if she knew more questions would come, she added, "My husband died in an…accident. I was taking in laundry, but it weren't enough to pay for our lodgings. So we was turned out."

"'Cause that doxy would give her more," said Ned.

"Ned!"

"Well, she would," the boy mumbled.

"Will he send us to the workhouse?" whispered one of the children behind his mother. She made it sound like the pits of hell.

"We ain't going there," declared her mother. "I'll find some-place. Never you mind." She sounded deeply frightened and yet stalwart. James had to admire such determination against the odds.

He'd never hired a staff. Hobbs had come to him without effort, on a friend's recommendation. He'd employed no other servants. This forlorn family was hardly suitable for a duke's household. But his household was not exactly ducal at this point, was it? Rather the definition of *not* in fact. Perhaps this woman was sent by Providence? On both sides of the transaction? Coincidence at least, he acknowledged. To be considered surely? "Can you cook?" he asked her.

"What?"

"I am in need of help in the house. Particularly cooking." After the toothsome scones, he simply could not face another greasy pie. "As well as some help shifting things." James examined the skinny boy. Not much muscle there, but once he was properly fed… "Perhaps Ned could do that. And run errands. Accompany you to the market, I suppose." The other children peeking out from behind the woman's skirts were girls. Smaller. James was no good at judging ages. "What are your names?" he asked them.

They ducked out of sight. "Jen and Effie," said their mother.

"Too young to be working, but…"

"I kin work," said the larger one, reappearing. "I kin scrub. And peel taters. And tend chickens. I ain't afraid of chickens." Her small face was taut with anxiety, every muscle visible.

James felt a pang. "How old are you…Jen?"

"Eight. Plenty old enough to work." She spoke as if she'd heard this phrase very often in her short life.

"I see. Well, would all of you like to work for me?"

The desperate hope that appeared in the woman's eyes pained him. "The house is in a poor state," James added.

"It's daft," said Ned.

"You've been inside?"

The whole family froze like rabbits spotting a snake.

"I looked through the winders, like," replied Ned.

"Ah." The boy seemed quick. James imagined that he'd slipped in to see what he could pilfer. James didn't blame him, though that must stop now. "Well then, you have seen that there's much to do."

"I'll take any sort of work, milord," said the woman. "We all will. Don't matter how hard." Her breath caught in her haste to assure him. "I can cook plain dishes. Not like you're used to mebbe." Her face creased with distress.

"They must be better than what I've had lately." James made up his mind. This had unfolded felicitously. More for the Gardeners perhaps than for him, but…he would try it out. Where was the harm? "Come into the kitchen where it's warmer, and we will set out a plan. Wages and so on."

Mrs. Gardener took a step forward as if she still didn't believe he meant it.

"I have scones," James said.

The smallest child burst into tears.

❧

"Ah, there you are. Just in time for the waltz." Prince Karl offered his arm as if Cecelia belonged to him. She wanted to say that she was already engaged for this dance, but it wasn't true. She had only just arrived at the ball, and he was the first to approach her.

Cecelia looked up at the tall, blond figure. The prince's dress was always vaguely military, without being a uniform. He was undeniably handsome, with his pale skin, jutting cheekbones, and hazel eyes. The satirical set of his lips was…intriguing. He appeared constantly, distantly amused, as if the world was a comedy presented for his entertainment. It made her wonder about his opinion of England.

With James's disappearance, society seemed to have decided

that there was an agreement between her and the prince, even though nothing had been settled or announced. Prince Karl's attitude certainly encouraged this view. His proprietary air annoyed her, but she also felt a lingering enjoyment at her new status in the *ton*. To become an acknowledged belle at this stage was a guilty pleasure. Cecelia felt she shouldn't savor it, but now and then she still did. She accepted his arm and walked onto the floor.

The music began. Prince Karl pulled her slightly too close—not quite to the point where a young lady might complain. But very nearly there. A quick glance told her that he knew this. He had judged it to a nicety. And he was enjoying his own skills.

He was a good dancer. He added turns and flourishes that drew admiring glances. His arm at her waist was masterful. His conversation was more interesting than many another man's. He seemed truly interested in her ideas. She couldn't say if the partiality he exhibited was love. She didn't know him well enough.

But there were quite a few points in his favor, and he seemed primed to offer for her. Briefly, she contemplated accepting him. To actually become a princess would have been unimaginable a few short weeks ago. But the title wasn't the chief temptation. Prince Karl opened the possibility of a more adventurous life than she'd thought to have. She would live in another country, learn a new language and customs. She might even contribute to the welfare of a different people. The prince seemed ready to listen to her. That was an interesting thought. If James had not existed, she might have…

But he did. And Cecelia wasn't certain she would ever feel as deeply about another man. Even though that was folly.

"Daydreaming, Miss Vainsmede?" Prince Karl asked. "Is my dancing…insufficiently exciting?"

The look he gave her promised more earthy attractions. Cecelia's cheeks heated. "Not at all."

"Ah. That is good. I am pleased I have the ability to…excite you."

This was more than light flirtation. It skirted very near the line. "Dancing is always invigorating," she replied.

He smiled down at her, acknowledging an evasion. That was another thing: he was intelligent. She could never pledge herself to a stupid man.

The music ended. Prince Karl held her for a moment longer than was strictly proper, releasing her just as she might have protested. Cecelia gave him raised brows. He laughed as he stepped away. His games were an innovation in her life. She had to admit that.

Cecelia turned toward Sarah and Charlotte, who were standing on one side of the ballroom. When they reached them, the prince bowed over her hand. "Alas that I must dance with another," he said. Nodding to the other young ladies, he moved away.

"Not one of us apparently, Sarah," said Charlotte.

"Shh! He'll hear."

"I don't think he or I would care if he did," replied Charlotte.

"You don't like Prince Karl?" Cecelia asked her.

Charlotte started to speak, paused, then said, "I'm not certain whether it's that, or merely pique at being so thoroughly ignored."

"He is extremely…focused," said Sarah.

"You are excessively kind," replied Charlotte. "I have always said so."

"Thank you."

"I did not mean it as a compliment."

Cecelia laughed as the two exchanged grimaces that had surely originated at a much earlier age.

Another set was forming. They were all invited to join it, and the ball made its stately, predictable way through the night. Prince Karl did approach Cecelia for a second dance, but this time she *was* spoken for. He received her refusal with gratifying regret.

Cecelia danced. She partook of the delicate supper provided. She danced some more. She missed James, whose absence was still a sensation among the *ton*. They had stood up together at nearly every ball in the last two seasons. It was odd to attend one without his suave presence. At least people had stopped asking if she knew where he'd gone. She'd honestly denied it at the beginning. Now that she knew, she preferred not to lie.

She was still thinking about him the following morning when a footman found her in the drawing room and handed her a folded note. Opening it, she recognized James's handwriting. "Who brought this?"

"A street urchin pushed it into my hand and ran away," the footman replied disapprovingly.

Aunt Valeria looked up from her notetaking.

Nodding a dismissal to the servant, Cecelia read the words. James wanted more money. He asked politely, promising to return any sums advanced. This meant he was still at the ducal town house. She let the sheet of paper fall to her lap.

"What has a street urchin to do with you?" asked her aunt.

"My…friend merely employed him to carry the message."

"Lacking a servant?"

"I suppose," Cecelia said, conscious that it was an evasive answer.

"And which friend would that be? Surely not one of your young ladies? That makes no sense."

Aunt Valeria gazed at her, waiting for an answer Cecelia did not wish to give. Not for the first time, or the hundredth, Cecelia noted how much her aunt resembled Papa. Both of them were plump and blond, with a bland air that disguised acute minds. She recognized the glint in her aunt's blue eyes now, from years of seeing it in Papa. Aunt Valeria was curious, and she wanted her curiosity satisfied. She would not stop until it was. She didn't care particularly about the underlying issue, but she would not be mystified. "It is a request for aid," Cecelia tried.

"Some charitable endeavor?"

Could James be defined so? Hardly. Unless one theorized that exile amid piles of discarded furnishings was good for him? Cecelia allowed herself a nod.

"It is no use giving money to street children," said her aunt. "That is a bottomless pit. You will make no difference."

"I know that you think so." Aunt Valeria had no interest in philanthropic endeavors, though she could sometimes be brought to feel for individuals.

Her flicker of interest exhausted, the older lady waved this aside and returned to her work.

Cecelia reread the note. Procuring the funds was no obstacle. She managed her father's affairs and was well known to his banker. But if she refused wouldn't James have to go home? And was that not best?

In the end she decided it wasn't her decision to make. She would do as he asked one more time.

∽

Later that day, once more in her drabbest gown, Cecelia returned to Tereford House, retracing her previous route. She found the stables empty and was disappointed that James had turned the poor family out. The back door was again unlocked, and she slipped through, to be surprised by sounds of conversation from the kitchen.

Quietly, she pushed the inner door open and discovered the woman she'd last seen in the stables bent over the hearth. A little girl of perhaps five stood next to her, staring at whatever was sizzling in a pan with avid anticipation. The woman poked at it with a toasting fork.

The child turned her head and noticed Cecelia. She gasped and clutched her mother's skirts. "There's a lady."

The woman straightened and turned. She looked better. Her

clothes were still ragged, but her face and hands were very clean and her hair was braided and coiled into a tidy bun. She dropped an unpracticed curtsy. "Good day, miss. His lordship said you might come."

"He...did?"

"He said he expected you would." She set aside the fork, wiped her hands on an apron that was more substantial than her gown, and added, "Go and fetch him, Effie."

The child rushed out.

"Would you care to sit, miss? It ain't proper, being the kitchen and all, but there's no other room, er, suitable. And I scrubbed everything clean."

"Thank you." She examined the low stools and rejected them. "I am Cecelia Vainsmede."

"Emmaline Gardener," the woman replied with another bob. "Missus," she added as if Cecelia might have some doubt.

"You've moved in from the stables?" Was it possible that James hadn't even noticed? No, of course not.

"To work for his lordship," was the reply.

"I've hired the whole family," said James's voice from the doorway. He came in, wearing the same clothes as before, only dustier. He had shaved and washed, however, and brushed back his dark hair.

The first little girl trailed after him. Two older children followed. They congregated around their mother. "Mrs. Gardener, Ned, Jen, and Effie," James added, pointing at each one as if to prove he knew their names.

"Hired them?"

Mrs. Gardener looked apprehensive at Cecelia's sharp tone.

"Yes."

Was he actually proud? Who was this new James?

"I take it you've brought what I asked for," he said.

"I have." She touched her reticule, which bulged with a roll of banknotes.

"Splendid. We've nearly cleared out one room, thanks to my new helpers." James gestured at the two older children.

"I got a pony," said the girl. Jen, Cecelia recalled. She pulled a small china horse from the pocket of her gown and displayed it.

"Come, I'll show you." James beckoned Cecelia, then held up a hand when Ned started to follow them.

The room where Cecelia had found him the last time was indeed nearly empty. A pile of discarded items could be seen outside the window. It rose in an untidy mound to just below the sill. "I shall hire someone to haul that away," said James when he saw Cecelia looking at it.

"This remains your method? Throwing things out the window?"

"Why not? They are refuse. And it is impossible to maneuver inside the house."

She had to admit that was true.

He extended his hand. She pulled out the money and gave it to him.

"Splendid. I've given Mrs. Gardener everything I had left to buy provisions. I think she's worried that I'm as poor as she is."

"James."

"The whole family is staying in the servant's old room in the basement. It's rather a hole, with a single cot. I'm surprised anyone tolerated it. We unearthed some cushions for the children to sleep on." He looked around. "I shall move them up here next, until we can clear more space. There's no lack of furnishings, of course." He offered a wry smile.

"James."

"The children are more help than I'd expected. This seems like a treasure hunt to them. They make a game of it. I've let them keep a few trinkets to encourage that idea. It rather keeps one's spirits up."

"You can't mean to stay here," said Cecelia. But she wondered.

She tried to remember when she'd seen him in such a carefree, ebullient mood.

"I can do as I like." He turned away from her. "I have found some real treasures. Come, I'll show you." He walked out.

Cecelia followed. They edged along the cluttered corridor to the entryway and then up the stairs and down another hall. James disappeared through a doorway.

Entering behind him, Cecelia found a bedchamber with a canopied bed and conventional shaving stand. It was old-fashioned, but a relief compared to the oppressive crowding in the rest of the house. Three massive wardrobes lined up along one wall were the only reminders of that.

A table on one side held an array of objects. Cecelia spotted a beautiful silver creamer, an inlaid snuffbox, a tiara worth a great deal if the jewels were real. Surely they couldn't be? There were some carved jade figurines and a small, exquisite cloisonné vase.

"Look here," said James, opening a wooden box. "These are very old, I think." He displayed a set of stone blades that looked as if they belonged in a museum.

"All of these things were in the jumble?"

"Stuck in nooks and crannies," replied James.

"That's idiotic. The old duke must have had *some* system." The idea of none at all appalled her. Chaos made her brain reel.

"After sifting through the contents of just one room, I can state definitively that he did not," James replied. "He seems to have had the mind and habits of a demented pack rat."

"He needed help. But no one knew." Cecelia wandered over to one of the wardrobes. She reached for the clasp.

"Don't open that!"

But she already had. A landslide of clothing tipped out and fell over her. She was engulfed by a flood of fabric and the overpowering smell of camphor.

James caught her around the waist to steady her. "Every chest and wardrobe in this house is crammed to bursting," he said. "That happens whenever one opens a wardrobe. Be grateful it was only cloth. Ned was battered by a hail of gravy boats."

Garments continued to fall. Cecelia batted at them.

James pulled her from under the onslaught. She leaned against him, soft and fragrant in his arms. The top of her head was just at his chin. She felt delightfully curved and pliable.

She turned in his embrace and looked up. Their lips were inches apart. James became aware that they were in a bedroom. In their long association, they had never been alone together in a bedroom. The sheets beckoned. All these years and he had never kissed her. In these last few weeks, everything had changed. Desire flamed through him. He wanted to, desperately.

His arms started to tighten of their own accord. His head bent. Cecelia gazed up at him, unmoving. Anticipating? Could she be wondering what it would be like to kiss *him*? She blinked. Her lips parted. She drew in a breath.

And James suddenly became conscious of his disheveled state. He might be fragrant in quite a different way from her subtle perfume. He'd probably smudged her gown with dust.

He let go of her and stepped back.

They faced each other, drifts of the old duke's clothes around their feet. Cecelia's cheeks were flushed. Was her breath as quick as his? Did her heart pound? James was uncharacteristically speechless. He'd asked her to marry him, but he couldn't bring himself to ask whether she might wish to kiss him. That was ridiculous. But somehow still true. He neither understood nor appreciated the dilemma.

He looked away, and his gaze immediately encountered the bed. Right there, seductive as a siren song. He dropped his eyes to the sea of fabric on the floor, and saw them as the scattered garments of two lovers in the haste of desire. If he picked her up and carried her to… No. *That* was unacceptable.

He took a step back. His left foot tangled in a dark-blue coat and nearly tripped him up. He reached down to pull it away. The cloth and workmanship were very fine. "Hah," he said, holding it up as a diversion. "This might be one of Weston's."

Cecelia moved out of the mass of cloth. "I can't quite imagine your great-uncle going to a tailor." She sounded breathless.

James was glad to hear it. "He had to get clothes somewhere."

"If it was his. Surely all this cannot be." She gestured at the sea of fabric.

"I wonder." James was very weary of his own dusty coat. Unthinking, he shed it and pulled this new one on. "It doesn't fit like one of Weston's, but it might do."

"Do? You look like a stripling who has outgrown last year's wardrobe."

James swung his arms. The coat *was* tight.

"The sleeves are too short, and the shoulders clearly bind," Cecelia added. "I wager you can't button it."

James tried. The coat wouldn't close. "Uncle Percival was a wiry old fellow," he acknowledged.

"You look silly, James. If you are actually staying here, send for your own clothes."

The briskness was back in her voice. He had missed his moment. The kiss—the compelling possibility of a kiss—was gone. "Hobbs is incapable of keeping his mouth shut," he replied. "He would bring all of society down on me." He quickly slipped off the coat and resumed his own. "I suppose we must cram this back into the wardrobe," he said.

"Why not take some down to Mrs. Gardener?" asked Cecelia. "It is all fine cloth. She can use it to make new clothes for her family."

He thought of their ragged layers. "A good thought." He started to gather up an armload of fabric.

"I wonder if she has sewing supplies?" said Cecelia as she followed suit.

"I believe all that exists in this house somewhere," said James.

Together, they made their back to the kitchen with their spoils.

But Mrs. Gardener didn't seem grateful for the offerings. "You should sell those garments if you don't want 'em, milord," she said. "I know a place you could get a good price."

"That's not necessary. You can alter them."

"Cloth that fine? I'd look a fool. And I couldn't work in such stuff."

"But Effie would like a silk dress, wouldn't you, Effie?" James asked.

The smallest Gardener, who had been fingering a silk dressing gown, dropped it guiltily.

"Effie don't need any such thing," said her mother.

James dug out the coat that hadn't fit him. "Here, Ned, try this."

The boy hesitated, not quite believing but clearly drawn. His mother made an uneasy sound. Ned couldn't resist. He put the coat on. It was large on him, but not excessively so. "You'll grow into it," James told him.

"This is a good weave, this is," Ned said, fingering the cloth. "And ever so well made. Look at that stitching." He preened.

His mother and sisters went very still, giving James nervous sidelong looks. He was puzzled by their reaction. It was almost as if they expected an attack.

"He can't have a coat that fine," said Mrs. Gardener then. Her voice was tight. She frowned at Ned, seeming to convey a message.

"Of course he can." James looked from one Gardener to another.

Ned was swiftly removing the coat. "Somebody'd steal it off me," he said. His voice was tight with regret and something more. Fear?

"They wouldn't dare." James was irate at the idea.

The entire Gardener family looked back at him as if they despaired of explaining the truth of their world to someone who'd never experienced it.

"Those who belong to my household will be properly clothed," James declared. "We will present a proper appearance, one that warns off thieves." He met each Gardener's eyes in turn. "Is that understood?"

Mrs. Gardener curtsied. After a moment Jen copied her. "Yes, milord," said the woman. "I'll get to work soon as I find some thread."

"You might want to hire a seamstress," murmured Cecelia.

He turned to her.

"Mrs. Gardener might well know of a suitable one," she added.

James thought that Cecelia was looking at him as if she'd never seen him before. Which was odd because he was feeling rather the same about her.

Ten

CECELIA COULDN'T RESIST. THE NEXT MORNING SHE SLIPPED out while Aunt Valeria was in the garden checking her beehives and took her customary circuitous route to the Tereford town house. Finding the back door locked, she knocked, waited for a stir at the kitchen window, and knocked again.

The lock turned, and the smallest Gardener opened the door. "Mam says you can come in," she said.

"Thank you, Effie."

Mrs. Gardener was in the kitchen, which looked even cleaner and tidier than before. The woman wore a muslin dress that had probably come from the store of clothing in the wardrobes. It was loose on her thin frame, and Cecelia thought she looked self-conscious about its suitability for kitchen work. Cecelia saw her run reverent fingers over the fabric, however. Effie had settled on a stool in the corner and wrapped herself in the blue and scarlet silk dressing gown she admired. There was an enticing smell of baking. "His lordship is clearing out," Mrs. Gardener said. "Next room down from where he was."

"Thank you," said Cecelia.

She made her way there and found James, Ned, and Jen maneuvering a large disintegrating wardrobe out the window. Bits of chewed wood flaked off as it teetered on the sill, threatening to fall to pieces in their hands. Jen started to lose her grip on the massive thing, and Cecelia hurried over to lend a hand. The four of them managed to tip it over and out. It landed with a crash on a new pile in the walled garden, next to the one from the cleared room.

"Thank you," said James. "That one was rather nasty. We found yesterday that it had a large rat's nest inside."

"Made Jen scream," said Ned. "She hates rats." His sister shuddered. "On account of one bit her once," Ned added.

"A rat?" Cecelia was shocked.

"Long time ago, when I was little," Jen said.

She couldn't be more than eight years old now.

"We are sure the rat has abandoned the house now that its den is gone," said James.

Neither of the children seemed convinced, and Cecelia didn't blame them. She'd heard that seeing a single rat meant that there were many more unseen, but she didn't say so. She did eye the corners of the room for signs. Then she noticed that her gloves were smudged from the worm-eaten wood. She removed them.

"Never mind," Ned said to his sister. "I got a plan. Fixed it up first thing this morning, before you was awake."

"What plan?" asked James.

"A first-rate one. You'll see." Ned grinned up at him.

"You need more help," Cecelia said to James. The sooner the house was cleared, the better.

"Yes, I think I must hire some workmen so that we can go faster. And certainly to haul away the rejected bits." He pointed at the discarded furniture outside, which was beginning to fill the walled area.

Belatedly she realized he was wearing different clothing—his own. "Have you been to your rooms?"

"I sent Ned over with a note for Hobbs. My landlady said he'd packed up his things and gone." James had been annoyed and then relieved at this news. "I expect he was lured away. Bingham was always trying to poach my valet." He shrugged. "It's just as well. Hobbs gossiped like a washerwoman."

"You don't care?"

"Strangely, I don't, much." James had wondered about this himself. A few weeks ago he would have been livid. Now it didn't seem terribly important.

"What is happening to you, James?"

It was true that something was. He didn't know what. So instead of answering, he said, "Come and see our room of oddities."

He led Cecelia to the first room he'd emptied, the children trailing behind. "See here," he said, picking up an item from the long table they'd set up there. "This clever implement combines a spoon and a fork. Good for stews, I suppose."

"We're calling it a foon," said Ned.

"Foon," Jen repeated with a giggle. She wore a pink gown that had been chopped off at the hem to fit her small stature and tied around the middle with a scarf. Ned had on a billowing lawn shirt with the sleeves rolled up. It hung nearly to his knees and was liberally streaked with dust.

James set the implement down and picked up a large pair of calipers. "Didn't that fellow who told fortunes use something like this?" he asked Cecelia.

"He predicted temperaments, not fortunes. He was a phrenologist."

"Ah, yes." James moved on from this unfamiliar word. "We have powder horns for muzzle-loading muskets, and look at this." He whirled an ornate, rotating bookstand carved with miniature gargoyles. "You can spread your book open here and read sermons to a reluctant audience. The carvings show what becomes of the inattentive." He grinned at her. "Ned thinks it's better than a museum."

"Never been to a museum," muttered Ned.

"We got knives, too," said Jen. She held up a long, slender dagger in a tarnished silver sheath.

"Indeed, Jen." James pushed the bookstand aside and revealed a litter of knives. "Uncle Percival seems to have been particularly fond of short blades. We've found them stuck in everywhere. Daggers, poniards, dirks, a stiletto. I would call it a collection if I could perceive any organization."

"I was thinking the old man was afeard for his life and wanted a knife to hand wherever he was," said Ned with a ghoulish relish.

"An intriguing idea," James replied. "But a bit too adventurous for Uncle Percival, I fear."

"You said you didn't know him so well," Ned pointed out.

"That's true." James grinned at the boy. "It is gratifying to picture the old fellow skulking through the place always ready to whip out a dagger."

"Mebbe he had secret passageways underneath the piles," added Ned.

"No, Ned, now I am seeing him as an oversized rodent."

"Like a rat-man? Ugh." Jen shuddered.

"Exactly. But he wasn't, Jen. He was a perfectly…" He stopped. Cecelia could almost hear him running through descriptive words in his mind—normal, no; kindly, no; sane, no.

"Quiet old man," James finished. His eyes laughed into hers.

"Who are you?" Cecelia said to him. "And what have you done with James Cantrell?"

He laughed as if she was joking, though he knew she wasn't. Indeed, he scarcely recognized himself lately. For example, if anyone had told him a month ago that he would rather enjoy sorting through broken-down furnishings with two street urchins, he would have told them they were demented. He had been a creature of the *ton*, and now he was…what?

Cecelia was staring at him. She wanted an explanation. He had none. Like him, she would have to wait until one emerged.

He set that puzzle aside. Cecelia was here, just as he'd planned. They were nearly alone together. Turning to the children, he said, "Why don't you go and ask your mother for some of her splendid muffins."

Ned and Jen didn't hesitate. Their history had left them susceptible to any offer of food. In a twinkling, they were gone.

"I have nowhere to ask you to sit, do I?" James surveyed the room. "If I pull that chair out, the rest will fall on us. And I'm certain it's as dusty as all the rest." There were seats in his bedchamber, but he didn't think he should invite her there again. He was not made of steel.

"I don't need a chair," Cecelia said.

"What do you need?" The question popped out of his mouth, surprising James almost as much as it evidently startled Cecelia.

"I..." She blinked. Her cheeks reddened. Her lips parted, then closed again without a word.

James very much wanted to know what she was thinking. What had made her blush? She'd come back, as he'd known she would. But could he hope that more than curiosity had brought her? "What are you..."

"I passed one of Lady Wilton's footmen as I was coming here," she said at the same time.

That was clearly not the answer to his question. She had not been thinking of a footman a moment ago. "Yes, he'd been pounding on the front door," James said. "I ventured a look and recognized the livery."

"He didn't try the back?" she asked.

"No, the fellow was clearly hired for his appearance rather than his intellect. I can't imagine what he wanted."

"Lady Wilton is concerned about her lost earl."

"Ah, that. Concerned or incensed at the fellow's rebellion?"

"Both?" said Cecelia.

"I shall have to talk to her. And set some inquiries in motion, I suppose. I believe there are people who do that sort of thing. I will do so, in a few days." He couldn't face it yet.

"You've decided to take up your familial duties then?"

She seemed to be marveling at the idea, which rankled. "I don't have much choice," James said.

"You do, you know. Look at Fleming or Pendle. You could be a wastrel like them."

James acknowledged the point with a shrug. "I find that I can't, actually. Perhaps it is due to your example."

"What?"

"Through all those years, while you more or less managed my affairs, you never drew back from necessary tasks. Even those you disliked the most. And now for your father, it's the same. I understand better than I did."

Cecelia's mouth hung open in astonishment. James savored the expression. He hadn't ever confounded her before, not that he could recall. It was quite enjoyable. "You've been calling me selfish for years," he added.

"Because you are!" She frowned. "You have been."

"Perhaps so. But I never really had a job, did I? Now that I've inherited, many people are looking to me."

"As I told you!"

"You did."

"And you scoffed. What has changed?"

She seemed fascinated, which was good. But James didn't have a proper answer. The only thing that occurred to him was, "Did you know that children like Ned get no schooling? He can barely read."

She blinked, bewildered. "There are charity schools, I believe."

"I have heard of them. But according to Mrs. Gardener, there are difficulties."

"What sort?"

"I couldn't quite understand that. I suspect a patron is needed to procure a place. And on that front, I am increasingly convinced that the late *Mr*. Gardener was a criminal. A housebreaker perhaps or a footpad. And that the 'accident' he died in was a stabbing."

"Good heavens. Why do you say so?"

"Things the children have let drop. And then looked anxious about revealing. Particularly about the array of knives we've found. Mrs. Gardener's marked silences are also suggestive."

"Do you think they're in danger?" Cecelia asked.

James shook his head. "Only of starving in the street. Which they are *not* going to do!" Was that admiration in her eyes? He discovered that he hoped so.

"That is good of you," she said.

"Do you think so?"

"Anyone would."

"But do *you*?"

"Yes, James. I said so. What is the matter with you?"

"I believe your good opinion matters a great deal to me," he found himself saying.

Cecelia stared. "You have never seemed to value it much," she replied.

Had he not? He had brushed off her criticisms. That was true. He had resented them. But was that because he disagreed or because they stung? He'd had to fight back. "Did I hope for something else beneath the surface?"

"What does that mean?" Cecelia asked.

"I have no idea. I've begun to speak quite at random, without any idea what will come out next."

"That makes no sense, James. And it sounds like an affectation."

"Which concerns me far more than it possibly can you."

"I think this disordered house is affecting your brain."

"Could that be it?" He felt an urge to take her hand. But she'd refused him that. Her hand remained her own. "Or perhaps the interminable sorting is uncovering treasures within as well as without."

She stared at him.

"Not knives," James added, and then wondered if she was right that Tereford House had addled his mind.

"I've never heard you sound so cryptic."

"Is that how I seem?"

She hesitated. "Not exactly. But you are much changed. It's… unsettling."

He knew that she worried about him; that had long been

evident. Didn't that mean she could not dislike him? "It's all this seeing things in a new light. You, for example. What would I have done without you?"

"I thought I was the bane of your existence."

"You did not."

"Well, you always said so, James."

"Fortunately, you never listened to me."

Cecelia laughed. The lilting sound made James smile, join in, and then realize that he wanted to laugh with her for the rest of his days. This had nothing to do with estate work. He cared for her far more than he'd ever understood. He opened his mouth to say...something.

Jen hurtled in and spoke in a rush. "Mam has made the tea and wonders if you'd like to come to the kitchen for a cup as she's very sorry there's no place for her to set a tray up here." She took a breath. "We have raspberry jam for the muffins!" Her eyes sparkled with longing.

"Well, we must have some of that," said Cecelia.

She followed the girl out before James could summon words to deflect the interruption. It was an acute disappointment. With every step, he was more conscious of the lovely young woman ahead of him.

The tea, muffins, butter, and pot of jam were arrayed on the scrubbed kitchen table. Mrs. Gardener hovered, looking proud and anxious in equal measure. They had just sat down when they were interrupted by a sharp rapping on the back door.

Their circle reacted with varying degrees of alarm. James wondered if his grandmother's footman had developed some inconvenient initiative.

Ned jumped up. "That'll be Felks."

"Who?" asked James. He had not sanctioned any visitors.

"He's a champion ratter," said Ned over his shoulder.

"What? I didn't..." James glanced at Mrs. Gardener. She shook her head, looking frightened.

Ned returned with a squat, seedy-looking man who held the leashes of three short-haired terriers. The little dogs vibrated with energy. "I told Felks we got rats here, and you'd pay to have them killed," said Ned.

"Penny a rat," said the newcomer.

"Well, but…"

"My boys is the best in the business," continued Felks, indicating the eager dogs. "They'll find your rats and bring them back to me, dead. Every last one."

"Commendable," said James. "But I do not think that this house is suit…"

As if feeling his payment slip away, Felks bent and released the terriers. They sprang away and out the kitchen door.

"Wait," said James, far too late.

The scrabble of paws faded. There was a pause that James felt to be ominous. Then, somewhere in the house, a large object hit the floor. A clatter of smaller items followed the thud, punctuated with excited barks.

"What the devil?" said Felks.

The sounds of toppling furniture nearly drowned him out.

"Was that a pianoforte?" asked Cecelia.

There had been a trill of notes as if from a keyboard. James had not noticed an instrument, but a small animal could go where he could not.

The cascade of noise continued. James pictured three trails of mayhem.

"My dogs do not knock things about," said Felks. "They're trained right, they are. No climbing on the sofas or pulling at draperies."

"As I tried to say, this house is unusual," said James. "Not…not suited for dogs."

"How many rats is in here?" asked Felks, scowling.

Cecelia choked. On a laugh, James thought. "Can you call your dogs back?" he asked their visitor.

"I'll go and fetch 'em!" Felks went out. "What the hell?" came floating back in his wake.

There was a good deal more banging and crashing and creative cursing before Felks returned with the terriers leashed once again. One held a large rat in its teeth and did not seem inclined to give it up.

"Ugh," said Jen.

"What sort of place is this?" Felks glared at Ned and then at James. "It's no better than a rubbish heap."

"Thus the rats," James couldn't help but say.

"My dogs couldn't keep from knocking into things," Felks went on, belligerent. "This ain't their fault."

"No. I don't think this is a good place for them to, er, work," said James. "Too constricted."

"Well, they can dig through most anything," replied Felks, recovering some of his balance. "But there might be damage, like."

"I think we will try another method."

"You owe me a penny for this 'en." Felks pointed at the dead rat hanging from the terrier's mouth.

"Take this for your trouble." James handed him a sovereign.

The man looked delighted. "Thank your lordship and no hard feelings about the misunderstanding, I hope."

"None."

Pulling on the leashes, Felks made his way out. James turned to Ned.

To find that the boy looked absolutely terrified. "I'm sorry," he cried, cringing under James's gaze. "You kin throw me out, but let Mam and the girls stay. It's not their fault. I never said anything to them about Felks."

Mrs. Gardener stepped in front of her son. "If you try to beat him, we will all go," she said, her voice shaking.

"I'm not going to beat him," said James, shocked.

"You have no right to touch him. You ain't his father." Mrs.

Gardener trembled and blinked back tears but stood her ground, a thin, careworn woman in an ill-fitting muslin gown. But adamant.

"James would never beat a child," exclaimed Cecelia. Her tone held absolute certainty. It was a voice that left no room for question or argument.

"Of course not," said James. "Not under any circumstances."

The change in the atmosphere was marked. All the Gardeners slumped with relief. Ned was clearly fighting tears with all his might.

"Let us sit and have our tea," said Cecelia.

Mrs. Gardener wrung her hands. "It's likely gone cold."

"I will make a fresh pot." Cecelia put a hand on the woman's shoulder. "Sit down."

"That ain't right."

"Of course it is." Cecelia took up the teapot and turned toward the fire.

"Jam," said James. "We all require a good deal of jam. Don't we, Effie?"

The smallest Gardener nodded tearfully. They settled again at the table. Muffins were buttered and slathered with raspberry jam. Large bites were taken.

"So," said James after a while, and wished that his staff did not stiffen and shy at the sound of his voice. "Your impulse was right, but the method was wrong, Ned."

"Yessir," replied the boy, eyes on the tabletop.

"You should have consulted me first."

"Yessir. Milord, I should say."

James could not understand why the lad looked so deeply anxious. "In the future, you will do so about any arrangements that, er, occur to you," he continued.

The mention of a future seemed to hearten Ned. He looked up. "Yessir. Milord."

"So here is what I think we must do."

Ned crouched, and the whole family froze again as if awaiting a blow. Even though he'd *said* he would never hit a child. What did they expect was going to happen? And then an answer occurred to him, and James decided that it might be a good thing the father of this family was gone. What had Mrs. Gardener said—that he had no right to touch Ned as he wasn't his father? Did she think a father had such rights?

James felt a sudden fierce longing to show these children, and their mother, too, that there were other sorts of men in the world. He almost said so. But words were cheap, and often deceptive in their world. Only actions would convince them, over time.

Ned straightened and raised his chin. "I'm ready to take my punishment," he said.

"Not a punishment," exclaimed Cecelia, who had brought hot water to warm the tea.

"Rather a change of strategy," said James quickly. "Or is it tactics?"

His small audience stared at him. Jen's mouth hung open.

"In either case, I think a stealthy approach is better suited to our...situation," he continued. "So, Ned, you should find us some cats. Large fierce cats who are accustomed to hunting rats. Several, I should think. Though not vicious, of course."

Ned didn't look much heartened. "I'm not partial to cats," he muttered to his half-eaten muffin. "Can I get Effie to help me?"

"Effie?" James glanced at the smallest Gardener. She had raspberry jam smeared all around her mouth.

"She loves cats," Ned explained. "And they all love her, even the meanest, scraggliest ones."

Effie nodded enthusiastically. She clawed the air with her hands.

"I suppose," said James. "If you take care."

"Course I will." Some of Ned's customary spirit resurfaced. "She's my sister."

"I kin do it," declared Effie. "I'll find proper mousers and bring 'em back. I can't do much work, like, in the house. But I kin do that."

James felt an odd tremor in the region of his chest. "Right. Good. Well, you may commence the, er, cat hunt when ready."

Ned stood at once. Effie followed suit, with a mournful glance at her remaining muffin.

"After you have finished eating of course and are, ah, fortified for the task ahead," James added.

They brightened like the sun and sat back down.

Cecelia walked out of the kitchen. Startled, James followed her. He found her in the room they'd first cleared, with its table of curiosities. Her eyes were bright with tears. "What is it?"

"I couldn't bear to see them look so happy about something so simple. A muffin, James. Some jam."

"Not being beaten for making a mistake," added James.

Cecelia nodded. Her breath caught on a sob, and she began to cry.

James moved to put an arm around her. She turned within it, buried her face in his shoulder and wept—a thing she had done only once before in all the years they'd known each other.

He put his other arm around her and held on while she cried. He hoped it was a comfort. Oddly, her tears were a comfort to him, because they were *right*. The scene they'd just witnessed ought to be mourned. It had left him raw—having children flinch away from him in fear, thinking of the circumstances that had made them act so. It was wretched, outrageous, insupportable. They deserved tears.

Cecelia's didn't last long. James could feel her struggling to shake them off. She stopped on a long, shaky breath and took another, deeper one.

James expected her to pull away, but she didn't. She lingered a moment in his arms, nestled there. Triumph shot through James at that small confiding motion. He felt as if he'd won a great prize he hadn't known he was vying for. He hadn't even been aware that it existed. Which made the gift even more precious.

They stayed together. Cecelia sighed, and the feel of her body changed, softened. Her hand moved on his back.

James's arms tightened of their own accord. Need flamed through him. He wanted Cecelia as he'd never wanted a woman before. She was all a man could desire.

Cecelia straightened, drew back, and stepped away. She didn't meet his eyes. He had to let her go. She brushed at his coat. "I've soaked your shoulder."

"No matter." He looked for a sign that she'd felt what he did. She pulled out a handkerchief to wipe her eyes and blow her nose with a ladylike snuffle.

"Our fathers were not easy," she said then. "But…"

James nodded. "Words can lash, but my father was merely cold and dictatorial."

"And mine distracted and self-centered."

"Beatings are something else entirely," he finished.

"Yes. Despicable!" She tucked her handkerchief away. "Do you think it was only Ned?"

"From the way the family reacted, I would guess so. I've gathered from other things they've said that Ned's father did not approve of him."

"Approve? What do you mean? He is an eleven-year-old boy."

"Who is interested in types of fabric and details of design. He let drop that he knows how to use a flatiron, and the whole family blanched as if he'd admitted to being a murderer. Such a clamor to change the subject!"

"But why?"

"I cannot say. But after today, I judge they were expecting an explosion of temper from me."

She shook her head. "I suppose Mr. Gardener was one of those who despises anything labeled women's work."

"Perhaps." James remembered incidents at school, when sensitive boys had been teased and bullied. So often the victim of his father's sarcasm, he'd never joined in. But he hadn't helped them either. "I do know one thing," he added.

"What?" asked Cecelia.

"I shall prove to them that their late unlamented father is not the only kind of man in the world." James was surprised at the ferocity of this resolve.

"What sort will you show them?" she wondered softly.

With such a strong feeling, he should have an immediate answer. But he did not. James struggled to put words to the impulse and realized that it had been spurred on by many things that had happened in the last few weeks. A proposal and a humiliation and a change in perspective. He spoke slowly. "One who knows that strength includes, is rooted in, kindness." He remembered Ned cringing away and nearly cringed himself. "One who appreciates those who are not like him."

Cecelia put a hand on his arm. She looked up at him with a tenderness he'd never seen in her eyes before. Her lips parted, but she didn't speak.

He bent his head. She raised her chin. They moved as one.

The kiss was soft and confiding at first. Gradually, it grew deep and exploratory, inflaming James to the core. It seemed that she did want to kiss him, noted the tiny part of his brain that still functioned. He certainly wanted to keep on kissing her—today, tomorrow, and for the rest of his life. James pulled her against him, every line of their bodies melting together. She laced her arms around his neck and matched his ardor. This was what he'd been looking for, James thought. This was the missing piece.

"Mam wonders can we order a roast beef from the butcher," declared a small female voice.

Cecelia jerked back. James protested wordlessly, but she stepped out of his arms and away. He turned to discover Jen standing in the doorway. She didn't seem shocked by the kiss. But neither did she make any allowance for privacy. How could it be so hard to achieve with only six people in a large house?

"She says it's more economical, like," added Jen. She waited, unconscious of awkwardness.

"I must go," said Cecelia. Her face was flushed. She looked gloriously disheveled, even though her clothes were scarcely mussed.

"Not yet," commanded James. He had to speak to her.

"No, I must." Cecelia turned and rushed out.

He started to go after her, then conceded that he couldn't settle matters between them while chasing her through the streets.

"Mam reckons a big roast would last us four days," said Jen. "With a stew at the end iffen we get more taters and carrots."

He would not be angry. Hadn't he just vowed as much? Or at least he would not show it. He could manage that. "Tell her yes."

Jen's eyes shone. "I never had a roast beef before."

"Then you are in for a treat." James made a shooing motion, and the girl ran off. He went to relieve his feelings by chucking some large items out the window.

Eleven

THOUGH CECELIA SAT IN HER FAMILIAR DRAWING ROOM, hearing the usual scratching of her aunt's pen in her notebook and occasional carriage passing in the street, her mind and heart were not there. They remained some streets away with James and his kiss. She could think of nothing else. His touch, his manner, his passion—these were all that she'd dreamed of. She felt that the heat in his eyes had been tinged with tenderness. Might she dare to love him?

Or, that was a silly question. Rather, might she admit that she did? Because the issue was beyond dispute. Her feelings were stronger than ever. His touch had ignited them.

She'd hidden her love in self-defense to keep from being hurt, but deception was becoming impossible. When she saw him again, she would want to kiss him again. And more than that. He seemed so changed. Perhaps they could…

"Lawks!" cried Aunt Valeria.

Cecelia jumped and turned to stare at her.

"I've spoken to you three times, and you have not answered," said her aunt. "What is the matter?"

"I was thinking."

"Indeed? I approve of cogitation. What weighty matter occupies you this morning?"

"I was…wondering about…" She certainly couldn't speak of melting kisses. And she didn't want to mention James, since all paths led from him to…melting kisses. Only one subject was guaranteed to divert Aunt Valeria. "About, ah, whether bees can…fly in the rain."

This earned her a look of blank disbelief. Well deserved, but she was launched on this course now. "I have seen raindrops almost as large as their entire bodies," she went on.

"True." Her aunt's thoughts were being pulled into her favorite topic. Cecelia could almost see it happening, like the ineluctable pull of gravity.

"They fly easily enough in light rain," she said. "Though from my observations I would say they don't like it. Well, who can blame them? A heavy rain is another matter. A very large drop is capable of breaking a bee's wing."

"Goodness."

"There is nothing good about it if they are caught out during a downpour. They must scramble then!" Aunt Valeria nodded emphatically. "Individual bees have been known to shelter under large leaves."

"That's clever."

"Of course." Clever was the nature of bees, her expression said. And apparently not the nature of nieces, it implied.

Cecelia was groping for something more to say when her father walked into the drawing room.

This was practically unprecedented. Papa's daily routine encompassed his study, the dining room, and his bedchamber. He might be seen in the corridors or on the stairs between these stations, but almost never anywhere else.

"I came to speak to you about the roast of pork at dinner last night," he said without preamble. He fixed Cecelia with a censorious glare. "It was not up to your usual standard. One might even say tough as old boots."

This explained his visit. Food and philosophy were her father's joint obsessions. Cecelia could not have said which was the more important to him. "It was rather," she acknowledged. "I did suggest a ragout, you know, because the joint seemed…"

He waved this excuse aside. "No dinner is complete without a decent roast. I trust this lapse will not be repeated. I would rather not send a reprimand to Cook."

"Please don't, Papa." That would cause an uproar and upset the household for days.

"There will be no need if you see to the matter," he answered loftily.

"I will." Cecelia wondered, not for the first time, what her mother had seen in him, particularly now that she knew Mama had chosen him for a husband. "Papa, where did…"

He held up a hand to stop her. "If this is something to do with the estate, I have no time today."

He never had time for matters of business. A roast of pork, on the other hand, riveted him.

"You manage it," he added. And then even he seemed to realize that more was called for. "As you always do so well."

"It's not about that," Cecelia replied. "I was wondering how you and Mama met." How could they have, when he never went out?

Papa stared at her as if the words made no sense. Aunt Valeria looked equally startled.

"Where did you meet?" Cecelia repeated. "For the first time."

"What in the world makes you ask such a question?" he replied.

"I want to know." She used a tone she employed when telling her father that she would not be fobbed off, no matter how hard he tried.

"Ah, er." He frowned. "Met."

"First," Cecelia repeated. Should this be so difficult to recall?

"Oh yes, the park," he replied. "They'd sent me out to walk. Two hours till I was allowed back. Not so much as a pamphlet to read."

Cecelia had noticed that her father and her aunt usually referred to their parents as "they."

"I went looking for a bench in the park. Someplace out of the way. But when I found one hidden in a shrubbery, Eloisa was already there. A young lady all alone. Sobbing her heart out."

Cecelia caught her breath. Even Aunt Valeria looked concerned.

Her father shook his head. "I said, 'Have they thrown you out as well?' Silly remark, but there it is. Startled her, of course."

Cecelia tried to picture the scene. It was next to impossible. She'd never seen her cheerful mother sob.

"When she nodded, I sat down beside her." He sounded surprised by this even now. "She asked me where I'd been thrown out of. And I said, 'Hades.'" He glanced at Aunt Valeria, and then they both looked away. "Bit of a joke, you know."

Or not, Cecelia thought.

"We talked," her father continued, sounding nearly as bemused by that as Cecelia was. "Until someone came calling her name, and she ran away. It was rather like a fairy tale."

Both his companions stared at him.

"We kept meeting there," he said. "They were pleased with my new regimen." He looked sourly amused. "And one day after they were gone, Eloisa called here and…" He broke off, but Cecelia knew the ending of that story. "So, that is the answer to your question," her father finished.

"Thank you, Papa," Cecelia said.

He seemed surprised.

In the awkward silence that followed, a footman entered and announced, "Lady Wilton."

Cecelia's father seized the opportunity and fled. Aunt Valeria looked as if she wanted to follow him, though she did not. As Cecelia stood to receive the visitor, she wondered if all families were a confusing mixture of irritating and heartrending.

The old lady stumped in, acknowledged Cecelia's greeting with a nod, and sat on the sofa. "I have no time to waste on trivialities this morning," she said. "Prince Karl has asked me to chaperone a visit to Vauxhall to which you are invited. I have agreed."

Cecelia blinked in surprise.

"The prince tells me that he wrote to your aunt about this expedition. But she seems to have ignored the communication." Lady Wilton glared at Aunt Valeria.

"I never accept invitations," said the latter. "I rarely even open them."

"Indeed. The prince was not aware of your…obdurate eccentricity. But your presence is not required." Lady Wilton turned back to Cecelia. "You can use the opportunity to make matters clear."

"What matters?" asked Aunt Valeria.

"Whichever ones require it, Miss Vainsmede," replied James's grandmother. "You cannot flout your responsibilities and then expect to be informed about developments." She looked to Cecelia again. "I've asked those girls you appear to dote on. They seem agog to see Vauxhall. It is to be tomorrow evening."

"You seem to be ordering me to go," Cecelia said.

"Because that is what I am doing."

"And if I don't wish to?" Prince Karl seemed like a distant memory now. James had superseded him.

"Your friends will be quite disappointed," Lady Wilton said.

"I could arrange a visit for another evening."

"And I shall be *most* unpleasant if you do not come."

"Why, Lady Wilton?" There seemed no reason for the old woman to be so exigent.

"I hope that the news you are being seen with the prince will root Tereford out of wherever he has gone to ground."

Cecelia hadn't thought of that. Of course, James was unlikely to hear any gossip in his current location.

"You've *still* had no word from him?" the old lady asked.

Making a noncommittal gesture, Cecelia avoided answering.

"I've sent servants around to Percival's old town house, but they found no sign of him there."

They hadn't tried very hard. Lady Wilton's staff was not very enterprising.

"He *has* to return. I require him to take up his duties and find Ferrington."

It took Cecelia a moment to remember that this was Lady Wilton's errant great-grandson, the lost earl.

"I must give him a push. And I can think of no other way." She gave Cecelia one of her signature glares. "I don't think it is so much to ask, to go to Vauxhall with your friends and a prince. He's asked Henry Deeping and some other young man. I've forgotten his name. Really, I insist."

Although she didn't like being pushed, Cecelia thought, why not? Her new friends would enjoy the outing. And she could find an opportunity to tell Prince Karl that she wasn't interested. His marked attentions had become burdensome now that her heart was full of James. "Very well," she said.

Aunt Valeria muttered something. Cecelia didn't catch it. Lady Wilton didn't appear to try.

In the end, the Vauxhall party numbered ten—five young ladies; four young gentlemen, including Ada's promised husband; and Lady Wilton. They took two boats across the water to the gardens. "It looks like fairyland," said Sarah as they embarked among lantern-lit trees.

The prince had engaged a large box. He informed them that he had ordered all the delicacies for which the place was famed— the thinly sliced ham, the cheesecakes, and of course champagne. Lady Wilton established herself in the box like a minor monarch. "You may walk about," she said, flicking her fingers at the younger people. "Hear the orchestra. See the pavilion and so on. Together, of course."

"There are fireworks later," said the prince.

Ada clapped her hands in delight, and her fiancé teased her about adoring explosions.

The group set off to explore, and Cecelia soon noticed that Prince Karl was maneuvering them like a sheepdog chivying his herd. He pointed out the best routes and most admired exhibitions, gathered from others' recommendations, it seemed. He interposed himself between Cecelia and the other young men. Gradually, he drew her toward the back of the group.

And then, between one moment and the next, he'd steered her away from them and into a side path. "Watch your step, Miss Vainsmede. It is darker here."

"I see that it is." Cecelia was mostly amused. His tactics to get her alone were transparent. This path was still peopled, though she noticed no one she knew.

"Do mind that rock." Prince Karl took her arm as if to help, though the stone in question was several feet away. "Have you been to Vauxhall often?" he asked.

"A fair number of times."

"It is a pleasant place."

"Indeed."

Her arm firmly in his grip, he veered left and onto another narrower path. The entrance to this one was scarcely visible among the bushes. Cecelia began to suspect that Prince Karl had explored this route in advance. The area was deserted. "We must go back to the others," she said, pulling away.

He pivoted, grabbed, and then she was in his arms. Cecelia looked up, startled, and he captured her lips with his own. It all seemed like a much-practiced move.

His kiss was hard, insistent. His hands on her waist and back pressed her against him. He was very strong.

For a surprised instant, Cecelia didn't move. Prince Karl's kiss probed and demanded. His grip seemed designed to crush and subdue. It was the opposite of James's embrace in every way. Most particularly, he did not arouse her. She felt merely mauled.

Cecelia shrank back and pushed firmly against the prince's chest. He resisted. She shoved harder, several times, until he released her, and she could step away. "I'm sorry, Prince Karl. I hope I have not roused false expectations. I can't marry you."

"Marry?" He sounded puzzled.

This pathway was dim. The nearest lamp didn't illuminate his expression. Cecelia frowned.

"You presume, Miss Vainsmede," he continued.

"I...what?"

"There can be no question of marriage between *us*. I shall wed a lady chosen by my father to make a useful alliance. Naturally. That is the duty of a prince."

His patronizing tone was offensive. "You have been courting me," Cecelia pointed out.

"I have signaled my interest in a connection," he said, as if correcting an erring student.

"Connection?" Society had certainly considered him a candidate for her hand. They had been a target for matrimonial gossip. She hadn't imagined it.

"An *intimate* connection. A pleasant dalliance while I am here in England." He reached out and moved closer. She stepped away.

"I cannot conceive why you would suggest such a thing." She started back along the path and caught her skirts on a protruding bush. The light really was dim here. The sooner she escaped the better.

"Come, come, Miss Vainsmede. Cecelia."

His use of her name was meant to be caressing. She found it presumptuous.

"You are no schoolroom miss," the prince went on. "You are past the age of silly romantics. You are a free thinker. We met at Lady Tate's house, after all. You attend balls alone."

Once, Cecelia nearly replied. One very much regretted time. But she merely jerked her gown free and moved on, fairly certain she'd torn the lace at the hem.

"You live with a lax chaperone, by your own contriving I have no doubt, so that your movements are free."

Cecelia stopped and turned to face him. "Have you been asking questions about me?"

"It is a sign of my interest," Prince Karl answered, as if he thought this was a compliment. "You are ideal for my purposes. As well as lovely, of course."

"Your purposes!"

"And your own," he said in a smug voice that was worse than patronizing.

"My..."

"You enjoyed the kiss," he said. Moving with unexpected speed, he slipped an arm around her again. "We are alone here. There is no need to be coy. I can fulfill all the desires you have been forced to deny. And show you passion you have never imagined."

She peeled his arm off and moved on. "I am never coy. You have made an error."

"After the way you melted in my arms in the waltz? And urged me on to fight for you? I think not."

"Urged?" She put all her incredulity into the word.

"Females enjoy a bit of violence," answered the prince. "They like to be won. Look at how the does watch the stags battle. I understood. Of course."

"You...you appear to understand *nothing*!" She couldn't throttle him. She couldn't shake him until his bones rattled. He was too large. She had to be content with escape.

"On the contrary." His voice was right behind her, practically in her ear.

She moved faster.

"I know what you would *truly* like better than you do," Prince Karl said with an odious air of certainty. "You need only let me show you."

Cecelia so longed to slap him. But that would prolong, and intensify, this encounter, and more than all else she wanted it over. She hurried toward the more traveled path.

A hand closed on her from behind. Outraged, Cecelia shook it off. His clutching fingers pulled the sleeve of her gown off her shoulder. She yanked it back in place and erupted onto the more traveled path, drawing looks of surprise from several strollers. She rushed along, too incensed to care.

The prince caught up with her. "There is no need to be ashamed, *Cecelia*. You succumbed, like every woman does when a man wakens her ardor. You need only give in."

"You...you arrogant lout."

"Is this how you English describe a masterful man?" He laughed.

He laughed! Cecelia wondered if anyone had ever actually burst with anger. It certainly felt possible in this moment. She experienced a state of perfect clarity. Of course James had not been able to resist hitting this man.

She couldn't keep him from accompanying her back to the box, not without creating a scene that would entertain the gossips for days to come. From the startled looks of people they passed, her expression was already causing speculation. She tried to smooth the scowl that tightened her features, with limited success, she concluded.

Everyone else was back when they arrived at the box, and their expectant looks suggested they awaited an important announcement. Cecelia made her way to a seat in the back and struggled to contain her emotions.

"We lost our way on the paths," said the prince jovially. "Vauxhall is quite a maze, is it not?"

"Often used to some advantage," said Lady Wilton. She gazed at him with raised brows.

"It offers a great *variety* of pleasures," he answered, glancing at Cecelia as if they shared a delicious secret. She ground her teeth. "Is that the ham for which Vauxhall is known?" he went on. "I shall take some. And champagne, of course."

"You have something to celebrate?" asked Lady Wilton, refusing to be diverted.

"Pleasant company," replied Prince Karl with a malicious twinkle in his eyes. He seemed to be enjoying the awkwardness. He took the glass Henry Deeping had poured and drank. "Ah, good."

"What's wrong, Cecelia?" murmured Harriet.

"Nothing!" She spoke too loudly. She couldn't help it. And her tone made all the young ladies in the box stiffen. Lady Wilton frowned.

Cecelia turned to watch the passing crowds. How she wished this evening over!

It went on. Cecelia fell back on established habits to play her part in the festivities. As her temper cooled, she began to feel less offended and more—not amused certainly, never that—but… analytical.

She'd met other people like Prince Karl, who inhabited worlds created inside their heads. They didn't listen. They could not be moved from their settled opinions. It was as if they wore a pair of blinders that shut out anything they didn't wish to recognize.

Cecelia didn't understand how anyone could remain oblivious in the face of other's needs and pains. Yet Prince Karl was only the most recent, and flagrant, example she'd seen. Looking up, she caught him gazing at her. He smiled with—smug anticipation? He really had no idea how intensely he'd infuriated her. He would refuse to believe her if she told him. Well, Cecelia didn't intend to bother. She would avoid him from now on. She wondered if he meant to stay for the entire London season.

As a first step, she made certain she rode in Lady Wilton's carriage on the way home, rather than the one the prince had hired to accommodate their large group. "I take it the prince did *not* make you an offer?" the old lady asked her as soon as they set off.

On the facing seat, Harriet and Sarah perked up like hounds who'd scented a fox.

Cecelia affected an air of mild surprise. "He is a prince," she said. "He will make a political marriage."

"Ah. He told you so?" Lady Wilton's eyes were piercing.

"It is only what one would expect for a prince," Cecelia replied, aware that the old woman saw right through her evasions.

"But he has been acting as if he meant to marry you," Sarah said. "Everyone thought so. They gossip about it."

"Let that be a lesson to you," replied Lady Wilton sharply. "One never knows what a man will do until he has actually proposed marriage. And sometimes not even then."

"What do you mean not even then?" asked Sarah.

"Precisely what I said," said Lady Wilton.

"But it wasn't precise," replied Sarah. "If a gentleman offers…"

"He might be hoping you will refuse," said Harriet.

Everyone in the carriage turned to look at her.

"That would be nonsensical," said Sarah.

"If someone was forcing him into the match, he might speak in a way that made it impossible to accept. In such terms that no female could agree."

"Did someone—" began Sarah.

"As a purely hypothetical case," Harriet interrupted. "In the spirit of rational analysis."

"We will talk about this later," declared Sarah, pinning Harriet with a stern gaze.

Lady Wilton gave a crack of laughter. "You girls are better than a play," she said.

Cecelia shifted in her seat. Had James hoped she would refuse his first proposal? She didn't think so. He was clumsy, not devious. She'd thought his regrets would come later. Now she dared hope she'd been wrong. When he'd kissed her…

She had scant experience of kisses. But James's had been as different from Prince Karl's acquisitive grab as anything could possibly be. Prince Karl was condescending and entitled. James was… not as she'd thought him?

A storm of emotion rose in her, bringing a strong desire to burst into tears. A small gasp, nearly a sob, escaped her. She struggled to suppress it, though she was fairly certain Sarah heard. Cecelia felt an irresistible urge to see James. To be with him, to discover what lay behind that searing kiss. Not to weep on his shoulder! Not again! She wanted to talk to him. She realized that she always wanted to talk to him. Even when they'd been at odds, over the years, she'd looked forward to their conversations. Was there anyone she knew better?

She would go to Tereford House in the morning and see him, taking advantage of her *lax* chaperonage. The idea was so comforting that her tears receded. Prince Karl was nothing to her after all. Less than nothing. All might still be well.

Twelve

CECELIA SLIPPED THROUGH THE EMPTY STABLES BEHIND Tereford House and across the cobbled yard. The back door was unlocked today, so she went in without knocking. She found the kitchen empty, though a fire burned in the hearth, and there were signs of baking under way. Mrs. Gardener was clearly making up for her children's previous deprivation with a steady supply of pastries. Cecelia was about to pass through to the corridor beyond when she felt a strong sense of being watched.

She looked around. There was no one here and no sound from the pantry. A vacant silence lay over the chamber. Yet Cecelia was convinced she was being observed. A flicker of movement led her to look up, and there she met the eyes that had alerted her. A very large brindled cat sat on top of a cupboard gazing down at her like a sentry at her post. The animal looked as if it had lived a hard life. It was thin and bore scars. But its steady stare held a marked aura of resolve, as if to say that this cat *would* succeed at this opportunity for a home. Cecelia nodded in acknowledgment as she started moving again. The cat's ears swiveled to follow her progress through the kitchen.

Voices reached Cecelia as she edged along the cluttered corridor beyond. She headed for the room James had been clearing when she was last here, and found it vacant. The sounds came from the one beyond. She followed them and entered another half-emptied chamber.

James and the whole Gardener family stood around a number of open trunks. Fountains of fabric erupted from them, silks and satins and beautifully embroidered cloth, a cache of clothes from earlier centuries. A miasma of camphor permeated the air. James bent over one trunk, his back to the doorway.

Jen paraded about in a blue satin gown that was much too large for her. Its hem dragged across the dusty floor like a monarch's train. "I'm Cinderella," she said.

"No I'm Cinderella!" exclaimed Effie. A silken shawl in rainbow colors engulfed her small frame, and she had a feathered turban balanced on her head. It nearly hid her eyes. "You're a wicked step-sister," she added.

"I am not!" replied Jen. "You are!"

"You're neither of you wicked," said their older brother. "You're princesses getting ready for the king's ball." Ned wore a dark-green velvet coat heavily embroidered with gilt flowers. Its full skirts fell to his ankles, and the sleeves hid his hands. He turned them back to free his fingers.

"You're getting dirt all over them fine things," said Mrs. Gardener, who stood a little apart looking anxious.

"No matter," said James.

"The dust will brush out," said Cecelia.

James turned so fast that he almost tripped. Then he smiled at her in a way that made Cecelia's heart pound.

"I wish gentlemen still wore clothes this fine," said Ned, finger-ing the embroidery on his sleeve. "I knew a lady near our old place that did this kind of stitching. She had to wear powerful spectacles. She'd ruined her eyes on the fine bits."

"You weren't supposed to be visiting her," said Mrs. Gardener.

"That don't matter now," replied Ned.

His mother threw a nervous look at James. James smiled sun-nily back at her.

Ned opened another trunk. It contained rows of smaller wooden boxes. He opened one of those. "It's wigs like the old people wore." The boy lifted out a powdered concoction of waves and whorls and put it on his head. The new frame changed his face into something much more solemn.

"You look like an ancestral portrait," said James.

"Or a high court judge," said Cecelia.

They exchanged a smiling look.

"We need a mirror," replied Ned.

"Ned," said his mother.

"There's a small one in my bedchamber," said James.

Cecelia noted that he seemed to be thinking of the room as his now, rather than his old chambers. "You must have a full-length glass," she said to Ned. "There has to be one here somewhere."

"Undoubtedly," said James. "But where?" He gestured at the rest of the house.

"Look at this 'en, it's purple." Jen lifted another wig from one of the smaller boxes. The powder on it did have a violet cast. She raised it and plopped it onto her head, but when she tried to turn and preen, the heavy mound of curls fell off. Powder whoofed out in a circle around her and streaked the satin gown.

"Jen, be careful!" cried her mother. "You've made a mess."

The three children crouched as if waiting for an explosion.

"No matter," said James again. "Look at this." He bent over the trunk nearest him and pulled out a long, dark velvet robe, slightly moth-eaten. He put it on over his clothes. The garment fell to his feet in a straight line with wide embroidered lapels turned back at the front edges.

Cecelia noticed a flat velvet cap in the same trunk and handed it to him. James gave her a wry look, but set it on his head.

"An ancestor of mine who served Henry the Eighth wore something like this in his portrait," he said. "I need a large gold chain of office though."

"And a sword," said Jen. "To chop off people's heads."

"What?" James turned to look at the girl.

"That old king Henry chopped off all his wives' heads," she explained. She made a broad cutting gesture.

"Not all," said James. "Only two out of six."

"Oh well, that's all right then," said Cecelia.

"I didn't mean…" James began.

"Look at the stitches here," said Ned, examining the seam of another coat. "So tiny you can't hardly see them. That's good work, that is."

"You like clothes, don't you?" Cecelia asked him.

Ned dropped the coat and ducked his head as if dodging a blow.

"He's interested in all manner of things," said his mother quickly. "He's a clever lad. He likes horses, don't you, Ned."

The boy nodded.

"I can see how clever he is," Cecelia replied. She hesitated, then decided to try out her idea. "I wonder if you might like to be a tailor?" she asked Ned.

"That's a feller who sews?" Ned asked.

She stared at James, willing him to catch her drift. He held her gaze for a moment, frowning, then gave a quick nod. "A fine tailor helps set fashions," he said to Ned. "He confers with gentlemen about the latest styles and makes certain they look their best. Someone like Weston or Stultz is highly respected and in great demand."

"Hah." Ned looked interested. "I don't see how I could ever do that."

"You would have to serve an apprenticeship," answered James. "Work hard and learn for some years, I suppose."

"Them costs money," replied Ned glumly.

James met Cecelia's eyes this time, and they held a quick silent conversation, noting that money could be found if it was wanted and that this topic should be set aside until the boy's mother could be consulted. Glancing at Mrs. Gardener, Cecelia thought that she was at least partly aware of the exchange.

She was more certain when Mrs. Gardener said, "Enough of this nonsense now. Tidy up and come see if my pie is finished, as it ought to be."

The tidying was a haphazard whirlwind. Effie retained the

silken shawl as the children rushed out. Their mother lingered in the doorway. "I ain't giving them too many sweets," she said, as if she'd been asked to defend her choices. "Only one time in the day. They've never had many treats."

"My dear Mrs. Gardener, feed them anything you like," said James.

She went out. Cecelia and James were left alone. Cecelia went to look into one of the trunks. "I never dressed up from the attics when I was young," she said.

"Neither did I," replied James.

She laughed, as he'd hoped she would.

He gestured at the wild spill of clothing. "And you didn't have this wealth of materials."

"No. Mama wasn't much interested in fashion."

"She always looked well."

Cecelia blinked, surprised or touched, he couldn't tell. "She did. Also Papa was trying to educate me in philosophy. Our amusements tended to be subdued."

"Was he? I didn't know." James was overjoyed to see her. When she hadn't visited for a day, he'd nearly left the house and gone to call on her. Another day, and he would have. But she was here now, not so very far from where she'd kissed him. The kiss had not kept her away. They needed to speak of it. And, he very much hoped, do it again. But mainly to get things settled between them.

"He'd given up by the time we met," she said. "He said my thoughts jumped about like grasshoppers." She sniffed. "I was seven years old!"

"I have always argued that your father's judgment is flawed. As you know."

"So very well." She glanced at him then away, seeming uncharacteristically shy. "You didn't have costumes at school?"

"Not like this." He ran his hand over the velvet robe.

"No troops of Eton boys dressed up as their illustrious ancestors?"

"None." James took off the robe and cap and replaced them in the trunk. "Grubby boots and skinned knees were more the fashion."

She wandered about the room examining the piles of garments. He couldn't simply sweep her into his arms. Could he? No. Something must be said first. The right words. James felt he had so much to say and so little idea of how to put it.

"You will have to find a way to curb the children without bringing up bad memories," said Cecelia. "Otherwise chaos will begin to reign."

"Chaos is already monarch here," he replied. "They fit right in."

"But you are trying to bring order."

"Am I? Yes, I suppose I am. But a bit of license can't hurt. And discipline is up to their mother, is it not?"

At last she met his eyes. "You can't bear to see them flinch."

James could not deny it. "Well, can you? Could anyone?"

"A good many people, I'm afraid. But not me. You're right."

"Well, we care nothing for those others."

The tender look she gave him then nearly destroyed his control. His hand rose of its own accord, reaching for her. How had he failed to see what she meant to him for so long? "Cecelia."

"I think Ned could be a fine tailor," she said.

"That was a good idea."

"I have them now and then." It was her old teasing tone.

"I have never said you did not."

"What about the time…"

"Cecelia." He repeated, moving closer. "I have been thinking about you nearly every moment since we last met."

She flushed.

"I hope that you had also… That you enjoyed it as much as I…" It felt as if the words were actual objects tangling his tongue, which had never happened to him before.

"I did."

The simple phrase loosed all bounds. They moved irresistibly together and into the sort of kiss that had flamed in James's memory since that day. She was soft and eager in his arms. He was wild with desire. Their bodies strove to melt into one.

"That is very much enough of that," said a scandalized voice from the doorway.

They jumped apart and whirled.

"Great heavens."

"Aunt Valeria!" exclaimed Cecelia. "What are you...? How did you find me?"

"How?" The plump blond woman looked exasperated. "I followed you, Cecelia. Which was not at all difficult to do. Your absences have been noticed by the servants, you know. And although the staff revere you, your maid thought it best to mention them to me. Rightly so." She let out an irritated breath.

Cecelia glanced at James. "I didn't see..."

"Of course you did not see me," interrupted her aunt. "I took care that you should not. That is how I lost track of you when you ducked into the alleyway behind this extraordinary house. Ducked into the alleyway, Cecelia! Do you hear the impropriety of that phrase? Does it have any effect on you? I found my way back and inside, lingering in the...disorder across the hallway to make my observations."

"Miss Vainsmede," began James.

She held up an admonitory hand, walked into the room, and turned in a circle, surveying the jumbled clothing before facing Cecelia again. "I have always trusted you to show good judgment," she continued. "I thought you were an intelligent, level-headed girl. And so I have never been a strict chaperone. But this is too much. Slipping off secretly to meet Tereford! Clandestine embraces." She looked around again. "Unacceptable. As well as inexplicable. It's not as if he is Romeo and you Juliet. He can call on you at home."

"Miss Vainsmede," James tried again. A rat flashed past the

open doorway; a large fierce-looking cat followed it down the corridor in hot pursuit. There was a clatter of falling objects.

A wordless exclamation escaped Cecelia.

Her aunt marched up to James and fixed him with a jaundiced gaze. "I am not one to criticize eccentricity, Tereford. Pot and kettle and so on. You are free to do as you like. However mad. But I will not allow you to involve Cecelia in…whatever it is you're doing here." She shook her head muttering, "A servants' costume ball?"

James wanted to say that he and Cecelia were engaged to be married. But Miss Vainsmede's inopportune arrival had prevented him from verifying this. Of course they were, with the way she'd kissed him. But he'd gone too fast the last time he'd proposed. He couldn't make such an announcement without speaking to Cecelia.

He tried to judge her thoughts from her expression. If she gave him some signal. But he could not be sure what she wished him to do.

"And I must say, abandoning polite society, which you purportedly enjoyed, to live in squalor is a bit much," said Miss Vainsmede. She frowned at him. "Could you find no other way of being a mystery?"

"Mystery?"

"The wonder of your disappearance after your abandonment of polite behavior," the older lady replied. "Has the disorder here turned your brain?"

"People are still talking of that?" James asked. The reason for his flight seemed so much less important now. He'd almost forgotten.

"Of course they are," replied the older lady. "It is much more than a nine-days' wonder. Everyone who calls on us has a theory. They have become increasingly wild."

The cat passed the doorway going the other way, the dead rat now hanging from its jaws. James wondered if she was taking her kill to the kitchen to demonstrate her prowess and solidify her position.

"And yet they do not quite come up to the reality," added Miss Vainsmede, her tone desert dry.

To announce an engagement when he had been absent from society without explanation would increase the gossip. Cecelia would be brought into it. James didn't want speculative whispers attached to their news. And Cecelia was still silent. Why had he wasted the chance to talk to her alone? He ought to have proposed and then kissed her. "If I could just have a moment to speak to C... your niece."

"You may do so whenever you like," answered her aunt. "At our house. Not here. She will not be coming here again. From now on she will be home for morning calls. As I informed the *horde* of people who came looking for details about her expedition with the prince."

"Expedition?" James asked.

Cecelia flushed. "Hardly that," she murmured. "A visit to Vauxhall merely."

The bolt of jealousy that went through James exceeded any that had shaken him before. It was like an earthquake. He realized that he'd imagined Prince Karl had dropped from her life, as he had from James's. Cecelia's visits to him here had created a small world of their own, apart from all that. He'd come to cherish it. He'd thought she did as well.

But she'd gone on with her life outside their hidden realm, and there she'd spent time with the prince. Gone to Vauxhall—with its dim pathways and hidden nooks! Prince Karl was just the sort of fellow to take full advantage of them. What was he to Cecelia now?

James felt furiously confused. She'd kissed him! And enjoyed it. She'd said so. Cecelia wasn't a girl who scattered meaningless kisses.

"Come, Cecelia, we are going," said Miss Vainsmede.

"I will just stay a bit longer, Aunt. A few minutes only."

She looked as if she wanted to tell him something significant. James clutched at the possibility. "Indeed," he began.

"No." The older woman's face fell into stubborn lines. "We have an agreement, Cecelia. Unspoken till now, I concede, but clear nonetheless. I stand in the place of your chaperone for propriety's sake, and you make it unnecessary for me to act as one. By being sensible! By behaving as you ought. *And* you deal with society. I am weary of them all. You will return home with me at once." She crossed her arms and glowered at them both.

"What about the free flight of the queen bee?" replied Cecelia. Quite inexplicably, to James.

"My dear girl, I know you are well aware that a metaphor is not to be applied *literally*." She huffed out a disgusted breath. "If only you were a bee. We would get on so much more easily. Come along!"

Cecelia's aunt practically dragged her through the door and away, leaving James alone in his wreck of a house, his mind seething with questions.

Thirteen

LADY WILTON WAS IN THE ENTRYWAY OF THE VAINSMEDE house when they arrived home, though it was past the conventional hour for morning calls. "There you are!" she exclaimed. "I was just going. I have been waiting an age." Not pausing for an invitation, she walked up to the drawing room with them, sat down like a one-woman delegation, and fixed Cecelia with a disapproving stare. Cecelia was strongly reminded of a raven she had once seen at the Tower of London. It had been pecking the eyes out of a dead pigeon.

The comparison nearly made her smile. But her thoughts were too full of James to be diverted. She could not have mistaken his kisses, or the look in his eyes when he said he had been thinking of her. She might have spoken up when Aunt Valeria berated her, but she hadn't wished for her future to be settled in such a scene. She would return to him, no matter what her aunt decreed, and they would do that together. Her heart sang at the prospect.

"What have you done?" said Lady Wilton.

Wondering if she'd discovered James's hiding place, Cecelia merely looked inquiring. Inside, she braced for a scolding.

"Prince Karl has been talking about you."

"What?" This was the last thing Cecelia expected.

"He is giving everyone the impression that you are his mistress."

"What?" Aunt Valeria turned on Cecelia as well. "What have you…"

"Hold your tongue, Valeria Vainsmede," said Lady Wilton, her expression and tone sour. "You are a travesty of a chaperone. Pretending to be deaf! Idiotic! You have no right to protest now that you have allowed disaster to befall your charge."

Aunt Valeria closed her mouth with a snap.

"Prince Karl dares to claim this?" Cecelia wished she had throttled him when she had the chance.

"Not outright," Lady Wilton admitted. "But he is dropping sly remarks among the gentlemen at their clubs. Which they then pass on to everyone they know, of course. Nothing overtly claimed, but everything smugly hinted. He is creating a strong, most unfortunate impression."

"He is a worm!" Cecelia exclaimed.

"Possibly. No one cares about that, however. What did you do at Vauxhall?"

"Nothing!"

"Your idea of nothing appears..." began Aunt Valeria.

"Quiet!" Lady Wilton gazed at Cecelia and waited.

"He led me onto a dark path and kissed me," she admitted. "And I pushed him away and told him I didn't wish to marry him."

"He proposed?" Lady Wilton looked surprised.

"No. I–I thought to forestall him. To prevent any awkwardness."

Their visitor's frown deepened. "I suppose this is when you learned that he plans a political marriage?"

"Yes." Cecelia bit off the word.

"And never meant to make you an offer."

Cecelia nodded curtly.

She got a sigh and a headshake in response. "So you had two fine suitors, and now you have none," said Lady Wilton. "One you have lost. The other you bungled. I am disappointed in you, Miss Vainsmede."

Aunt Valeria started to speak. Cecelia cut her off with a gesture. "*I* did none of that, Lady Wilton," she replied.

"It is always the lady's fault in these situations."

"That is the stupidest thing I have ever heard."

"Then you are fortunate in your conversations," replied the old lady dryly.

"I have done nothing wrong."

"You have done nothing right either, Miss Vainsmede. That is the problem." She turned to Cecelia's aunt. "And you. You're known to be very lax. Oblivious, in fact. You are the poorest vestige of an excuse for a chaperone. That is adding to gossip. People can believe you would overlook all sorts of unconventional behavior."

Aunt Valeria looked outraged. "They suggest I would allow Cecelia to become someone's mistress?"

Lady Wilton shook her head. "Rather that you pay no attention. And thus do not see what is going on under your nose. Which makes some believe that matters might have gotten out of hand."

A queasy mixture of fury and contempt gripped Cecelia and brought her to her feet. "So you have passed along your news. You have pointed out our supposed failings. And told me my fate. Are you satisfied?"

"What do you mean?"

"You have had your gossip. Perhaps you will go now."

"I beg your pardon? I came to help you."

"Indeed?" Cecelia ground her teeth. "If I am such a hopeless bungler, why would you wish to?"

For the first time in this conversation Lady Wilton appeared uncertain. "It isn't fair," she said finally.

"You do not say so!"

"Oh, sit down, Miss Vainsmede. Enacting a Cheltenham tragedy won't mend matters. We must think what to do."

"We? I still don't understand your interest."

"I…" The old lady shrugged. "At one time, I thought you might marry Tereford and become part of my family."

"Which time?" Cecelia couldn't help asking.

"It doesn't matter. You are a sensible young woman. I don't wish to see you humiliated."

Cecelia's turmoil had subsided slightly. "So you are here to… What? Offer advice?"

"It is a bit late to be asking my advice."

The sour response was almost welcome. It would have been strange if Lady Wilton had suddenly become all kindness and accommodation.

Female voices sounded from below. Cecelia would have told the footman to turn away visitors, but she hadn't known what news Lady Wilton was coming to deliver. Cecelia started to rise, but before she could act, the drawing room doorway was filled with bright gowns.

Her four new friends arrived like a second delegation. Sarah, Ada, Harriet, and Charlotte stopped a few steps in, clearly disconcerted to find Lady Wilton present. The looks on their faces suggested that they'd heard the gossip.

No one seemed to want to speak, so Cecelia broke the awkward silence herself. "Prince Karl is spreading lies," she said. "Lady Wilton has told me."

The young ladies looked at the old woman, surprised.

"The story must be everywhere if even silly chits are hearing it," said Lady Wilton.

"We are not silly chits," said Sarah.

"We came to form a scheme to help," said Ada.

The old lady made a derisive sound. "How do you imagine you could do that?"

"We don't know yet, but we are very resourceful," said Charlotte.

"Nonsense!"

"I don't know why you say so, since you don't know us at all," said Harriet.

"I know that society will not listen to girls fresh from the schoolroom."

"We don't intend to lecture people," said Charlotte. "We will develop stratagems."

"La, what a word." Lady Wilton shook her head. "You will not get far on vocabulary."

"I will. To the places I *want* to go," snapped Charlotte.

"I begin to feel like a charity project," Cecelia interrupted. "And I don't care for the sensation. I will manage this…difficulty myself."

"No, you won't," replied Lady Wilton. "Without allies you will be lost."

Cecelia felt a battery of eyes upon her. Allies were a fine idea, but she didn't see what any of them could do. They couldn't march up to people and deny hints and innuendo. That merely gave them strength. She didn't know what she was going to do. At this moment, she was mainly thankful that James had withdrawn from society and would not be hearing the prince's hateful lies.

❧

James was tossing a wad of mildewed tapestry out the window when Effie ran into the room they were clearing. "There's a man out back," the little girl said. She looked anxious.

"What sort of man?"

"A fine gentleman. He looked in the kitchen window and saw Mam and me."

"Why didn't you hide?" asked her brother, Ned.

"We didn't know he was there! He just…turned up. All of a sudden like. And he ain't going away. He went and knocked on the door!"

"I said as how we should fix that lock on the stables," said Ned.

Since James suspected that the boy had broken it in the first place, he said only, "I'd best go and see."

Effie looked relieved to have passed off responsibility.

Peering out into the cobbled yard behind the house, James saw Henry Deeping pacing there. He did indeed show no signs of leaving. With a sigh, James went to let him in the back door. "Did Ce… someone tell you I was here?" he asked when he opened it.

"I worked it out for myself" was the reply. "Who knows that you're here?"

"Never mind."

Henry craned his neck to see over James's shoulder. "Looks like a rum sort of place."

"You have no idea."

"Did you know there's a pile of furniture in your back garden?" Henry pointed to the wall at the side of the yard, and James saw that his discards had begun to show over the top. He merely nodded.

"And that Hobbs has gone to work for Bingham? Bingham's boasting all over town about luring your valet away from you."

"I suspected as much," James replied.

"Don't you care?"

James shrugged.

"What's happened to you?" asked Henry.

"I have more important things to think about."

His friend gaped at him. "More important than your valet? You always said…"

"A great many irrelevant things," James interrupted. "I'm touched by your concern, Henry, but I must get back to work."

"Work?" He said it as if he could not connect the word with James.

"My great-uncle left a monumental mess." James gestured at the pile over the wall. "It has to be gone through."

Henry gazed at him, at the discarded furnishings, and then back at him.

"And I'd appreciate it if you did not share my current address," James added. He indicated that his friend should go out the way he'd come.

Henry shifted from one foot to the other. "Something to tell you," he said. "My sister said I had to find you. And after a bit I thought of this place."

"Your sister?" James couldn't imagine what that spiky girl had to say to him.

Henry nodded. And then said nothing.

"Well, what is it?"

"Not quite sure how to put it." Henry looked around as if he feared eavesdroppers. "It's a bit sticky."

Seeing that his friend appeared genuinely concerned, James stepped back and led him inside. He took him through the house and up toward his bedchamber, the only livable private space.

As they walked, Henry voiced astonishment about the state of the house. "This is a rum place and no mistake. Is that a spinning wheel?"

James simply nodded. As they passed the room where he'd been working, Ned and Jen stuck their heads out. "Who's that?" asked Henry.

"My staff."

"Your... Is this some sort of joke, James? Because I'm not seeing the humor in it."

"It's Uncle Percival's jest, not mine." They reached James's bedchamber, and he closed the door. "What is this thing you must tell me?"

His friend looked uneasy.

"You see how much there is to do here," James added. "I should get back to it."

"Prince Karl is spreading rumors about Miss Vainsmede," Henry blurted out.

"What?"

"He's claiming...well, insinuating that she...succumbed to his advances."

The fury that swept through James then made him incapable of speech.

"He's doing it really well, too," Henry added. "If that's the word for slander. I saw him at a card party. He drops hints and then pretends to regret his slip. Claims far too vigorously that he meant nothing by it. Goes off with a sly, secretive smile."

"That foul buzzard," James growled. He was shaking with the need to pummel the fellow.

"Charlotte says it's not true," Henry added quickly.

"Of course it's not true!" James had no shred of doubt.

"But she's worried that some people are being convinced."

"I'll kill him!" said James. He turned to go and do so immediately.

Henry caught his arm. "A duel would just draw more attention to his story. People would say there must be some truth to it if you issue a challenge."

James jerked free. He hadn't been thinking of anything as formal as a duel. More along the lines of assassination. "People," he echoed with revulsion. But he had to admit that Henry was right. A fight—*another* fight—would add to the talk. There was also the fact that Prince Karl would skewer him in a duel. He struggled with rage and frustration.

"Charlotte and her friends want to find a way to squash the rumors."

"Ridding the world of the prince would be a good start," James answered.

"Not really," replied Henry.

"Stealthily, as a conjuror makes a rabbit disappear."

His friend almost smiled. "But that is not possible."

"You could not use your diplomatic connections to have him deported?" James was only half joking.

"My 'diplomatic connections' are no more than a slender hope at this point," Henry replied.

He'd known this. "I must return to society," James said. There was no question. Cecelia was more important than anything else, including his own position. He would return to his rooms today. "I don't suppose you can recommend a valet?"

"I…what?" Henry stared at him.

James had to look his best if he was to come down on Prince Karl like the avenging Furies from the old Greek story. Didn't they rip evildoers to pieces? That must have been a satisfying role. He would make the fellow sorry he'd dared to malign Cecelia. More than sorry. He would see him crawl. "Never mind. I will call on your sister tomorrow morning," he added.

"On Charlotte?"

James nodded. "Perhaps you could arrange that her three friends are also present?" He couldn't recall their names in the heat of the moment, but Henry knew who he meant.

Henry had not moved.

"Well, go!" James commanded.

His friend started and went.

James wanted nothing more than to run to Cecelia and sweep her out of harm's way, but in the circumstances that was no simple task. There were preparations to make.

He went downstairs to inform Mrs. Gardener that she would be watching over the house until he could return. "The stable lock will be repaired," he told her. "And you will be given a key. The front door you can ignore."

"How long will you be away, milord?" she asked.

"I'm not certain just now." At her anxious look, he added, "Is there anyone you would like to have with you here? A relative perhaps?"

"Uncle Will," said Jen. "He could fix the lock. He can fix anything."

"Jen!" said her mother.

"Your brother?" James asked her. He was recalling remarks about the children's father and wanted no criminals brought into the household.

"Yes, milord," said Mrs. Gardener.

"He's a good man, brave as a lion," said Ned as if he understood James's worries. "He fought in the war."

His mother nodded. "He lost a leg."

There had been so many such soldiers in the last few years.

"But he don't go begging in the street," she added quickly. "He finds work, here and there. Like Jen said, he's a whiz at fixing things. And he has a peg. He can move about right well."

Her tone was a further recommendation. James didn't believe she would advocate for a lawbreaker after the hardships she'd experienced. "Would you like to invite him to stay here?" he asked Mrs. Gardener. "We certainly have much that needs mending. And he could watch over things."

"I can do that," protested Ned.

"That'd be fine, milord," said his mother at the same time. "He'd work hard, he would."

"Let us do that then." James turned to Ned, who looked sulky. "You said you could use a flatiron."

The whole family looked surprised by the change of direction. And uneasy. "Yeah," said Ned.

"Could you press a coat? Properly?"

"I reckon I could," answered Ned, his expression shifting to puzzlement.

"Milord," put in his mother.

"Milord," muttered Ned.

James examined the idea that was forming in his mind. He was perfectly capable of tying his own neckcloths, and a laundress could manage his linen. But there was more to it if he was to appear in all his old perfection. His landlady would pitch in, but… "Have you ever shined boots?" he asked Ned.

"I could make 'em look better than that," the boy replied, indicating the ones James currently wore. "Milord," he added at his mother's frown.

James looked down at the dusty, scuffed leather. How had he let his footwear come to this? Hobbs would have been horrified at the state of his boots. He made up his mind. It was nothing more than an experiment after all. "My valet has scarpered," he continued. "I need someone to help with my clothes. Perhaps you could try."

Ned stared, then grinned, then nodded with wide-eyed enthusiasm.

James noted that the boy's mother appeared to have doubts. Well, so did he. They could only see how it went.

Fourteen

THE GENTLEMAN WHO STROLLED INTO THE DEEPING DRAWING room the next morning was that paragon of fashion and elegance, the Duke of Tereford in full glory. Ned had done quite well with the boots, using tips about Hobbs's practices from the woman who provided James's rooms. He'd also proved adept with a flatiron, as promised. The intricate neckcloth was all James's achievement, of course. But Ned had done well with his hair. He'd also been greatly impressed by the result of their efforts.

James found Cecelia's four new friends waiting as he had requested. He also found no one else, which was a relief. He'd been scheming over how to be rid of a crowd of duennas and had not developed a satisfactory plan. When greetings had been exchanged, he said, "I have come to discuss Miss Vainsmede's situation. It is not quite proper for me to…"

"We don't care about that," interrupted Charlotte Deeping. "We want to help."

"Cecelia is being exceedingly brave," said Miss Ada Grandison.

"Perhaps because she has nothing to be ashamed of?" replied Harriet Finch dryly.

James decided that he liked the redheaded girl more than he'd thought. "Henry told me you wished to help," he said.

"We do," said Miss Finch. "But there are difficulties."

James raised his eyebrows.

"We've all been ordered to avoid being seen with her too often," said Sarah Moran with a woeful expression. "Our mothers say that if there is even a hint that she is an unsuitable companion…"

"Ridiculous!" exclaimed Charlotte Deeping.

"We intend to defy them," added Miss Grandison.

"We *wish* to do so," said Miss Finch. "We would be happy to do so. But if we all disobey our parents to sneak out and visit Cecelia… That may not do her any good."

"She could be accused of inspiring impropriety and rebellion," said Sarah Moran gloomily.

"Which we are not permitted to exhibit," muttered Ada Grandison.

James had not foreseen this obstacle. Matters had gone further and faster than he'd expected. Fury at Prince Karl burned through him.

"Also, we are not allowed to defend her in conversation," said Charlotte Deeping, who looked bitterly angry. "Because we are not supposed to know about 'such things.' I tried to tell Lady Harte that the story wasn't true, and she had a nervous spasm."

"She is a foolish widgeon," said Harriet Finch.

"Who relishes her spasms," added Ada Grandison.

"I know," replied Miss Deeping. "But that does not alter the situation."

James realized that he hadn't quite understood the limitations young ladies labored under. Clearly they had thought this through, and he had not. "I see," he said. It seemed he must abandon this line of assistance. But he wanted a plan to offer before he called on Cecelia.

"Lady Wilton wants to help," said Miss Moran. "And she can do as she pleases."

And thus it was that James found himself, half an hour later, at the door of his grandmother's house, an address he'd been told he visited far too seldom.

He knocked, was admitted at once, and followed a footman up to the drawing room. He wondered if this was the same servant who'd been sent to Tereford House to find him. He might have asked if not for a slender hope of preserving his refuge for the future.

The old lady already had morning callers, and James's arrival caused a stunned silence, and then a murmuring sensation. Two elderly women and a matron with a debutante daughter in tow gazed at him as if he'd appeared in a magical puff of smoke.

"Tereford," said Lady Wilton.

"Hello, Grandmamma."

"How pleasant to see you. You know everyone, of course." She nevertheless named her guests. The sardonic glint in her eye told James that she knew he'd forgotten half of them. He made his bow and took the chair he was offered.

"You are fully recuperated?" asked the matron.

James frowned at her, at a loss. Had his grandmother spread some tale of an illness?

"From the…contretemps with Prince Karl," the woman added, mockery in her gaze.

For a moment James couldn't think what she meant. His concern for Cecelia had pushed that regrettable episode out of his mind. The sword bout, which had felt like such a deep humiliation, hardly seemed to matter anymore. Though he could wish that he'd punched the fellow much harder. But apparently the incident was still fresh to others. He'd fed the fires of gossip with his flight, and now these ladies were waiting for his response like carrion birds hanging over a carcass. They would spread their gleaned tidbits throughout the *ton*. Best to dispose of this matter at once. "Contre…?" he mused. "Ah, I had forgotten." He tried to sound as if she'd mentioned some silly, rather stupid matter. From the look on her face, he'd succeeded.

"The prince has made quite an *impression* in society," said one of the old ladies.

She was referring to Cecelia now, James had no doubt. It was a pity that one couldn't simply tell people they were idiots. It would save a great deal of time. Except that they wouldn't listen. And they would take it as a twisted sort of corroboration. "Has he?" James replied in a bored tone. "People seem to enjoy every sort of ridiculous spectacle."

The old lady bridled. "Some appear to be *enjoying* more than others," said her companion sourly.

He could not shake a septuagenarian with the bones of a bird, or simply order her out of the house. Declaring that he had private business to discuss with his grandmother would merely draw attention. James settled for a blank, world-weary look, as if he couldn't imagine why she was speaking to him about something so tedious.

"Do you call the prince ridiculous?" asked the matron.

The callers bent closer. Again James imagined beaks poised to snatch up gobbets of well-aged scandal. "Of course not," he said.

They waited. He added nothing.

"Have you heard whether Lady Goring is recovering from her illness?" asked Lady Wilton.

It was her drawing room. Visitors could not demand a return to the previous subject. They responded. James remained silent, offering them no more nuggets to share. Finally, after what seemed an eternity of maddening chatter, the callers departed.

Lady Wilton waited until they were well away before saying, "You did well on the matter of your unfortunate sword fight."

James brushed this aside. "I don't care about that."

His grandmother examined him. "Do you not?"

"No. I've come to talk about Miss Vainsmede and Prince Karl, though their names should *not* be linked."

She nodded. "Go and tell the footman that I am not receiving any longer."

James did so. When he returned, his grandmother eyed him. "Where have you been?"

"That doesn't matter."

"Perhaps not, now that you are back again. But I am curious. And since I suspect that you want my help, you must indulge me."

Refusing to grind his teeth, James said, "At the town house, clearing up."

"I sent a servant to look for you there," she said.

"Well, the next time you want a thing found, you should send someone else."

"Hah." She sat back and gazed at him. "It seems you have heard about the rumors Prince Karl is spreading."

"The man is scum," James said from between clenched teeth.

"One would expect a royal personage to be more of a gentleman. But then look at our own English princes."

James snorted. "He must be stopped."

"How do you intend to do that? Not more swordplay. I hope?"

"It's well known that you are a mistress of sarcasm, Grandmamma. You needn't demonstrate your skills on me."

"I am rather annoyed with you, James."

He ignored this. She was so often annoyed. "I have formed a plan." It had come to him as he endured the callers. "I shall escort you and Ce…Miss Vainsmede to a play first of all."

"To sit before everyone and show that we don't care a snap of our fingers for the whispers?"

"Precisely." Lady Wilton was irascible, but no one had ever called her slow.

"She has agreed to attend?"

"I haven't told her yet. I came to you first. But she will."

"Can you be so certain…"

"You may leave that to me!"

She gazed at him as if she was trying to see right through to his depths. "You understand that such a small party—just the three of us—will look marked. As I am your grandmother."

James decided that was an advantage rather than a drawback. He nodded.

Lady Wilton did the same, as if he'd confirmed some suspicion. "Very well," she said. "I will make a pact with you."

"What do you mean?"

"I will join in your scheme if you do something about Ferrington."

"Ferrington?"

"Why can no one remember that he exists?" asked his grandmother irritably. "My great-grandson who is now the Earl of Ferrington."

"The one who has disappeared," said James.

"So you *do* recall that much. Yes! I seem to be plagued with disappearing descendants."

"I will set inquiries in motion," said James.

"This is a meaningless phrase."

"I will hire agents to search for him."

"What sort of…"

"I don't know, Grandmamma! I have never done such a thing before. I will have to discover where one finds such people. But you have my word that I will do so."

She gazed at him. "I don't believe you've ever given me your word before."

James didn't remember. She was probably right.

"But I think that it is good," his grandmother added.

"Thank you." The words were sarcastic, but he found that he was also gratified by her trust.

"Very well then. I shall do all I can to help you."

James rose. "I will send word of the details for the play."

In the street, James paused to gather his thoughts. He ached to see Cecelia but wanted to get it right, as he had not been doing so far. Should he speak of marriage first? He longed to hear her say that she would marry him, that she wanted to as much as he wished it. He wanted to protect her from all harm. He indulged in a brief fantasy of sweeping her away from London to some perfect realm where they could…

"Tereford!"

James turned to find one of the leading lights of the dandy set approaching, resplendent in a heavily padded tailcoat, a neckcloth that appeared to be choking him, and a glittering wealth of fobs. "Hello, Crawdon."

"Where the devil have you been, man? You know Bingham snabbled your valet."

"I heard."

"Want me to cut him? Serve him right, the sneak. I never liked the fellow."

"That isn't necessary," said James.

This earned him a critical look. "If you say so," replied the dandy. "But I must tell you the shine on your boots is not up to your usual standard."

James marveled at how much less he cared about this than in the past. Which was not to say he cared *nothing*. He would find someone to give the Hessians a proper gleam.

"Care to toddle along to the club with me?" Crawdon asked.

"Sorry, I have an engagement."

"Very well. Oh! That prince of yours has been kicking up a fuss."

"Hardly mine," said James in his most thoroughly bored tone.

"You did have that set-to."

"A momentary lapse." James made a dismissive gesture.

"Right. Foreigners, eh?" Crawdon touched his hat brim and walked off.

James turned in the opposite direction and set off for Cecelia's home. He couldn't remember when he'd made so many morning calls. In the past he'd found them tedious beyond belief. How strangely things changed.

Cecelia was surprised when the footman announced James. At any other time her heart might have leapt at the news of his arrival. But today he was the last in a string of visitors who had tried her patience to the breaking point. All of them had been sly gossips probing for tidbits about Prince Karl, looking for cracks in her facade. And there seemed nothing she could say to dispel the miasma of innuendo. Whatever she did, the ground shifted beneath her feet. If she denied, she was protesting too much. If she pretended nothing unusual had occurred, she was evasive and deceptive. Blank incomprehension only roused more probing. And feigning stupidity was both foreign and repugnant to her. Aunt Valeria had actually tried to help. But she was abrupt and clumsy. And the sudden abandonment of her pretended deafness bewildered several visitors. She had finally fled to her beehives.

This had made for an extremely trying morning, and yet Cecelia hadn't thought it wise to refuse callers. To shut herself away would look like cowardice, or guilt. And so she'd put on her brightest gown, had her hair dressed in careless ringlets, and spent the morning stifling her anger. Now it hovered like storm clouds about to break.

So when James strolled in, wearing an impeccable dark-blue coat and pale pantaloons, with a fresh haircut, looking every inch the nonpareil, Cecelia's heart did not melt. Rather she resented his careless nonchalance. "You're back," she said.

"I am." He sat down beside her on the sofa as if he'd naturally been invited to do so.

No one would have associated this man of fashion with the dusty, disheveled fellow throwing broken-down furniture out a window. He looked like the old James, and Cecelia felt a tremor of unease. The old James had not noticed the plight of poor children or been full of gratitude for scones or dressed up in old-fashioned robes and paraded about. He had certainly never kissed her. He had looked down his nose and called her the bane of his existence. Had that James returned? If he had, she frankly could not bear it just now. And why had he chosen this inopportune day to emerge? When he was all too likely to hear things. "I am rather tired," she said. "What do you want?"

He looked startled, as well he might, she supposed. "I beg your pardon," she added. "I have a wretched headache."

He seemed about to speak, hesitated, then gave a slight shake of his head. "I've come to invite you to attend a play tomorrow evening with me and Lady Wilton," he said.

Words slipped out before Cecelia thought. "Going to Vauxhall with Lady Wilton created this whole tangle in the first place."

"What?"

She hadn't meant to say that. She didn't want him to know… anything. Particularly not about Prince Karl's kiss. He mustn't ever… And then something in James's expression showed Cecelia that he'd already heard the gossip and was here because of it. She flushed as a host of implications raced through her mind. "You need not do this," she said.

"Ask you to a play?"

She was sick of sly implications and fencing with words. "When you never have before? We both know why you're doing it, James."

"I'm doing it because you need help," he answered.

He might have said something that heartened or soothed her. Cecelia imagined that was possible. This was not it, however. Had she become a charity case now for the Corinthian, the newly minted duke, the handsomest man in England? "I will manage for myself."

"How do you propose to do that?"

She heard the old James in these words—the impatient, dismissive James of so many of their disputes. "That is my problem, not yours."

"Brazen it out until the talk passes, I suppose."

"Brazen…" A lady did not curse. Another unfairness imposed by the so-called polite world. She gritted her teeth instead.

"While an active…opponent adds fuel to the fires of gossip." His expression had gone hard with this reference to the prince. "That's no good."

Cecelia silently consigned Prince Karl and the gossips and just everybody to perdition.

"Don't you want to fight? You never had any difficulty opposing *me*."

His smile goaded her. But then she thought she glimpsed something else in his eyes. They seemed sympathetic rather than satirical, warm instead of combative. Cecelia's throat grew tight. Over the morning, she'd been feeling very much alone.

"You always argued matters of principle. Are they not involved here?"

The soft look was gone. No doubt she'd imagined it. "That was about estate business and your trust. This is rather different."

"Is it?"

"Yes!" Cecelia sat straighter, closed her hands into fists. "How does one combat whispers and sneaking lies, James? I have spent the morning trying. It's like trying to strike fog."

"Difficult," he agreed. "However, you don't need to battle it alone. Perhaps your father would come to the play as well?"

"He never goes to the theater."

"So would his presence signal solidarity or panic?"

The mere question goaded her further. "I don't wish to tell him about this matter," said Cecelia. Papa would be distressed, yet still reluctant to bestir himself, guilty about his reaction, resistant to any shift in his routine, and then annoyed. She didn't care to deal with any step of that process.

"You don't think he would want to help you?"

"What have you ever observed in him that makes you think so?" She heard the brush of bitterness in her voice and clamped her lips down upon it.

"And so you took up his tasks for my benefit," James replied softly. "You must allow me to reciprocate. I insist that you come to the play."

"Insist? What makes you think you have the right to do that?"

"*That* is the Cecelia I know," he answered with a smile that shook her to the core. "I don't have the right. But I have a sincere desire to enter the lists at your side."

The soft look was back. She hadn't imagined it. Perhaps the man who had kissed her so tenderly had not vanished into the old James.

"Unless you will give me that right?" he added.

He moved. It almost looked as if he meant to kneel at her feet.

"Ah, they told me you were here, Tereford." Aunt Valeria strode into the room and plopped down in a chair directly across from Cecelia. She gazed at them, her round face disgruntled. "I told the servants to inform me if any gentlemen called."

Now, *now* she was going to play the chaperone? She'd left Cecelia to the spite of the gossips, but she chose to interrupt James. This was to be a day when nothing went right, Cecelia concluded.

James sat back. "I came to invite Ce…Miss Vainsmede to a play tomorrow."

"I don't care for the stage," said Aunt Valeria. "All that silly prancing and ranting while one stifles in a reek of perfumes and pomades. The stench of a crowd! I don't believe I can…"

"Lady Wilton will accompany us," James interrupted.

"Ah." Aunt Valeria's complaint was arrested. "Well, I suppose that's all right then." She brightened. "She can't complain about my chaperonage if she's taken charge. I will allow it."

"Al…" began Cecelia.

"Very good of you," said James.

His tone and the understanding look he gave Cecelia cut off her explosion. She throttled her temper and refrained from telling her aunt that she had no right to allow—or forbid—*anything*. She was going to have to deal with this new, infuriating Aunt Valeria. Who sat staring at them, showing no sign of turning to her notebook and her customary oblivious state, nor any vestige of enjoyment. Clearly, she was willing James to go.

He rose. "Until tomorrow," he said. He held Cecelia's gaze for a heart-stopping moment, and then he was gone.

Fifteen

JAMES MADE CERTAIN THAT HIS PARTY ARRIVED WELL AHEAD OF the start of the play the following evening. His goal was to be obvious to the entire audience. Cecelia looked lovely in a pale-rose gown with a spray of flowers twined in her blond hair. She appeared poised and serene. He didn't think anyone would spot her anxiety. Lady Wilton was her usual imperturbably fashionable self. James dared anyone to challenge *her*. He was prepared to do social battle and to triumph this time. They settled in their box, ignoring the stares and whispers that rose around them.

"So now we must look carefree and chat," said Cecelia. James heard strain in her tone.

"Indeed," said Lady Wilton. "And I have a good deal to say." She was clearly pleased to have James cornered for an entire evening. "Ferrington," she added with a steely glint in her eye.

James held up a hand. "I have found an inquiry agent to set on his track. He wants a place to begin. What can you tell me about your lost earl? Where should I send this fellow first?"

"If I knew that, I would already have looked there," replied his grandmother acerbically.

"Sent your enterprising footman perhaps?" asked James, unable to resist.

The old lady scowled.

"Smiles, Grandmamma," said James. "Don't forget." Not that the entire *ton* wasn't accustomed to Lady Wilton's glowers.

"Insufferable boy," she muttered. But she smiled for their observers.

"Could Ferrington have gone back to America?" asked Cecelia.

"America?" James had not thought to send anyone so far.

Lady Wilton snorted. "Of course he hasn't. No one walks away from an earldom."

"And yet he seems to have done so," James pointed out.

"Unless something happened to him?" said Cecelia. "What if he was attacked by footpads?"

"All of his things and a horse I had purchased for his use disappeared with him," said Lady Wilton. "Hardly the work of footpads."

"So why and where has he gone?" James asked. "Let us begin at the beginning, Grandmamma. He was here in London."

"The beginning is my daughter's marriage to the earlier Earl of Ferrington," Lady Wilton interrupted. "Sixty years ago."

"Yes I know, but…"

"She had two sons," Lady Wilton continued, in the tone of one reciting an oft-told tale. "An heir and a scapegrace instead of a spare. Ralph. We had to send him off to America before he was eighteen."

"Had to?" echoed James. He felt a surge of pity for the lad. He saw the same emotion in the Cecelia's eyes.

"He was intractable," Lady Wilton went on. "Plunged into every vice from a scandalously early age. It was the best solution."

"Until you needed him again," murmured Cecelia.

James glanced at her.

Lady Wilton merely nodded. "Because my elder grandson got himself killed on the hunting field without producing an heir. So we had to go looking for Ralph."

"You didn't know what had become of him?" Cecelia sounded shocked.

"We heard he made a dreadful marriage. Years ago. After that…" The old woman made a brushing motion. "But we finally tracked down his son."

"Ralph's?" James had rather lost track of this proliferation of people.

"Yes, Tereford. Have you not been paying attention?" Lady

Wilton bared her yellowed teeth in what might have appeared to be a smile, from a distance. "I had this *American* fetched. A shabby, rag-mannered fellow. Prone to *lounging*. Wished to be called Jack, if you please! But I informed him that I was willing to lick him into reasonable shape to fit his new position. Despite his dreadful mother. The next day, he was gone."

"How very odd of him," said James. He saw Cecelia catch his tone. They exchanged a look of mingled humor and sympathy for his grandmother's victim. "Might he have gone to his mother's family?"

"She had none."

"Everyone has a family, Grandmamma." James was rather wishing that he did not.

Lady Wilton waved this aside. "The worst sort of riffraff."

"What was her name?"

"I have no idea."

"Then how do you know...?"

The old woman leaned forward and spoke softly, as if fearful of being overheard, and murmured, "Her people were Travelers."

James frowned. He had heard of this rambling tribe. "They are rather like gypsies?"

"Quiet!" hissed his grandmother. "We do *not* want that known!"

James's pity for the new earl increased. If he did return to London, he was not going to have an easy time of it.

"I wonder if he might have gone to see Ferrington Hall?" Cecelia asked.

"To take a look at his inheritance?" said Lady Wilton. "But if he saw the place, why has he not come back to claim it? It's a substantial estate."

"I'll send the agent up there to look around," said James.

"And what else?" demanded the old woman. Impatience was an inadequate description of her tone.

"What do you suggest?" James asked her.

"I don't know. You're the head of the family now. Think of something!"

All the responses that occurred to him were ones his grandmother would not appreciate. Thankfully, the play was beginning, and he was able to drop the conversation to listen. But James wondered if this new earl *had* returned to America. Faced with Lady Wilton's scorn, he would have been tempted to do so. Presumably the fellow had a life of some sort across the sea.

Laughter at an actor's antics filled the theater, including a ripple from Cecelia at his side. James turned to gaze at her delicate profile. He could trace signs of strain in her face, though they would not be visible from other boxes. He hated to see it. Throughout their long association she had been the calm solver of problems, the one who found a way to untangle the worst snarls. She'd never turned away from a dispute. To see her shaken by this wretched excuse for a prince was dreadful.

She turned, noticed his gaze, and smiled. The trust in her blue eyes, the lovely curve of her lips, led James to a moment of stark clarity. She mattered more to him than anyone else in his life. There was no one he knew better, none he valued so much. He realized that he couldn't imagine his life without Cecelia. He... *required* her. He had for years, all unaware. But what did she feel? She'd refused his proposal. When she was in trouble, she hadn't turned to him. Had he ever been more than a burden to her? A void seemed to open in James's chest at the question.

But she'd kissed him. She'd wanted to. She'd melted in his arms. She was not the sort of person to do that lightly. She must feel the bond that linked them.

Unsettled by the demanding intensity in James's face, Cecelia turned away. She watched the actors go through their speeches and tried to ignore the audience all around, many of whom continued to stare at her rather than the drama. Lady Wilton's lost earl had temporarily diverted her from her own predicament. But now she was again conscious of innumerable sharp eyes focused on her. Much of society attended the theater to socialize and gossip rather than follow any action on the stage, and Cecelia felt that tonight she was the play. She was pretending nonchalance, presenting a picture of ease while emotion roiled unpleasantly inside her. She felt that she was succeeding, but the strain was considerable.

Some people loved being the center of attention, craved it even. But she had found over the course of this unusual season that she did not. Her early excitement had given way to unease. And now she had learned that a reigning belle was the target of envy and malice as well as admiration. She hadn't quite understood that before, from the outside. There were many in society avid to see her fall. And one, of course, who was trying to ensure it.

She'd misjudged Prince Karl so completely. Any shame she felt was for her own blindness. Had her head been turned by the flurry of social success? Had the thrill of James's offer addled her wits? She'd had no experience of a man like the prince, but this was no excuse in her eyes. She'd made an idiotic mistake.

Did Prince Karl really expect that she would now make another? Yield to him under the threat of disgrace? Could he be so blind? No, he was punishing her for refusing his advances. He was a smug, vindictive blackguard.

Cecelia diverted herself by imagining that she could challenge Prince Karl to a duel. It would be so very satisfying to slap his smug face with a glove. Did anyone do that these days? It was a sad loss if not. Think of his surprise and chagrin.

She would accuse him of tarnishing her name with lies. Bid him name his seconds and give her an opportunity to redeem her honor. And then to pace off the steps in some misty dawn, to turn, and take a shot at him. She had never fired a pistol, but it didn't look difficult. She couldn't kill him, but surely she could wound him a bit, drain off some of his infuriating complacency?

But the prince would choose swords, Cecelia realized as she

embroidered on this fantasy. Of course he would. He'd delighted in besting James, who knew how to handle a blade. Prince Karl would make her look like a clumsy fool on the dueling ground. He would thoroughly humiliate her. She could not…

Cecelia shook her head. She was pretending she could actually fight him. In fact, she could only sit here, as decoratively as possible, looking as if she didn't care. It was no wonder that beleaguered ladies of the past had resorted to underhanded weapons, like poison.

"Now we are for it," said Lady Wilton.

Looking up, Cecelia saw that the first interval had arrived. This was an opportunity for visitors to come and interrogate them. No doubt they would do so. She braced to offer bright confidence and carefree delight.

But the very first to appear at the door of their box was an unwelcome surprise. Prince Karl stood there, tall, blond, and arrogant in one of his vaguely military coats. How dared he? James rose to face him. Cecelia remained where she was. She would *not* speak to him.

The intruder bowed. "Lady Wilton, one sees you everywhere," he said. "And the so charming Miss Vainsmede." His smile became a leer. She tried not to see it. "Milord duke has reappeared also. To hit me again perhaps? Since his first effort was so…feeble?"

James longed to plant a facer on that sneering countenance. He could almost feel the gratifying crunch of the blow, the welcome pain in his fist. It would be splendid to see this knave reel back and fall. But that would simply cause further scandal. Some might see it as the prince's vindication.

He struggled with his temper. The prince had put them all on display. Those in nearby boxes had certainly heard what he said. He was here to embarrass them as publicly as possible. James needed to defeat him with his own weapons. He groped for the right phrase.

And then indecision subsided as the idea came to him. James

said nothing at all. He looked Prince Karl straight in the eye and then slowly and ostentatiously turned his back. James sat down, catching the eyes of his companions. He nodded at them. His grandmother looked startled, Cecelia shocked. But they both took his cue and turned away from the visitor as well. And then the three of them acted as if Prince Karl did not exist. He had, metaphorically, vanished from their lives. He would never be recognized in their ambit again. The cut direct.

Murmurs washed through the theater, a susurrus of delicious horror. It seemed as if every eye was now upon them. James listened for movement from behind. The prince might decide to retaliate with words or even a blow, which he would have to answer. But there was nothing for what seemed like an age but was in reality only a few moments. Then the swish of cloth suggested that Prince Karl had left their box.

James did not lean back or sigh. He made sure to show no reaction whatsoever. But he was relieved. He had put his social position and credit up against the prince's. It was a different kind of duel, and it remained to be seen whether his adversary was as skilled at this type. But he had won the first throw.

"What have you done?" murmured Cecelia.

James turned, smiled as if she'd made some commonplace remark, and quietly said, "We will not discuss it here."

"No indeed," replied his grandmother, smiling like a sated vulture. "We will…rampantly enjoy the play. But I must say, James, I didn't think you had that in you."

"Reckless audacity?" muttered Cecelia.

"Resolute daring," said Lady Wilton. "We will see what comes next."

"What will the prince do?"

"We will not speak of it here," James repeated.

"No, we will leave that to everyone else," replied his grandmother, running her eyes over the chattering crowd.

Few audience members paid attention to the play after that. They talked through the action at a level that made some of the actors sulk visibly onstage. James knew that people would take sides. His action had set off a kind of war in society, but it was one he thought he could win. He'd been an admired member of the *haut ton* for years and had a host of friends and acquaintances. He'd recently been elevated to one of the highest titles in the land. Prince Karl, on the other hand, was a foreign stranger. He would be leaving England at some point, so there was less future advantage in backing him. Some might be spiteful just because they could be, but James thought they would be few.

James's party endured the stares and watched the rest of the evening's program in their roles as carefree playgoers. They laughed as much as was reasonable. No one else visited them. "Afraid to," Cecelia murmured to James. "Who knows what you might do?"

He smiled at her. Not sardonically. He was feeling something very like joy after acting strongly in her defense.

They lingered after the end of the performance, letting the room empty out, which allowed them to reach their carriage without pushing through a crowd. Once inside the vehicle, Lady Wilton said, "I haven't seen that tried since the Regent cut Brummell."

"Which did not go well for the Regent," said Cecelia.

The old lady shrugged. "He had less reason for the snub. And Tereford is rather more popular than the Regent."

James grimaced. "Please do not say that where anyone else can hear you, Grandmamma." The Prince Regent was notoriously jealous of his consequence. And petty when he felt it threatened.

She snorted. "I cut my eyeteeth before you were born, my boy. You do not need to tell me." The vehicle slowed. "Here we are, Miss Vainsmede. You may tell your aunt I delivered you home safe and sound." Her eyes gleamed with sarcasm in the dimness.

James handed her down and escorted her to the door. There

was time for nothing but a squeeze of her fingers. And then she
was gone, and his grandmother was summoning him back.

∽

Sitting alone in her drawing room early the next morning, Cecelia
was still prey to jumbled thoughts. She'd enjoyed snubbing the
prince. There was no doubt about that. After the way he'd treated
her, he deserved it. And she'd been touched by James's decisive
defense. "He might have consulted me," she murmured. "Although
I don't believe he planned it in advance." The cut had been an
impulsive rejection, an automatic response to Prince Karl's intru-
sion and sneering remarks.

The problem was, the way things had unfolded made this seem
a fight over her between the two men. Again. Still! Like their mock
fencing battle and the rivalry they'd exhibited before the *ton*. So
many people insisted on seeing her as a prize to be won. It made
her think of the conversation she and her friends had had about
their role in society. "Young men roam, young ladies stay home,"
she muttered. Yet for much of her life she'd managed her father's
affairs. She dealt with tenants and tradesmen and servants. She'd
played the diplomat when James and her father wrangled. She'd
planned projects and seen them completed. There had to be some
way to take control of her situation herself.

Aunt Valeria came in. "Cecelia, you are up early today." She
didn't look pleased.

Her aunt was accustomed to having the drawing room to herself for the first hours of the day, before it was invaded, as she put
it, by Cecelia and the threat of callers. She went to her customary
chair by the table and set out her notebook. Next she would open
it and become immersed in something she'd written there. She
would pretend that Cecelia did not exist. After a bit, her presence
would actually fade from her aunt's mind, Cecelia believed. The

pattern was engrained. Aunt Valeria's sporadic new attempts to be a chaperone would not affect it.

Aunt Valeria did as she pleased. So had her mother, Cecelia remembered, on at least one important occasion. She had not sat waiting with folded hands for her fate to find her. The seed of a radical idea took root in Cecelia's mind. "Aunt Valeria, do you think my mother was happy?" she asked.

"What?" Annoyance at being interrupted filled the word.

"You told me that Mama chose her own future like the queen bee."

"That is *not* what I said. I told you that the queen flies high and fast to test her suitors and find the strongest."

"Is that not a choice?"

"Not as I understand the word," replied her aunt.

Cecelia waved the distinction aside. "You said that Mama decided she wanted Papa and went and got him."

Aunt Valeria nodded, her eyes straying to her notebook.

"Do you think she was happy with her choice?"

"I really do not…"

"You knew her for more than fifteen years," Cecelia said. "You stayed with us often during that time. You must have formed some conclusions."

"I am not particularly adept at deciphering people, as I'm certain you have noticed."

That was true.

"She loved you very much," Aunt Valeria added. "She was delighted to have a daughter. She told me so."

"I know." Cecelia examined her memories. "I think she *was* happy, mostly," she said. "I don't think she regretted her choice."

Her aunt examined her, frowning as if Cecelia was a knotty conundrum. "From what I have heard, I do not think this prince would be open to the sort of arguments that…"

"Him!" Cecelia could imbue a single word with emotion also. In this case, contempt.

"We are not talking of…?"

"He is an irrelevant annoyance," said Cecelia. "Like a wasp buzzing about one of your hives."

"Wasps are not irrelevant. They can be quite dangerous."

"Not a wasp then. Some inconsequential thing." Cecelia's brain was full of another topic entirely.

"Then I am not sure what we're talking about right now."

"There is no need for you to be."

"I would so like to agree, Cecelia." Her aunt's gaze moved to her notebook again. She set a yearning hand upon it. "But I fear I cannot. I may be a poor excuse for a chaperone, as Lady Wilton said. Yet I can see that something has agitated you."

She ought to know. Cecelia told her what had transpired at the play.

Aunt Valeria sighed when she finished. "No more than the fellow deserved, but it will raise the talk to an intolerable pitch. Humans are such exhausting creatures."

"At least they don't have stingers," Cecelia joked.

Her aunt's round face creased with rare concern. "But they do, Cecelia, and I do not wish you to be hurt."

"I know." Aunt Valeria did care, in her peculiar way, even if she was not very good at it. "Why don't you go out to your hives? You will feel better there."

"I wish to. Very much. I cannot help it. But I won't abandon you. You know we will have a flood of morning callers after the events you have described to me."

It was true.

"I won't leave you to be…swarmed by them." She smiled at her feeble jest.

Must she be? Cecelia had faced down the gossips before the play. She'd shown them she wasn't cowed. She'd cut the prince in public. She had nothing more to say to the *ton* and much to ponder. "I believe I will tell the servants that we are not in to visitors today."

"Really?" Her aunt looked absurdly hopeful.

"Really."

Cecelia went down the stairs to give the order and encountered Sarah, Charlotte, and Harriet, arriving at the earliest possible moment for a morning call. Cecelia beckoned to them before telling the footman to admit no one else.

"Oh, Cecelia," said Sarah when they'd settled in the drawing room. "Such a furor. We had to come. We said we were going walking in the park."

"You shouldn't visit here secretly," Cecelia replied. "I don't want to cause trouble in your families." The idea was mortifying on a number of levels.

"We don't care!" replied Charlotte Deeping.

Harriet Finch's expression suggested to Cecelia that this wasn't true for all.

"Ada was sorry not to join us," Charlotte added. "She is arguing with her mother about bride clothes today."

"Still! With the wedding only two days away," said Sarah, shaking her head.

"Ada wants garments suitable for restoring a moldering castle," said Charlotte. "Her mother is partial to delicate gauze and lace."

"Peter made the mistake of getting between them," said Harriet dryly. "Social skills not being part of his...charm."

"Who is Peter?" asked Aunt Valeria, looking interested for the first time since their visitors arrived.

"Ada's future husband."

"A groom should never intervene in wedding plans," said Aunt Valeria, as if it was an adage she'd heard and committed to memory with no expectation of ever needing herself.

"I believe he has learned that," replied Harriet.

Sarah leaned forward. "But Cecelia, the play last night! How I wish I had been there."

"It was too bad of you not to warn us so that we could observe," said Charlotte.

"It wasn't planned," said Cecelia. "It was more of a spontaneous…"

"Combustion?" finished Harriet.

Cecelia had to smile. "Of a sort."

"Prince Karl must be dreadfully angry," said Sarah.

"Well, I am extremely angry at *him*," said Cecelia. "Should my anger matter any less?"

She received three surprised looks and a frown from her aunt.

"Do you remember those jokes we made?" Cecelia continued. "Young men gamble, young ladies amble. Young men drink, young ladies shrink. Why should it be so?"

"It's not a case of *should*," said Harriet. "But rather of *is*."

"Unless one wishes to be…" Sarah broke off self-consciously.

"Gossiped about?" replied Cecelia. "Criticized, even ostracized?"

"Well, yes," said Sarah. "I find malice very hard to bear."

"Who does not?" answered Cecelia. "That is what they count on. But if one…" Her voice trailed off.

"Cecelia," said Aunt Valeria.

They were all looking at her with varying degrees of concern, Cecelia saw. "Don't worry, I shall think before I act."

"Act how?" asked Charlotte.

"I'm not completely certain. Yet."

There were sounds below and a moment later, James strolled into the drawing room, every inch the handsomest man in London. He stopped and surveyed the company. "A footman keep me out? Really, Cecelia?"

The three young callers broke into a round of applause.

James looked startled, then acknowledged their reaction with a smile and a bow.

"The cut direct," said Charlotte. "Delivered with great style, it seems."

"Indeed," he said. "And this morning I am here to take the consequences."

"Consequences?" echoed Cecelia.

"The onslaught of hideous harpies," James replied. "The morning callers ravenous for scandal. Present company excepted, of course." He turned to Cecelia. "You didn't think I would leave you to face them alone?"

The look in his eyes made Cecelia's heart pound. The idea that had sprouted in her mind produced branches.

"We can plot strategy in the intervals of routing the enemy," he added.

"I have decided not to receive visitors today," she said. "Any more visitors, that is."

"Ah." James looked thoughtful. "Thus my...discussion with your footman. Do you think that wise?"

"I don't care. Let them wonder."

"Our adversary is unlikely to be silent," James said.

"The prince? What can he do? Whine that we turned our backs on him?"

"He does seem rather more...resourceful than that."

"He's already done his worst," said Cecelia. She felt somehow certain of that. He'd expected to frighten and cow her. He was a bully unused to opposition, and he'd gotten far more than he'd imagined.

"It seems I have no reason to stay then." James waited, but Cecelia didn't protest. She needed to speak to him. But it must be alone, and Aunt Valeria had begun making that difficult. He acknowledged all of them with another bow and took his leave. Had he looked regretful? She thought so. She'd discover the truth soon.

"You sound so confident," said Charlotte.

"Do I?" Cecelia looked at her three younger friends. She so appreciated their steadfast support. "You should go," she told them. "You shouldn't call here when you've been forbidden."

"We want to help!" said Sarah.

"If we can," added Harriet.

"I shall help myself," said Cecelia, her mind suddenly made up.

Sixteen

"A FOOTMAN BROUGHT THIS NOTE," NED SAID TO JAMES, making a small, rather elegant obeisance as he held out a folded sheet of paper. James received the page appreciatively. Despite his youth, Ned had settled into Hobbs's position and small chamber with enthusiasm. He had examined James's entire wardrobe with great pleasure and absorbed information about the latest men's fashions. He watched and learned bits of polite behavior and observed every move James made like a scholar presented with original sources. Given what seemed to James an absurdly small sum, Ned had outfitted himself in a decent coat, shirt and breeches from some mysterious source of used clothing. Handed one of James's neckcloths for his own, he'd achieved a creditable waterfall style on the second try, and his hair had been brushed into something resembling a Brutus. Roughly. Even his way of speaking had begun to shift. He was a remarkable mimic. Clearly, with just a bit of help, Ned was going far.

James unsealed the note. Cecelia asked him to call on her at eleven the following morning. His pulse accelerated. Could she want to see him as much as he wanted to see her? Unless... But no, he'd heard of no new outrage from Prince Karl. The fellow had gone quiet. Perhaps ominously. They would see. But before that, *he* would see Cecelia. Alone. He would push her aunt out of the room and lock her in a wardrobe if he had to. He would *make* this the opportunity to settle matters between them. He tucked the note into his waistcoat pocket.

He looked up to find Ned slowly folding a stocking, as if he savored the feel of the smooth knit under his fingers. "That is worn with evening dress," James said.

Ned started, froze as if fearing retribution, and then relaxed. "Knee breeches and pale waistcoat," he answered, repeating an earlier lesson.

"Correct."

The boy grinned, pleased and proud.

It was so easy to cheer him, though it seemed few had ever bothered. "Is all well with your mother and sisters?" James asked.

"Yes, milord. Uncle Will mended the stable lock."

"Ah, he's arrived then."

Ned nodded. "Staying in a room above the stables. He reckons it was the head groom's."

James started to say that the man could sleep in the house. But where would he find proper quarters? The stable was probably more comfortable for now if it was fitted out for a head groom.

"He said to tell you thankee—thank you." Ned enunciated the last two words carefully. "And if you have any other work that wants doing, he's ready and able."

There was so very much do. But first, always first, there was Cecelia.

James arrived precisely on time the next day. He was taken up to the drawing room at once and found Cecelia waiting for him there. Alone.

"My aunt is with her bees," she said. "And I have given orders that she is not to be disturbed."

He scarcely heard through the exultation racing through his veins. Now he must retrieve the words he'd been rehearsing. He'd botched this the last time. He wouldn't again. Even though she looked so lovely that he could think of little else.

She sat down. He took a chair opposite. "I was wondering if you still wish to marry me," she said.

This was such an unexpected beginning that James stumbled over his answer.

"Considering recent…occurrences, I thought you might. But it's best to be sure of these things, is it not?"

Was she calling their kiss an occurrence? That made it sound like an encounter with footpads or a carriage accident.

Cecelia frowned. "If you have changed your mind, of course there is nothing more to be said."

"I have not!" All his careful phrases now escaped him.

"Oh, well, good. Then I think we should."

"Should?"

"Get married," she explained, as if he was being purposely slow.

"Dash it, Cecelia."

"What? I thought you said…"

"I spent half the night trying to find the right words to convince you to marry me."

"You did?" Her tone was softer.

"Yes, and now you jump in before I've used any of them. You have a pronounced autocratic streak."

"So you have often said."

"Because it's true. What about the time you shoved a quill into my hand, and it spattered ink all over my favorite waistcoat? Those spots never came out. I had to dispose of it." James's errant brain wondered if the garment had gone to the sort of place where Ned had acquired his refurbished wardrobe.

"Well, you and Papa had been wrangling for an hour," said Cecelia.

"*I* was wrangling. Your father was wishing himself elsewhere and, unless I am mistaken, emitting very soft moans." He shook his head. "I am not mistaken."

"Yes, and we all knew how it was going to come out, with you signing the deed." Somewhat oddly, she was smiling.

"Well, I know, but I wished to be…argued into it."

"Did you?" Cecelia sat straighter, with folded hands. "Very well. The points of the case then. You wanted my help with your estates. Which appear to be in disarray."

"Yes, but…"

"And so you suggested that we should marry in order to acquire my services."

"I did not put it as well as I might…"

"Which are quite valuable, if I do say so," she interrupted with calm conviction. "In return I will have an advantageous social position, as you mentioned."

"That was before," replied James. He had said any number of idiotic things. But much had happened since then. She'd been there for most of it.

"Before?" She raised her eyebrows. "Ah, the prince and the gossip have changed my situation, of course."

"That wasn't what I meant!"

"I had thought you didn't care about the rumors." For the first time, she sounded tentative.

"Less than I do about a flea in the coat of a mongrel dog," he replied.

She blinked, startled. "So we shall go ahead then? We will make an agreement."

"Agreement?" This was not the term James would have chosen.

"Considering the points in favor and of…mutual benefit."

"You are going to marry me, Cecelia? You promise." He heard the plea in his tone.

She met his eyes. "Yes."

That was all that mattered, really. They could set aside this odd conversation, adding it to the litany of others they'd had over the years. "Splendid! I'll send a notice to the *Morning Post*."

"I suppose we must," she replied.

"Why not?" Was she drawing back?

"There will be talk." She sighed. "I'm so weary of talk. I believe a special license and a quiet ceremony would be the best course of action."

"You've thought about this, I see. Are you in a hurry to be wed?"

She blushed. James thrilled to see it. He was beginning to be amused as well as bemused by this exchange. "I find that *I* am, rather."

"So that I will take over your work," Cecelia said.

She'd rallied. Cecelia always rallied. It was one of the things he admired most about her, James realized. "So that you are my wife." He said the last word caressingly, trying to make her blush again.

She disappointed him. Except that she didn't. He appreciated the raised chin and the steady gaze. Had Cecelia ever actually disappointed him? She'd irritated him and surprised him and made him laugh. But disappointment? No. Never that. "I'd best go see the archbishop," he said.

"Archbishop?"

"I believe one must apply to the Archbishop of Canterbury for a special license."

"How do you know that?"

"A man on the town picks up these little tidbits of information."

As James had hoped, she laughed. He looked forward to seeing her laugh often in the years that lay ahead. And to so much else as well.

❧

Cecelia attended Ada Grandison's wedding with her aunt, a grudging but surprisingly solid presence. Tereford and Prince Karl were not invited, not being friends of the couple, and this was a relief. It was the reason she'd chosen this as the first occasion to appear since the public announcement of her engagement. Easier to be gaped at without their contentious presence, she'd thought, and so it proved. She also found the gossips' attitude changed, now that she was about to become a duchess. The past was not forgotten, but the general consensus seemed to be that she had triumphed over it. Decisively. Some were glad; some were sourly envious. But no one snubbed her. These were the ups and downs of society.

She couldn't help but compare Ada's lively festivities with her own plans, about which she evaded all questions. She had decreed a small ceremony with just a few people in attendance. The date—tomorrow!—and place were not precisely secret. They simply hadn't told anyone. The distinction without a difference made her smile. She'd decided on this course because she thought Prince Karl the sort of person who enjoyed revenge, and she did not want some disagreeable scene enacted at her wedding. Why give him opportunities when she needn't?

Perhaps it would not be the lavish celebration girls dreamed of, but that didn't matter. Her greater wish had come true; she would be James's wife. She'd wished for that since she was seventeen, and the knowledge made her heart sing.

Yes, she had doubts. It was not exactly the love match she'd longed for. But the last few weeks had convinced her that something sweet could grow between them. And that was enough, was it not?

Cecelia pushed this concern aside. She'd taken her future into her own hands; that was the important thing. She'd reached out for what she wanted and secured it. She would find a way to success. Hadn't she often done so in the past? This wasn't some estate problem or financial issue, of course. She was still not certain what James felt, for example. Except that he had easily agreed.

She wondered if her mother had felt as if her heart was in her throat when she arranged her future. James's blank look when she'd begun had nearly stopped her cold. But then he'd said that he'd spent half the night trying to find the right words to convince her. She clung to that. With a wisp of regret that she had not waited a little and let him speak.

"How do people bear the tedium of these things?" asked her aunt. "Chatter, chatter, chatter, all empty."

Cecelia turned to the small fair-haired woman at her side. As she so seldom had been before. Aunt Valeria's presence had actually caused a small stir, since she never appeared in society. "Well, you won't have to endure it again. Your job is nearly over. After tomorrow, I shall be gone."

Her aunt looked startled. "I hadn't thought of that."

"Now you can, and be glad," replied Cecelia.

"Will your father wish me to leave, do you think?"

Aunt Valeria, and Papa, would always consider themselves first, Cecelia acknowledged. It was their nature. "He will need someone to manage the household," she answered.

"Deal with Cook and the coal merchant and...all that sort of thing?" Her aunt frowned. "I suppose I could. A bit. You will be nearby to help out."

This was not a happy prospect, and Cecelia nearly denied it. But she was silenced by the sudden realization that she didn't know where she would be after tomorrow. She would be married. That was certain. But where would they go after the ceremony? Where would they settle? Not in the shambles of Tereford House surely? James couldn't mean to do that. Did he have a plan? When had he ever had a plan? She was the planner everyone relied upon. But she hadn't. She'd leapt without really looking, and now life was rushing forward at a frantic pace to...where? This was so unlike her familiar self. They should have talked. They should have discussed...everything. Something!

Charlotte and Sarah approached, each carrying two plates heaped with wedding delicacies. "Lobster patties," said Charlotte, holding out one.

"Oh splendid," said Aunt Valeria, taking the plate even though Charlotte had clearly meant it for Cecelia.

"Are you all right?" asked Sarah.

"I feel...sightly dizzy," said Cecelia.

"Oh dear. It's probably the heat. It's dreadfully close in here." Sarah handed a plate to Charlotte and took Cecelia's arm. "Come and sit down."

"I don't think that will help."

"Are you ill?" asked Aunt Valeria. "Can we go?" She ate two lobster patties in quick succession.

"I don't know where," muttered Cecelia, too distracted to notice their stares.

◆

James tracked down Henry Deeping at his lodgings preparing to go out for the evening. "Henry, you've been a hard man to find lately."

"I've been out of town for a few days. Stanley wanted to see a mill. My brother, you know."

"Yes, Henry, I remember that your brother is called Stanley. One of them. The others are Cecil and Bertram, the youngest."

"Well done, James." Henry made a final adjustment to his neckcloth.

"I am going to be married tomorrow, Henry. I hoped you might stand up with me at the ceremony."

"Is it tomorrow? I saw the announcement of your engagement, of course."

"And sent a note of congratulation. Very proper. Diplomatically so. I answered it, with my request for your support at the wedding."

"Oh. You did?"

"I did." James examined his old friend. Henry's gaze seemed evasive. "What is the matter?"

"May I ask you a question?"

This was odd. Did Henry not wish to stand by him at the wedding? James found that idea curiously lowering.

"Are you marrying Miss Vainsmede because of the prince?" Henry asked. "Out of a chivalrous impulse to save her reputation?"

"I am marrying her because I wish to. I told you that weeks ago."

"You did. But much has happened since then."

"Nothing to the purpose," said James, pushing back a quiver of anger.

"That's good then. Of course Miss Vainsmede is a fine choice."

James thought of saying that it had not been entirely a choice, but he didn't. Cecelia's proposal would be a secret he cherished all his life.

"It's just that…"

"What is it, Henry? You're not usually so…oblique."

Henry sighed. "I'm not sure how to… You know I've become rather friendly with Stephan Kandler during their visit."

"Who?" James wondered what this had to do with anything.

"Stephan Kandler, Prince Karl's aide. I introduced you. He was at Lady Tate's evening as well."

James supposed he might have been. But he didn't see why Henry wanted to talk about the fellow.

"He may be of some help with the prince."

"I have no need of help, since I don't intend to ever think of him again."

Henry went on as if James hadn't spoken. "This is not the first time Prince Karl has…behaved in a shameful manner. He has a habit of bullying people, particularly women, with false stories. He was sent on this trip to see the wider world, understand that he cannot ride roughshod over everyone, and modify his behavior. With a view toward becoming a wiser ruler when that time comes. But it has not worked."

"Obviously," said James. "And I don't really care a fig about his future, Henry."

His friend held up a hand. "His father is not pleased with his progress, and he has given Kandler permission to do something about it."

"Take Prince Karl away from England, I hope."

"He has no power to do that."

"Too bad."

"He will act, however. In case that should make a difference in your plans."

James struggled with his temper. It seemed that Henry was trying to discourage him from marrying Cecelia. Why would he do that? Did Henry—Henry!—think that Cecelia had been tainted by the gossip? If so, he thought less of his friend. He didn't want to do that. "I would be glad to see Prince Karl paid back for his infamy, through some other agency than mine," James said carefully. "I shan't have anything to do with it."

"That's very…astute of you."

Did he sound surprised? "Were you still expecting that I would waylay him some dark night and beat him senseless?" asked James dryly. The man who'd struck Prince Karl after their fencing bout seemed distant to him now.

"I simply thought you should know about Kandler's plans. In case…that is."

James waited.

Henry looked uncomfortable. "You began talking of marriage to Miss Vainsmede as a kind of…contest with the prince."

That wasn't right. He'd asked her before he knew the fellow existed. He thought he'd told Henry that. But Prince Karl had… altered his courtship. That much was true. As well as unfairly maligning Cecelia. Suddenly, James wondered if she'd changed her mind because of that. She'd refused him, rather firmly, and then she'd turned about and proposed to him after the prince tried to ruin her reputation. Many thought Cecelia very fortunate to have "snagged" him and redeemed her social position. He'd heard that said of her, perhaps had been meant to overhear it. She'd mentioned the rumors, of course, in case he wished to withdraw. But had it been a maneuver? To goad him into moving ahead?

No! Cecelia wasn't that sort of person. She possessed the highest moral character. She'd changed her mind because…

James realized that he could not definitively complete this sentence, and that, unlike all the rest, worried him. She'd tossed his foolish arguments back at him and spoken of a deal, the advantages to them both. But she'd rejected those ideas the first time. Was she really marrying him to save her reputation? He was happy to do so, naturally. He would have eradicated the prince if that had been possible. But there was more involved in their union. Was there not?

He was having doubts, James realized. He wasn't accustomed to doubts. He never had them. And he didn't like them. At all. It was ridiculous. This whole match had been his idea. He refused to doubt.

"Hasty marriages do go wrong," said Henry.

His match was not hasty. He'd known Cecelia for years. Yet never thought of marrying her until the responsibilities of a dukedom descended upon him, a dry inner voice pointed out. And a rival appeared. The last few weeks had felt rather…headlong. Henry thought James was marrying out of pique, or an irresistible desire to win a competition. He suspected his grandmother thought the same. And others? Perhaps. All of society thought they could have an opinion and exercise their wagging tongues, it seemed. Marriage was not simply an agreement between two people. "The prince has nothing to do with my wedding plans," he said in an even tone.

His friend nodded. "All right."

"Do you not wish to stand up with me, Henry?" James was conscious of a mournful annoyance. Why had Henry thought it necessary to roil the waters in this way? "If you would rather be excused…"

"Of course I would not."

"You seem reluctant."

"I just wanted you to know…to be certain."

"And if I wasn't?"

"Then I'd help you get out of it."

How had Henry imagined that might happen? A gentleman could not draw back from an engagement. He'd procured a special license, engaged a parson. And he didn't *wish* to cry off. He couldn't imagine being married to anyone other than Cecelia. He would simply like to understand that she felt the same.

Seventeen

CECELIA WOKE LATE ON HER WEDDING DAY, THOUGH SHE WAS always up early. She came swimming up from a sea of dreams she did not remember. Thus it became a rush to dress in the sea-green gown she'd chosen for the ceremony, find bonnet and gloves, and ride over to the church. There was no time to wonder if she'd made the right decision or worry about the future.

Her father and aunt, who accompanied her, added a sense of disconnection as the three of them so seldom traveled anywhere together. They commented on the fine weather and the sight of a climbing rose as if this was any carriage ride on any late spring day. They did not seem concerned that with this ceremony she was leaving them forever. Though Cecelia had felt rather differently about her father since his story of meeting Mama, he remained exactly the same.

They came to the church and found James and Henry Deeping waiting there. Cecelia hadn't invited anyone else. Once she was married, at some future time, she would celebrate with all her friends. For now she preferred that word not get out.

The priest was ready. They stood before him and heard the familiar phrases of the wedding service. Cecelia spoke her vows clearly, as did James. She'd chosen this, she thought as she signed the register. There was no cause for unease. And yet, with a few words spoken and a signature on a piece of paper, she'd taken on a lifetime of duties and expectations. Perhaps pleasures and joys as well. Of course, those. She loved James. She'd dreamed of being his wife. But she hadn't thought it would feel so…tentative even as it was also a personal revolution.

And then, in less than an hour's time, it was done. In the eyes of society, her status was changed. She was a married woman and a peeress of the realm. Their small party came out of the church and paused on the cobblestones before it.

"Where are you off to now?" asked her father, once again as if it was any ordinary morning and she might be planning to make calls or take a walk in the park.

This was the other dilemma. Cecelia didn't know. Ned had picked up a valise she and her maid had packed and taken it away, but he hadn't known anything about James's plan. And James had evaded her questions about it in the most vexing way. The immediate future was a blank. A touch of dizziness assailed her. She had never been in this position in her life. She was so accustomed to making order.

"Your chariot awaits," James said. Looking terribly handsome under the midmorning sun, he offered his arm.

Feeling oddly in need of the support, Cecelia took it. He led her to a smart traveling carriage. The others trailed after them. "Why does it have someone else's coat of arms on the door?" she asked.

"I borrowed it," James said.

"Rather than hire a post chaise?"

"As you see."

Did he sound irritated? She didn't want that. Their years of disputes over a wide variety of issues came back to her. More than a few had ended with one of them—or, James really—stomping out and going off to cool down. He hated losing an argument. But they no longer had separate homes to retreat to. Or any livable home at all, Cecelia noted. What did that mean for discussion?

Suddenly, every word seemed more of a risk, weighted with signs for the future. Would she be less at ease married to him than she had been when single? Did one have to be more…polite once married? If she lost the ability to talk easily to a man she'd known, and debated, most of her life… That would be distressing.

He handed her into the vehicle and climbed up to sit beside

her. They said their goodbyes, the coachman signaled the team, and they set off. Cecelia watched her father and aunt and Henry Deeping recede and then disappear as they rounded a corner. She turned back, and became acutely conscious of James's broad shoulders against the seat back, his pantaloon-clad leg not far from her skirts. They'd sat as close as this on drawing room sofas, she supposed. But they'd never traveled alone together in a carriage. They would be side by side here for…she had no idea how long.

"Where are we going?" she asked him.

"It's a surprise."

"I don't like surprises."

"Of course you do."

How could he say that? Could he have failed to notice that most surprises in Cecelia's life had been near disasters? Times when her father had neglected some important business matter, which had then become a full-blown emergency. Times when James himself had descended like a horde of marauders, full of exigent demands. If he didn't know her any better than this, how were they to get on together?

"What about the jugglers on your birthday that time?" James asked. "You were delighted by them."

"Because I arranged for them to come."

"*You* did?"

"Yes. And then I pretended to be surprised."

James stared at her. "That's…a bit…sad."

It probably had been. But she'd been missing her mother so much, and it was the sort of silly thing her mother would have arranged. So she had done it instead. It hadn't helped with the grief, of course. It had surprised her father. And in the end he'd liked the performance more than she did. "Who did you think had hired them?" she asked.

"Well, I…"

She saw consciousness of the timing occur to him—the

year after her mother's death. She saw him recall her father's heedlessness.

"I suppose I didn't think about it," he replied.

Of course he hadn't. It wasn't the sort of thing James considered. He'd called that day, she remembered, in the midst of the juggling and stayed a while to admire the performers' skills. He'd given her a bracelet for her birthday, a gift more suited to a grown-up lady, which someone probably should have ordered her to refuse. Fortunately, no one bothered because she'd adored it. It was years later that she discovered his birthday visit had been accidental. He'd come to wrangle over some trust matter and found himself at her sparse festivities. The bracelet had been intended for someone else—the kind of female she was not to know about. She'd meanly enjoyed taking it from that faceless lady. But today she found a familiar annoyance with his self-absorption threatening to creep in. "You still haven't told me where we're going."

"To the estate of a friend of mine. I thought the place would amuse you."

Cecelia was puzzled by the word. How should an estate be funny? "Amuse?" she echoed.

"It's a bit out of the ordinary."

"Will your friend be there?" She hadn't planned to share her honeymoon with a stranger. But then she hadn't been allowed to plan anything!

"In the house," James replied with an airy gesture.

"*In* the..." Cecelia frowned. "Do you mean that we will *not* be in the house?"

"Not the main house."

"A guest cottage?"

"I really think it would be better as a surprise. Descriptions don't do the place justice."

"Is this like the time you took Papa and me to see that string of racehorses you wished to buy? And the black one tried to bite me?"

"Nothing like that!" James was half-laughing, half-insulted. "I really think you might trust me."

She had promised to have and hold, to love and cherish, but not actually to trust him. She met his blue eyes and nearly lost herself in them. She supposed that trust was implied in those other vows. In this case, she had no other choice. "How far is it?"

"Three hours from London. Probably a bit less with this team."

She nodded and settled back.

"You'll like it, Cecelia. I promise."

It was a day of promises. And after all, she had never known James to break his word.

He reached under the seat and pulled a large basket from behind his feet. "I have not forgotten the wedding breakfast."

He set the basket opposite them, opened it, and began pulling items out and unwrapping the napkins that held them like a magician performing tricks. "Bread rolls, ham and hard-cooked eggs, a flask of tea and one of lemonade, strawberries." He set things in the upturned lid of the basket so that they wouldn't fall. "And of course a wedding cake." He unveiled a small round cake with white icing, slightly smudged by the covering.

His triumphant expression made Cecelia smile. "Where did you get all this?"

"I ordered it from Gunter's."

"They have a set wedding breakfast basket?"

"Not at all. I carefully chose each and every item. Give me some credit."

He had planned. She hadn't trusted him to, but he'd obviously taken some care on arrangements.

"You adore strawberries," he added.

This was true.

He held one out to her by its stem, wiggled it a little.

Cecelia leaned forward, took the berry in her teeth, and bit down. It was sweet and a little tart and completely delicious. She licked her lips. "Perfect." She looked up and found James staring. Not into her eyes. Was he looking at her mouth? The heat in his gaze made her flush. They had habits of talking, and disputing, built over the years. These fell into place automatically when they were together. But after this morning, they had a new relationship as well. He might sweep her into his arms. Now, if he wished to. And his expression suggested that he did, very much. Then tonight...

James smiled—lazily, teasingly—as if he knew exactly what she was thinking.

Cecelia's pulse quickened. She'd married him for this, too. She cared about him. But no other man had ever roused her as James did—his presence, his wit, the paltry few kisses they'd shared. She would demand many more of *those*. She met his gaze with that certainty.

He blinked. His smile widened, becoming more warmly appreciative. He gave her a small nod before saying, "Perhaps a bit of ham on a roll?"

Cecelia had a moment of acute disappointment. Then she realized that embraces in a moving carriage were probably awkward. Particularly with a basket of viands ready to spill. She had a sudden picture of the two of them, wildly entwined, crusted with bits of wedding cake and crushed strawberries. That would certainly enliven their arrival at his friend's home. The idea was ludicrous, and strangely stimulating.

"Does ham amuse you?" James asked.

"Not ham." Perhaps she would tell him her vision, later. When carriages and clothing were irrelevant. Her breath caught. "I should like some, thank you."

He sliced the roll with the knife provided, added ham and a dab of mustard from a tiny china pot that closed with a ribbon tie, and held the result out to her. Cecelia took it and bit down. "Good." She was hungry.

James served her a neatly sliced egg, more strawberries, lemonade from the flask. Gunter's had foreseen all their needs, providing small cups without handles.

"We must have the cake," said James. "It's bad luck not to eat a wedding cake."

"I have never heard that."

"Well, perhaps it's not true. But it should be." He cut a morsel of the cake and held it out as he had the strawberry.

Cecelia leaned closer and took it, feeling his fingers on her lips as a shivery caress. The confection was dark and chewy, dense with dried fruit. "Aren't you having any?" she asked when she'd swallowed.

He gave her the knife.

Cecelia cut a bit of cake and offered it to him. His taking of it felt like a kiss on her fingertips.

He licked a trace of icing from his lower lip and said, "Good."

She was not the sort of woman who would ever swoon, Cecelia told herself. But her surroundings seemed to be swaying more than could be accounted for by the bouncing of the carriage. Was this what people meant when they said their senses were reeling?

"Tea?" James asked. His eyes were laughing.

"I–I don't care for it without milk."

"Oh, there is milk. Gunter's would not let us down." He showed her a small jar.

"They have thought of everything."

"*I* made them a list," he replied. "Detailed. Comprehensive. One might even say meticulous." He raised dark eyebrows.

Cecelia laughed. Lists had been a point of contention between them for years. Cecelia found them critical. James claimed that truly important matters stuck in one's brain, and anything else deserved to be forgotten. She had called him scatterbrained. He had called her obsessive. "I commend you," she said, adding a dollop of milk to the cup of tea he had poured for her. She sipped. It was only barely warm, but she would not complain.

"What is this place?" asked Cecelia.

"It was a ruin from some centuries ago," James replied. "My friend's grandfather had it restored for…his own purposes."

"Nefarious, I assume?"

"He was apparently rather a loose screw."

"Is that slang for a libertine?" Cecelia asked.

"Ah, yes. I shouldn't have…"

She waved his scruples aside. "Oh, I may know these things now that I am a married woman. So your friend keeps it up?"

"Well, he has not torn it down. I believe he occasionally lends it to…"

"Friends who require a secret retreat," Cecelia finished when he hesitated. "And how do you know that?"

"Not from personal experience, I assure you."

Yet he had experience, Cecelia acknowledged. He'd had mistresses; she knew that, though he had never flaunted them. She, on the other hand, had been circumscribed by the rules of society, which wanted her to learn as little as possible of physical passion. Though her aunt had given her more freedom than most, she was still unequal in this.

"Shall we go in?" asked James.

He led her through the door into the ground level. It was one large round room with walls of bare stone, a flagstone floor, and a wooden ceiling. The space was very plain. It held a large table with several chairs around it. Their basket was set on top. The only other furnishings were several closed chests. There was a small empty fireplace on the right and a stone stair curving up on the left. This was not promising. James's friend had told him that the tower was quite comfortable. James began to worry that they had very different definitions of what that meant. "This is where the servants creep in to leave meals and take them away," James said.

"Creep?"

"They are instructed not to talk to guests unless they are addressed."

Cecelia looked around. "That is a bit…odd."

He had thought it sounded romantic. Marvelously private. Now that they were here, he wasn't so sure. Had he brought her to a medieval hermitage for their honeymoon? Well, if it was no good, they would return to London, which would be an exhausting first day for a marriage. "Let us look upstairs," he said.

They walked up the curving steps and, to James's relief, came out into a luxurious sitting room on the next level. Comfortable-looking sofas and armchairs stood on lush Turkish rugs. There was a small table with two chairs under a narrow window and colorful tapestries on the walls. James threw his hat and gloves onto its surface. Though the day was fine, a fire burned in the small fireplace, counteracting the chill of the thick stone walls.

The stair continued upward, and James ran quickly up to the top story. It held a great, carved four-poster bed, wardrobes, and a dressing table, all in dark wood. More fine rugs dotted the wooden floor. A fine chamber, and a relief.

"Someone has left us lovely flowers," Cecelia said when he returned to her. She was bent over sniffing a bouquet on the table. She'd removed her bonnet and gloves. "Your friend's wife?"

"He has none. The housekeeper, I suppose." There had been flowers upstairs, too.

"Ah." Cecelia straightened and looked at him.

An awkward silence fell. Some married couples were alone for the first time on their wedding night, James thought. He and Cecelia were far more fortunate, being so well acquainted. And yet… He knew her as confidante and adversary, not as wife or lover. And the change felt more complicated because of their long history than it might have been with a near stranger. They'd had countless emotional discussions but hardly ever touched. Perhaps four times in thirteen years. There were those kisses though!

"Shall we walk in the garden?" Cecelia asked.

"If you wish."

"Only if you want to."

"I am happy to if you would like…" James stopped. They never stumbled about like this. Their exchanges had always been forthright. He'd simply said whatever he liked. Perhaps he had done so without giving enough thought to her feelings. He'd been more concerned with how to alter her position and make her do as he asked about the trust. And she'd more than held her own. That was one of the things he admired about her. But now their situation was different. Uncharted territory, he thought, and wondered if a honeymoon far away from all they knew was a mistake. She was gazing at him, as if waiting for some important word.

"Is something wrong?" Cecelia said.

"Why did you change your mind about marriage?" he asked her.

She looked surprised, started to speak, then closed her lips again.

It didn't seem such a difficult question. Should she need to think it over?

Cecelia moved across the small distance between them, put her hands on his shoulders, and kissed him.

James's pulse leapt in response. Desire shot through him, and he pulled her close. Cecelia laced her arms around his neck and melted against his body, her lips eagerly responsive. Here was the answer to all his questions. This was their new way to be together, and a glorious way it was. He gave his hands license to explore as he urged her toward the stairs.

The damn steps were so narrow that they had to go up single file, but when they reached the top he swept her up and carried her to the bed. Setting her down in a froth of silk, he joined her there and plunged them into another dizzying kiss.

They pressed close, held tight. Their legs grew tangled in her skirts and petticoats. When they drew a little apart, panting, she said, "I never knew that clothes could be so inconvenient."

Not to mention his boots, James noted. He had to be rid of the things, and he wasn't used to pulling them off himself. "The best approach is to be ruthless," he said.

"Rip them off, you mean?"

James laughed. She was a wonder, a marvel. He stood up beside the bed and shucked off his coat, tossing it over the back of an armchair. He pulled away his neckcloth and sent it flying in the same direction. In shirt and pantaloons, he went to a chair, sat down, and yanked off his wretched boots. Then he rose and faced her again.

Cecelia had slipped off the bed, a little wide-eyed, but smiling. She stepped out of her shoes. Her fingers went to the buttons at the front of her gown. James wondered if she'd chosen that garment because it fastened in front. The idea of such forethought enflamed him further.

She wriggled out of her dress, letting it fall at her feet. She reached around and caught the string of her stays, pulling on it. Once, and again. "The knot is stuck," she said.

He went to unfasten them, letting his fingertips trail along her arm and shoulder as she pulled the stays off and untied her petticoats. Muslin and ruffles fell away, and there she was in only her thin shift, which was nearly transparent in tantalizing spots, and her silk stockings.

James pulled his shirt over his head and discarded it before he knelt at her feet. He let his hands slide gently up her right leg. To the garter that held up her stocking and then higher. Her breath caught in the most satisfying way. Slowly, his eyes on hers, he eased the garter down and off, flicking her stocking away. Then he repeated the maneuver with the other. Cecelia gripped his arm and urged him upright, pressing herself into his arms once again.

His kisses were more intoxicating than anything she'd

experienced before. As his hands strayed over her, Cecelia felt as if every part of her body flamed to life. It didn't matter that she'd never done this before. Her impulses seemed a reliable guide.

He took hold of her shift and raised it. She lifted her arms like a dancer in the ballet and let him take it away. She was naked before him—James, her longtime love, her maddening friend, and now her husband. He shed the rest of his clothes and was the same, so very handsome in his natural state. She'd seen him in all sorts of guises but never this way. There was nothing between them but curiosity, history, and desire.

He lifted her onto the bed again. They twined together, burning skin to skin. And now his kisses trailed down her neck and shoulder to her breasts while he ran his hands along her sides. Cecelia shivered with longing, the sensation almost too intense. She yearned for him, ached for him.

As if he knew, his touch went to the center of that craving and tantalized until he fulfilled it in a dazzling, shuddering wave. The glory of it still echoed along her nerves when he came to her and found his own release. Holding him afterward, she hoped it had been as wonderful.

She had married the man she loved, Cecelia thought in that moment. She had no more to ask of life.

Eighteen

OR PERHAPS SHE DID, CECELIA THOUGHT FOUR DAYS LATER AS she once again brought up the subject of their future plans. James continually put her off on this subject, making it clear that he had no scheme for where they would live until Tereford House could be made livable. And he had a new weapon in his arsenal now. When he wished to divert her, he would make love to her until Cecelia felt like one of the honeybees lolling in the center of flowers in the tower garden, dazed and sated with sweetness. Physical passion was a lovely addition to her life, and it most often left her thinking that she didn't care where she lived as long as it was with James. Then, when her wits returned, she would note that they did have to go to an actual place, eventually. "Your friend will expect us to leave his tower," she tried.

"He doesn't need the place," James replied. "He spends the summers in Brighton."

"We brought very little clothing with us," she said another time.

"We can send for whatever you like," he answered. "I'll dispatch the coachman."

"James."

"Are you not content?" His gaze was sultry.

"I am, but…"

He waved her caveat aside.

In the end, the outside world resolved this issue for her. Word arrived from Mrs. Gardener that a team of thieves had raided the pile of discarded furnishings in the garden at Tereford House. In the dead of night, they had passed a good portion of it over the wall and spirited it away.

James's first reaction was careless. "They are welcome to all of it," he said. "I wish them joy and encourage them to return for the rest."

"We can't allow thieves free rein," Cecelia replied. "Mrs. Gardener's note sounds anxious. And if the gang is not opposed, they will very likely go beyond the garden into the house. We must return and do something."

"I should not have left my direction with Ned," James muttered.

"James."

This grumble was inaudible.

"You know we can't stay here forever." Cecelia reached across the breakfast table and put a hand over his. It was lovely to feel free to touch him whenever the impulse arose.

He turned his hand over and laced his fingers with hers. "Let us go upstairs," he said.

"We just came down."

"But I am ready to be up again." His blue eyes danced wickedly over her.

Cecelia flushed. It was just as well the servants kept their distance here. Her father's placid staff would be shocked by such a suggestive remark. "I think we must go back and put a stop to the thieving."

"I am a duke," he said. "I should be able to do as I wish."

"You know a high position brings responsibilities," Cecelia replied, and then thought she sounded horridly prim.

"I do now."

"We must get on with clearing out Tereford House." It was only the truth, though she didn't relish being the prosaic one. Must she always be? And yet the tasks ahead nagged at her. She tried to estimate how long the sorting would take. "And you said your uncle's former man of business sent boxes of documents."

James groaned, a bit theatrically.

"As well as all those piled up in the library."

"Oh my God." He pulled his hand away. "Very well. We will go back. I suppose we could stay with your father for a while."

"No."

"You don't wish to do that?"

"I do not! Aunt Valeria would try to push the household duties back on me. In fact, I would wager a good deal that she'd urge us to remain, so that I take them up again. And the servants would encourage her, I imagine."

"Poor Cecelia. You are far too competent. Everyone wants you to do their work."

The remark came with a smile and a caress, as though it was a joke. But was it? James had married her for this precise reason. A few days' idyll didn't change that fact, and she shouldn't forget it. James would be expecting her to take up the burdens of the duke-dom. "The season will be ending soon. There will be many houses coming available in London."

"I suppose we could go to a hotel for a while, though we will be rather cramped."

"Yes, good, and then we will hire a furnished house to use until Tereford House is ready. It needn't be grand."

"Whatever you think," James replied. His attention had wandered to his breakfast.

"You will leave the choice to me?"

"Of course."

Of course he would. This was the real beginning of their marriage, Cecelia thought. The reality of it wasn't towers and gardens and sated honeybees. She would settle down to work, and James would no doubt resume his indolent habits, with an occasional objection to the decisions she'd made when he had paid no attention to the process. This picture gave her a sinking feeling. But she'd known about it beforehand. She had nothing to complain of; she arranged this life herself. And look at all she'd gained!

❧

They drove back to town the following day in the same carriage that had brought them. Cecelia had not realized that the vehicle and driver had waited on their convenience. "Your friend did not need his carriage?" she asked James as they started out.

"He has several."

He was as careless of this friend as of the one who owned the tower. He seemed to take no thought for their needs. Watching his handsome profile against the passing countryside outside the carriage window, Cecelia felt a wisp of apprehension about the future.

James engaged quarters for them at Brown's Hotel, a fine parlor and bedchamber as well as rooms for her maid and Ned, who were duly summoned. Cecelia immediately wrote to the efficient man of business who had helped her manage her father's affairs, and he called on them within hours, offering polite felicitations on their marriage. When Mr. Dalton heard that he was being asked to aid in management of a dukedom, he could scarcely contain his elation. He assured them that his firm was quite capable of handling the larger business.

"Matters are in quite a tangle," said James.

"We would be more than happy to put them in order, Your Grace," the slender, brown-haired man assured him.

"We should send him those boxes," James said to Cecelia.

"I think we must look through them first," she replied.

James's impatient gesture was familiar to both of his companions. They had seen it many times over the years of the trust. Dalton did *not* throw Cecelia a commiserating glance. He was far too circumspect for that. He'd always been careful to keep his opinions to himself. It was one of the traits that led Cecelia to trust in his discretion. He did promise to find suitable houses available for rent in London and bring Cecelia a list of candidates. He then went on his way with a bounce in his step.

Cecelia next sent notes to her close friends, letting them know she was back. She also encouraged James to pay a visit to his club, which would accomplish the same thing. Word of their arrival would spread. It was time to take up the duties of society.

James had gone out as instructed when a hotel servant informed Cecelia that she had visitors. Three young ladies, the maid said, handing over cards. Cecelia was not surprised to read the names of Charlotte, Sarah, and Harriet. She nodded, and in the next moment the three hurried in. They were dressed for walking.

After a flurry of greetings, Sarah said, "We had to rush right over to tell you. You won't credit what has happened!"

They waited, eyes sparkling, for Cecelia to say, "What?"

"There is a rumor flying around town that Prince Karl is not actually a prince," said Charlotte. "That he is an imposter, who has imposed himself on the *ton*."

"What?" repeated Cecelia in a far different tone.

"He is absolutely *livid* with rage," said Sarah. "Whenever one sees him now, he looks like he's going to explode."

"Or hack something to pieces with his sword," added Charlotte.

"Can it be true?" wondered Cecelia. It seemed so unlikely.

"No one knows," answered Harriet. "He denies it, of course. But we know how difficult it is to deny scurrilous talk." She gave Cecelia a wry glance as the other two girls nodded.

"Doesn't he protest too much," said Charlotte.

"No smoke without fire," said Sarah.

The four young ladies exchanged satisfied looks. These things had been said of Cecelia when she tried to counter Prince Karl's insinuations.

"You are completely vindicated, of course," added Harriet. "The victim of a deceiver."

"And now a duchess," said Cecelia dryly, knowing that this change was the important factor for society.

"And that," Harriet agreed.

"We all wish you very happy by the way," said Sarah. The others nodded.

"And we must go," said Charlotte. "Mama will be wondering what's become of me. We will see you tomorrow, Cecelia."

They rushed out again, leaving Cecelia bemused.

"I don't think it is true," said James when he returned to the hotel sometime later and discovered that Cecelia had already heard the rumors. The speed of gossip was always a marvel. If it could be harnessed for finer purposes, how much might be accomplished.

Cecelia nodded. "I didn't see how he could carry off such a large deception."

"Indeed." As soon as he'd heard the story at his club, James remembered what Henry Deeping had told him about the prince's father. He suspected that this slander was Stephan Kandler's move to curb the prince. And very satisfying it was, too.

"But why did it begin?"

He was uncertain about sharing what Henry had told him. He would ask him first. "Perhaps someone wanted him to see what fighting a false accusation feels like," said James. "Poetic justice."

"I'm afraid I won't be able to keep from enjoying his struggles."

"And why should you?"

"Overscrupulosity?" asked Cecelia. "If that is a word."

James laughed. "I don't think it is. Nor should it afflict you."

"Do you never worry about other people's feelings? Or pity their misfortunes?"

"Not those like Prince Karl, who richly deserve them." James was puzzled by her tone. She sounded almost melancholy when a touch of genteel gloating seemed more justified.

A knock at the parlor door heralded Ned, who brought a note addressed to them both. James broke the seal and opened it. "Grandmamma wishes to hold a ball in honor of our marriage," he told Cecelia. "I say 'wishes,' but it is clear that she has already planned it and sent out the invitations."

"I don't believe we received one," replied Cecelia with a smile.

James waved the page. "This is to be considered our...command to appear." He looked down and read, "'We don't want people to see anything furtive'... That word is heavily underlined... 'about the match. A ball is traditional, and I shall do my best to make it a grand occasion.'"

"Knowing Lady Wilton, she will certainly succeed. And we have no house in which to hold it ourselves."

For the first time, James heard this as a criticism. He had married her, made her a duchess, but he had no home to offer her. Tereford House could scarcely be called that, not for some time. Months, no doubt. Their honeymoon had been so sweet. Now life stretched ahead, and as far as he could see into the future, it was crammed full of meetings with Dalton and musty documents and piles of broken-down possessions to sort through. He feared a cascade of disputes, because he and Cecelia had always disagreed about business matters.

That was the old Cecelia, he told himself, the one who did not approve of him and was engrossed in boring tasks that he could not endure. But she was gone or, at the least, modified by the woman who responded so eagerly to his caresses. And yet, the former Cecelia had existed for much longer than the ardent wife.

James looked up to find her gazing at him. "Do you not want your grandmother to hold a ball?" she asked.

"I'm sure she has the right idea." He examined the lovely creature on the other side of the hearth—golden hair, serenely beautiful face, the body that he now knew so well. He had never satisfactorily answered the question of why Cecelia changed her mind about marrying him. When he'd hinted at it, she'd distracted him in the most delicious way. She'd done that more than once, he realized. Physical pleasure could have been an answer, but she hadn't known what that would be like, between them, beforehand. And oddly, passion was not enough of an answer for him. He wanted more. But what precisely? He didn't know how to ask in a way that she would tell him.

It was ironic that Cecelia's very slightly tarnished reputation was now restored by Prince Karl's fall from grace. If she'd married to save her good name, she must now see that was unnecessary. Might she regret her hasty decision? And surely this whole line of thinking was foolishness?

"I am eager to get to work over at Tereford House," she said.

"Are you?" James had looked in on his way to the club and reassured Mrs. Gardener.

"I was thinking we might involve one of the large auction houses," Cecelia added. "They have people accustomed to valuing property, and they will be eager to sell the things we don't wish to keep. They could probably provide workers able to sift through the piles and make judgments."

James felt a trace of nostalgia for his days with the Gardener children searching for buried treasures. They had looked endearingly ridiculous in the old wigs. This new method would take all the fun out of the process. And yet, he had been growing weary of sorting. "Very well," he said.

"You don't sound enthusiastic."

"I'm sure you know what's best. You always do."

She blinked, and her lovely lips turned down. Was she offended? Hurt? James realized that he had never paid such close attention to her reactions in past years.

"This is my part of the arrangement after all," she said.

"Arrangement?"

"As we agreed."

"I never used that word," replied James. His chest felt tight.

"It was implied in your proposal, when you pointed out what I would gain by taking on the estate management."

She kept reminding him. Yes, he had said that, because he had been an idiot. But now he was…less of one? Or even more? He didn't know. "You've said you like such tasks."

"Yes," she replied.

"Yes, you have said so? Or you do like them?"

"Those are one and the same," she answered. "You can trust me to do a good job."

He did trust her for that, but could he trust her with his heart? And where had that very odd thought come from? James noticed an array of bottles on the sideboard. "Would you like a glass of wine?" He intended to have one. At least.

"Yes, thank you," she said.

He rose, poured, and returned with the glasses. When he handed hers over, he noticed a list in her other hand. James groaned, only half teasing. "That is the longest list I've ever seen you make."

Cecelia smiled up at him. "There's much to do."

He sat. She sipped her wine. James took a gulp of his.

"We needn't discuss every item," she said. "Just a few of the most important."

"Suppose I simply declare that you are right about all of them."

"And then complain when the thing is done that you wished it otherwise? We have seen how that goes."

"That was…"

She waited, then said, "Yes?"

He wanted to say that was the past, and that everything was different now. But he knew she would ask him how things were different, and he had no answer.

Fortunately twenty minutes later, the hotel servants arrived with the dinner Cecelia had ordered, and she put the list aside.

Cecelia had seen James's restlessness growing as she discussed the tasks that needed their attention. He seemed even more resistant than in the past. She'd thought of this before their marriage. They could no longer wrangle over some bit of business and then part while the dispute faded. Or, if they did, this would be a sad sort of marriage. They must have more to talk about than estate management, and the truth was, she could manage most of it without bothering him. That might be best.

She changed the topic over their dinner, asking which friends he'd seen at his club and what fresh gossip was circulating. Since he could now tell her some of the more spicy stories, she heard some eye-opening tales. She raised her eyebrows at the right spots and let her shock amuse him.

And when the dishes had been cleared away and they were alone, she went to sit on his lap, suggesting he demonstrate one of those scandalous stories he'd been telling her. That made him laugh. Cecelia sank into delirious kisses with the realization that they were happy together in this. Soon, surely, they would be in other ways as well.

Nineteen

"WELL, I MUST SAY, YOU HAVE NEVER LOOKED BETTER," SAID Lady Wilton to Cecelia when they arrived at her home for the promised ball. "That gown is splendid."

Cecelia smoothed a hand over the froth of creamy silk and lace. She was pleased with her new ensemble. She'd judged that it was just the right combination of high fashion and elegance for a duchess, and she was glad Lady Wilton agreed.

"What about me?" asked James.

His grandmother waved this away. "You always look well. It is easier for gentlemen."

"If you think so, you know nothing about it," he replied with a rueful smile.

"Well, I certainly *care* nothing about it," said the old lady. "Have you any news from your agent about Ferrington?"

"I've been rather busy. Getting married and so on."

"Always thinking first of yourself. You haven't even thanked me for putting on this ball, you know."

"Thank you very much for setting us up on display to the *ton*, Grandmamma. And increasing your own consequence by issuing a coveted invitation, which will draw a great crush even so late in the season."

Lady Wilton sputtered. "Rogue."

"I suppose people will begin arriving soon," mused Cecelia, to distract them.

"They will," said James's grandmother. "Come along and display yourselves."

And so the Duke and Duchess of Tereford took their places beside Lady Wilton to greet a burgeoning stream of guests.

It was soon apparent that the ball would be very well attended. Many were curious or pleased about the new couple and eager to look them over. Some were undoubtedly envious and hoping to see cracks in their facade. Cecelia's swooping changes of reputation over the last few weeks added interest. People offered their congratulations and took in every detail of the Terefords' appearance as they passed along into the ballroom.

She and James opened the dancing with a waltz, and Cecelia couldn't help comparing it with the same dance at the beginning of the season, which seemed so long ago now. Outwardly, all was the same—his hand at her waist, his fingers warm on hers, the whirl across the floor. Their steps were still well matched, and it was still a delight, floating across the floor with him. But inwardly, all was different. The waltz was no longer the thing that brought them closest. The warmth in his blue eyes as he looked down at her spoke of bare skin and tumbled sheets. She felt her cheeks warm with thoughts of those caresses.

She danced with others and then with James again. They spent the supper interval together, sitting with Sarah, Charlotte, Harriet, and their partners, and then resumed dancing. The room grew very warm despite long windows that opened on the night. The scent of the flowers that decorated the ballroom was heavy on the air. James had just gone to fetch Cecelia a glass of lemonade when there was a flurry at the doorway. The murmur of the crowd rose in volume, and people started to stir like water being parted by the prow of a rushing boat.

A tall man moved aside, and Cecelia saw Prince Karl striding into the room, actually pushing people out of his way if they did not move fast enough for him, furiously scowling. He had, of course, not been invited. But he ignored the rising tide of comments and disapproving glances. He was aimed at someone, and when Cecelia met his eyes, she understood that she was his target.

He shouldered past Harriet Finch, nearly knocking her down, and came to stop a few feet from Cecelia. "You!" he said.

Cecelia wondered if he'd lurked at the door until he saw James leave her. She suspected it. The prince was tall enough to see over the heads of most of the crowd.

"I have come to confront you, you see," he said.

Though her heart beat fast, she was not afraid.

"To make you take back your scurrilous lies in the hearing of all." His hazel eyes burned with anger. "Tell the truth!" he snarled.

Cecelia took a breath to steady her voice and then let it ring out. He was practically shouting, and she wished to be as easily heard. "Are you suggesting that I have spread a false story about you, as you had done about me?" she asked.

"*Natürlich!*" snapped the prince. "What else?"

"So you admit that the things you said about me were untrue," Cecelia answered.

"Is this your cowardly plot? To force me to admit it?"

"Do you?"

He made a savage gesture. "I have no time for trivialities."

"Do you?" Cecelia repeated in a tone he could not ignore.

"Yes, yes. They were not true. And now you will say the same. This falsehood has sullied my honor!"

"As your lies did mine?"

"Women have no honor," Prince Karl said. "Not in the same way."

"I beg your pardon?"

"You are made for dalliance and pleasure. The rest is all nonsense." He came a step closer. He looked as if he longed to shake her. "Now you will tell the truth!"

Cecelia was so angry that she was trembling, but she managed to speak clearly. "I had nothing to do with the rumors about you. I have been out of town and only heard them when I returned. I know nothing about your background and would never presume to comment upon it."

"You cunning jade," he growled. "You planned this."

"Planned for you to intrude where you were not invited and make more false accusations. How could I?"

He clenched his fists.

"I do sympathize," Cecelia added. "I know how difficult it is to correct false stories. People aren't easily convinced, are they?"

Prince Karl raised a hand as if to strike her. Cecelia moved back. At the same time, in the corner of her eye, she saw James shove a glass of lemonade at a surprised young gentleman and rush toward her.

He would see this as a contest between two men. And it was not. She could defend herself. "I give you my word that I did not malign you," she said to the prince before James could reach them. "I do not know who did. I don't believe it was any of my friends."

"The *word* of a woman," sneered Prince Karl.

He really was a loathsome creature. "Do we not take oaths and sign legal documents?" Cecelia asked. "You can trust me to tell the truth." If her tone implied that the same could not be said for him, she couldn't help it.

James came to stand beside her. He looked thunderous. Whether because of this ally or some other factor, Prince Karl seemed to become conscious of the hostile murmur of the crowd around him. He looked, saw no sympathetic faces, and appeared suddenly bewildered.

A young man came through the crowd and went to touch Prince Karl's arm. Cecelia recognized him as one of the prince's entourage. Searching her memory, she came up with a name—Stephan Kandler.

The newcomer bent close to murmur to the prince. Prince Karl turned to him, seeming about to argue. There was a brief muttered colloquy. Then Kandler pulled at the prince's sleeve to urge him out. After another scan of the room, the prince yielded, and they went.

"Like a dog herding a willful ram," said James.

He prepared his own cup and drank. "Ugh. It's gone cold."

"The thought is what counts."

"Not with dreadful tea." He tossed the contents of his cup out the open carriage window and reached for hers.

She pulled it back. "I shall drink it."

"Nonsense." He pulled the cup from her and dumped it outside. "You may have more lemonade if you are thirsty."

"May?"

"You cannot really wish for cold tea, Cecelia."

She didn't. But she didn't care for his dictatorial tone either. She started to tell him so, then stopped. She didn't want to be always arguing with her...husband. James was her husband! She began placing the uneaten food in the basket. Surely, with time, they would find a way to settle points without contention.

৵৹

They arrived in midafternoon, sweeping through an open gate guarded by rampant stone lions in a long gray wall.

A gravel drive stretched ahead to a large manor house in the distance, but they took a turn into a narrower lane well before reaching it, passed into a thick grove of trees and through another smaller wall into a lovely garden. The scent of flowers followed them around a curve.

"There it is," said James.

Cecelia leaned out the carriage window and gazed at a round stone tower perhaps thirty feet across. It was three stories high with crenellations at the top.

James got out and handed her down from the carriage. A manservant came out of the tower and took their valises inside. When he returned with an inquiring look, James indicated the basket inside the vehicle. He took that as well. "They are expecting you at the main stables," James told the coachman. The driver touched his hat brim and drove away.

Cecelia choked back a laugh. She would not gloat. "If he had horns, he would have butted me," she said quietly.

"Undoubtedly."

"There was a moment when I thought he would hit me."

"And you evaded him."

James sounded irritated, and Cecelia didn't understand why. She thought she'd done rather well.

"I would have appreciated an excuse to strike him," he added.

Now she saw. "I could not provide it."

"Of course not. You had no need for protection. Clearly you don't need my help for anything at all. You are supremely competent." He turned away from her and addressed the guests. "A small contretemps, which should not stop our dancing." He signaled the musicians to resume and went to ask another woman to dance.

Cecelia stood alone as others slowly joined in, and couples began to form up around her. She felt reprimanded and did not see why she should have been. At last she was saved by Henry Deeping, who solicited her hand for the set. "That was very well done," he said when they were dancing.

"I thought so."

He nodded. "You were composed and reasonable. You routed your opponent. I wouldn't be surprised if Prince Karl decided to continue his tour elsewhere."

"James seemed annoyed though." The words slipped out, because she was perplexed and a bit disappointed.

"He prefers to flatten his problems with his fists. Those that can't be tipped a leveler are a challenge for him."

"What problems can you punch?"

Mr. Deeping smiled down at her. "That is a difficulty. Beyond the boxing ring, not too many at all."

She knew that James turned most things into a contest. He saw life as a series of battles to be waged, opponents to be vanquished.

But that would not do for a marriage! "You've known him even longer than I have," she said to Mr. Deeping.

"Since we were grubby schoolboys."

"And he was always that way?"

"I think he was born combative. I've often imagined James as a pugnacious baby, flailing at his nursemaid." He smiled in fond amusement.

Cecelia did not find the picture comforting. She hoped for fewer disputes, not more.

When the dance ended Mr. Deeping took her to his sister, and they were soon joined by Sarah and Harriet. Her friends were full of admiration and told Cecelia that she'd been magnificent against Prince Karl. Cecelia appreciated the praise, but she noticed that James did not dance with her for the rest of the evening. And in the carriage going home, he merely said the event had been tiring and leaned back against the seat with his eyes closed.

"Is something wrong?" she asked him.

"Nothing," he replied.

"But you seem…"

"Merely tired." His tone was flat, and he did not open his eyes.

She sat back, chilled. She knew how to argue with James. She'd won, and lost, any number of disputes with him. But this coolness was not familiar. It seemed designed to repel and silence her, and she didn't understand why he would wish to do that. "Are you angry?" she finally asked, just before they reached the hotel.

"I am tired, Cecelia," he replied in a voice that indeed sounded weary. "It is time for sleep. May we do that?"

She wasn't certain whether he took his own advice. But it was a long time, lying beside him, before she found rest.

◦∾◦

The next morning James rose early and took himself off to Gentleman Jackson's boxing saloon, where he spent a satisfying half hour pummeling the bag and then another in a sparring session with an acquaintance who was also looking for an opportunity to hit something. James was aware, as he perhaps hadn't been in the past, that these sessions made no difference to his current perplexities. But the hard physical exertion was a relief, even taking some blows that rattled his bones. It was like the steam that jetted from a boiling kettle, reducing the pressure. He welcomed the fatigue that came after as well and, more sheepishly, the fact that he'd clearly bested his opponent in the ring.

This was far better than the muddle in his mind, a hash of all the disputes he'd had with Cecelia over the last thirteen years. He'd been accused of laziness, extravagance, selfishness, excessive complaining, being too combative, and probably of other things that he couldn't recall at the moment. He didn't think these criticisms were true—at least, not lately. He'd felt like a changed man in the last several weeks. But how was he to convince anyone? Rather, how was he to show Cecelia, the only one who mattered? He remembered her struggles to counter false accusations. He could *say* he was different, but he wondered resentfully, who would believe?

And did she care? She'd faced Prince Karl without a glance at him. There hadn't been the vestige of an appeal. She was shouldering responsibilities right and left. She was taking over everything. Exactly as he'd asked her to do in his original proposal, suggested a dry inner voice.

James grimaced in the mirror as he made a final adjustment to his neckcloth. The James who had first offered for her had been such an arrogant, paltry creature! Puffed up with his own imagined consequence. He couldn't bear the fellow.

Nor could he blame Cecelia for doing as he'd asked. Or for being better than he was at nearly every task. Hadn't he admitted it? Didn't he *want* her to manage the ducal affairs? He put on his hat and left Gentleman Jackson's.

Generally he wanted that, James acknowledged. Mostly. Except for the important, interesting bits, suggested a sneaking inner voice. He wanted to decide those. And he'd rather thought that she would consult him more often. James struck a lamppost with his cane as he walked along the pavement.

A picture filled James's brain—Cecelia soliciting his opinion, praising his ideas, begging for his approval. Part of him found it disturbingly attractive.

No, that was not what he'd expected! He'd meant them to... He didn't know what. The man who'd requested her skills and the man who was married to her today were not in agreement. And so it was easier to hit things.

He turned a corner and walked toward Tereford House. They had an appointment to meet a representative from an auction house about the mass of items there. He'd snapped at Cecelia when she said she could receive him on her own. She hadn't sorted a single pile so far! Was his work to be dismissed?

He found her in the kitchen with the Gardener family, including Ned who'd come along to see his family and a stranger. Their vociferous welcome salved his feelings a bit. He was also glad to see that they all looked much less anxious and better fed. "This is my brother, Will Ferris, milord," said Mrs. Gardener.

The thin man with a wooden left leg below the knee gave him a half bow. "Milord," he said. "I thank you for the chance to work."

"Trooper, were you?" James asked him.

"Ninety-Fifth Foot, sir. Until Salamanca." He gestured at the artificial leg.

"A rifleman!"

He stood straighter. "Yessir."

Knowing the man had been a member of a crack regiment, chosen for special training, made James glad he'd moved him in.

He nodded acknowledgment and vowed to make Will Ferris's employment more formal in the near future. He noticed Cecelia's inquiring look. Here was something she knew nothing about.

"Ned's been telling us about his valeting," said Mrs. Gardener.

"He looks so grand," declared little Effie.

"Puffed up like a croaky bullfrog," said their sister Jen.

"You're just jealous." Ned fingered the lapel of his new coat.

Cecelia took a step nearer the center of the group. "We have been thinking of introducing Ned to a tailor who wants an apprentice."

Was this the royal we? James was unaware of these thoughts. Well, they had mentioned such a plan, but that was long ago. Days ago?

"I have talked to Ned about it…"

"You have?" James interrupted.

"Yes, and he is quite interested. We would pay the fees, of course."

Shouldn't he have been consulted about this? "Ned wishes to leave my service?"

Cecelia looked at the lad. When he said nothing, she replied, "He thought tailoring would give him…scope for his ideas."

James turned to Ned. "I gave you no scope?"

With an anxious frown, Ned said, "Yes, milord. I mean, no. You did. But you need a regular trained valet, which I know I ain…am not."

It was true. James had been wondering how to break it to the lad that he couldn't keep on. But that didn't mean he should be left out of this entire process. "I thought we were rubbing along well enough." His voice sounded sulky to his own ears.

Ned winced. "You said—about the shine on your boots. And the shirt."

A moment's impatience was not important. Everyone knew that. Then James noticed that the entire Gardener family looked worried. Even the former rifleman. He'd forgotten their lingering fears of retribution. Cecelia was frowning at him, too, probably adding to his faults on the list she kept. "Splendid," James said, taking care to speak heartily. "Apprentice tailor it is then. I'm sure you'll be all the rage in a few years, Ned. Probably refuse to make my coats because you're so fashionable."

"I would never do that!" Ned declared. "I'll make 'em for free."

"No, no, you must charge all the market will bear," replied James. "That is what cements your reputation as a top-of-the-trees tailor."

The sound of the front door knocker came down the hallway. "I'll go, milord," said Will Ferris.

"Never mind," said Cecelia. "We're expecting someone. We will let him in."

"I can do it, milady" was the gruff reply.

"Please do," said James. He observed Cecelia's raised eyebrows and questioning gaze as Ferris stumped out. Later he would explain to her about a man's pride. Another thing he might know more about!

They followed and thus got to see the visitor's surprise when a somewhat battered ex-soldier opened the door.

"Name?" asked Ferris, in the crisp tone of a sentry on duty.

"Reginald Nordling," replied the newcomer, handing over his card even though his eyes were on James and Cecelia at the back of the entryway.

Ferris turned, holding it. "Mr. Reginald Nordling of Drellinger's Auction House," he read out at parade-ground volume.

Perhaps he would appoint Ferris butler, James thought.

They moved forward to meet the visitor, who bowed low and said, "Your Graces." He seemed inordinately pleased to be in the presence of a duke and duchess.

James stepped over to the right-hand parlor doorway and pushed it open as far as the mass of furnishings inside would allow.

When he turned, he saw that Cecelia had done the same with the left-hand parlor door.

Mr. Nordling dithered for a moment before hurrying over to peer in. Left, then right, James noticed. "Merciful heavens," the man said.

"The whole house is like this," replied Cecelia.

Mr. Nordling grew more and more wide-eyed as they conducted him about the place. "I had heard whispers of this," he murmured. "But seeing it is…"

"Melancholy," said James.

"Overwhelming," said Cecelia at the same moment.

"No, Your Graces, it is fascinating. Who knows what treasures we might find in this?"

"Well, I have some idea," said James. "I sorted out two rooms. Nearly."

"With what result?"

"I found broken-down furniture, mostly, which I chucked out a window."

Mr. Nordling looked distressed. "It will be far better to have everything evaluated by an expert eye, Your Grace. Valuable things might be salvaged. But we can look outdoors as well."

"Much of it has since been stolen," said Cecelia.

Were they blaming him? Was he now to add incompetent to his catalog of faults? Cecelia had urged him to work, and now his methods were to be criticized.

"It is just that… With a few repairs, a piece can often be made quite saleable."

"Even when it has been thoroughly chewed by rats?" asked James.

"Rats?" Mr. Nordling looked around uneasily.

"Oh yes, we have quite a colony."

"The cats have taken care of them," said Cecelia. "Mrs. Gardener said they have not seen a single one in three days."

It was obvious that Mr. Nordling had never dealt with a property such as this. He goggled, and his mouth opened and closed twice, making him resemble a goldfish, James thought.

"So as to your methods…" Cecelia began.

James had to make a push to deal with this fellow, show her he wasn't useless. "I assume you will separate everything into categories," he said.

"Indeed, Your Grace. We will discard the, er, chewed-over and worthless items, and then you may decide what to keep and what to sell from the remainder."

"What about sentimental value?" James actually could not imagine feeling tender about any of his great-uncle's leavings, but it seemed a responsible thing to say. "I suppose some family relics might appear worthless," he added, as much to himself as the others.

"We will take care to set such things aside," replied Mr. Nordling.

"I came across some odd bits in the sorting."

Their visitor perked up. "What sorts of things, Your Grace?"

James struggled to remember. "Some old flint knives."

"Indeed. We count collectors of ancient artifacts among our clients."

"There were powder horns for muzzle-loading muskets," James recalled.

"A rotating bookstand carved with miniature gargoyles," said Cecelia. Was she laughing at him?

"And many knives," said James. "Daggers, poniards, dirks, a stiletto, just in one room."

"Perhaps it was the knife room," suggested Cecelia. Her eyes were certainly laughing. Part of James shared her amusement. Another part felt ridiculed.

Mr. Nordling seemed to be searching for a polite response to this catalog.

James was afflicted by a wave of stubbornness. "I find some of the stranger things interesting," he said to Nordling. "I should like them kept out for me to look over."

"Of course, Your Grace. Would you wish to come every day?"

When one put it that way, he didn't really wish to.

"So much of it *is* rather strange," said Cecelia.

She thought she knew what he was thinking. Blast it, she probably did know. But that didn't mean he had to confirm her conclusions. "I will call here each day at six," he declared. "And you may show me what you have found."

Cecelia looked surprised, which was gratifying.

"Yes, Your Grace," replied Nordling. "I will bring my people in first thing tomorrow to begin the work."

"Agreed." The word sounded official. James liked that. "I will see you out." As he herded the fellow toward the stairs, he turned to say to Cecelia, "I will see you back in the kitchen."

"My proper place, Your Grace?" she murmured.

James wasn't certain whether Nordling heard this, or understood the sarcasm if he did. But he hustled the man out, thinking that it was quite unfair of her to mock his efforts when she had been urging him to do more for years. In fact, it seemed she didn't care to give up an ounce of control. She was too accustomed to managing him.

Returning to the kitchen, James found the entire household there, digging into a pan of scones fresh from the oven. He couldn't blame them. There was nowhere else to sit in the house. He'd be glad when that was remedied. The hotel was feeling cramped as well.

"I'm going on to look over two houses for rent that might do for us," Cecelia said, as if she'd heard his thoughts.

It annoyed James that she could do that when he usually had no idea what she was thinking.

"I don't suppose you wish to come along?" she added.

"I do," he answered, clipping the phrase.

Cecelia could tell this was a lie. Or perhaps that was too strong a word. But he certainly did *not* wish to view houses for rent. That was plain in his face. Why not just say so? James was behaving very strangely. "I am happy to manage this alone," she tried.

He frowned as if she'd said something irritating. "That will not be necessary."

She couldn't ask what was wrong before the entire Gardener clan, and she was in no mood to suggest a retreat to the previous duke's bedchamber for private conversation.

"Now?" he asked, gazing at the scone in her hand as if it was a personal failing.

And with that, Cecelia realized he'd set up another contest, this one between the two of them. That explained his pushing forward with Mr. Nordling. As always, James was intent on winning, and he couldn't evade the house visits because that would be some twisted sort of defeat. So very typical. What she didn't understand was why James saw it so. He'd bargained for someone—a wife—to take on his work. He'd even admitted that she was more skilled at it. Hadn't he? Surely she hadn't imagined that?

In any case, she was playing her part. It was quite unfair of him to be contentious when she was trying to do as he'd asked. Also irritated now, Cecelia put aside her scone and rose. "We will need a hack."

James hailed one not far from Tereford House, and they rode in silence to the first address Cecelia had been given. It was a compact wooden edifice that looked newly painted.

"Not a fashionable neighborhood," James commented as they stepped down from the cab.

"It is quite temporary," replied Cecelia.

"But so out of the way."

"The season is nearly over."

"Indeed. So why stay in London?"

"Where do you propose to go?" Cecelia asked. If he wanted to be snappish, she could match him.

He had no answer. She knew he'd often visited his bachelor friends in the summer months. Before he could suggest Brighton, she added, "And what about your daily visits to Tereford House? At six sharp."

He frowned. "It is some distance away."

"You can get a horse."

"I have a horse, Cecelia. You've seen me riding in the park."

"Oh yes. So that's settled then." She went to knock on the door.

Mr. Dalton was inside, having procured the keys from the owner. Being an extremely efficient man of business, he'd also acquired details about the property, which he reviewed as they walked through. "Only one sizable reception room," he said. "The furnishing are new, however, and the kitchen has been brought up to date with a closed stove."

She would have to find a cook to make use of it, Cecelia thought as they walked up the stairs. As well as other staff.

"Two decent bedrooms," continued Mr. Dalton. "And two that are…"

"Small and shabby," said James, having barely glanced into them.

Mr. Dalton bowed his head in acknowledgment. He was familiar with James's dilatory manner from years of assisting with the trust. Still, Cecelia felt that James wasn't giving him enough credit. Mr. Dalton had gone to some effort to find possibilities for them. "It is very clean," she said.

James shot her a sardonic look. "There is another, I believe? Cecelia said two houses?"

"Yes, Your Grace."

"Let us go on to that then." James turned to the stairs.

The second candidate was a short walk away, further from the hub of fashionable London. It was larger, however, built of red brick with ornate stone lintels.

"Some merchant had aspirations," James commented.

Mr. Dalton had these keys as well, and they entered to look over two spacious parlors at the front of the house, a dining room and smaller one at the back. "There is a garden," Mr. Dalton pointed out.

Cecelia examined it through a window. The plantings were nothing special, but it was a pleasant walled space.

"Kitchen below, quite tolerable," Mr. Dalton continued. "There are four good bedchambers here and servants quarters on the third floor."

They went up to survey all of these. "I think this would do," said Cecelia as they returned to the entry.

"The furnishings are dowdy," James replied.

"But endurable until we get our own new things."

"Oh, if you are to be satisfied with the mediocre."

This was too much. He was deliberately provoking. "You know very well I am not!" said Cecelia. "But if you are concerned, we can go around all the warehouses together."

James couldn't quite hide a wince.

"I know of one that has *hundreds* of fabric samples for draperies and chair coverings," Cecelia added.

James looked queasy, and she felt a flash of triumph. The only sort of purchasing he cared for was at his tailor. And, she supposed, when he had bought his horse. All else had been provided by his landlady.

"There will be so very many things to choose from," she said.

One of James's hands jerked as if to ward off a curse. He closed it into a fist.

Mr. Dalton had moved a few paces away. During the years when Cecelia and James argued over trust business, he'd cultivated a sort of motionless invisibility.

"We will take this house," Cecelia told him.

"I have not made up my mind," replied James.

She glared at him. Silently. Challenging, not reproachful. *Certainly* not apologetic. She knew from long experience that she could outwait him.

After a time James looked away. "I suppose it will do," he muttered.

Mr. Dalton waited a moment, then said, "I will make the arrangements. The cost is quite reasonable."

James started to speak. But he seemed to think better of it. His jaw tightened, and he turned to the door.

"Very good. Thank you, Mr. Dalton," said Cecelia.

"Shall we go?" asked James, impatient now.

"I will stay a little longer," she answered, feeling contrary. "In case there is anything we need, I want to—"

"Make a list," interrupted her new husband, the phrase an accusation.

"Precisely so, James. A thorough and intelligent list."

With a sound rather like *pfft*, he swept out.

Mr. Dalton of course said nothing. And he had, of course, brought paper and pen, including a clever portable ink bottle. He arranged them on a table in one of the parlors, and then was good enough to sit there and note down items Cecelia called out to him as she paced about the house. Gradually, shouting mundane requirements up or down the stairwell—more saucepans, three proper vases, a larger wardrobe, and some oil lamps—she recovered her temper. James was undoubtedly using whatever method he'd created to do the same. The process was familiar.

But the circumstances were not. This was not the past. They were man and wife. She didn't want to contend with him. She certainly didn't want him to see her as an adversary. He looked at life as a continual battle—very well. She might not be able to alter his outlook. But she should be an exception. Surely he wished her to be?

Cecelia stood at the linen press, smoothing a pile of bedsheets with pensive melancholy. The pleasures of physical passion were entrancing, shattering, but they were not all of life. And apparently they did not change everything.

Twenty

THEY MOVED INTO THE RENTED HOUSE THE FOLLOWING DAY. Cecelia's maid and Ned came with them, along with James's things from his former rooms. Cecelia sent for her clothes and other personal items from her father's house. She thought it fortunate that neither of them had too many possessions, if one didn't count the mass left by his great-uncle Percival, which she refused to do.

When her trunks arrived on a cart the next day, Aunt Valeria came with them. She walked through the house as the carters unloaded, her round face sulky. "Really, Cecelia, I do not see why you have set yourselves up in this distant place. You might easily have come home."

"Papa's house is no longer my home," Cecelia pointed out.

"Of course it is. And if you would only return, you might be some help to me. Really, you are familiar with everything that needs to be done, while I am not. The servants miss you sadly."

Cecelia could easily believe that. Aunt Valeria was an erratic mistress. Cecelia experienced a brief, unworthy temptation to hire the staff she knew away from her father. Of course she could not be so underhanded. Except, there was Janet, the cook's assistant. She'd thoroughly learned her trade and begun to chafe under Cook's orders. She would be moving on to another position soon, no matter what Cecelia did. And Archie, one of the footmen, was on the verge of leaving as well. He'd told her he hoped to find a place in a larger household. He might like to come here, as the first of a ducal staff that would be much larger in time. Her father's household would carry on quite well without these two. Perhaps even more smoothly. And Aunt Valeria wouldn't even notice they were gone. She never could tell the footmen apart. "I'm sure you will settle in very soon," she said to her aunt.

"I do not want to settle in," replied her aunt. She might have meant to be plaintive, but the word came out sulky. "They *ask* me things. When I am trying to concentrate."

"Send them to Mrs. Grant," Cecelia suggested. Her father's housekeeper was extremely competent.

"Well, I do, but she seems to think I should have *opinions* on the most trivial things. New types of coal scuttles!"

"Tell her that you are happy for her to make decisions," Cecelia suggested.

"I have. She does not appear to believe me." Aunt Valeria pulled a long face.

Cecelia had liked to supervise, and Mrs. Grant was accustomed to working with her. But the housekeeper would actually relish the chance to take more into her own hands. "I will send her a note explaining that you are quite serious," she told her aunt. She would mention Janet and Archie in the letter. She suspected that Mrs. Grant would see losing two of her junior servants as an acceptable trade for greater scope.

All this proved to be true. Janet and Archie accepted her offers with alacrity and moved themselves in that very evening. Janet was delighted to rule her own kitchen and suggested two girls of her acquaintance to assist her. Hoping she was not establishing a tyranny, Cecelia agreed.

Thus, the next morning, there was expertly brewed tea and fresh baked bread, along with the dishes Cecelia customarily ordered. She waited for James to notice this minor miracle, but he appeared to take a fine breakfast in a completely new household for granted. "I found a cook," she pointed out.

"Ah? Yes. This jam is quite good."

Which of course had been purchased; there had been no time to make jam. This was the heedless James she knew. Testing him,

Cecelia added, "I shall be looking for other servants today. Would you care to join in the interviews?"

"What about Will Ferris for a butler," he replied.

"Mrs. Gardener's brother?" She was nearly certain he was joking.

"I like his style."

Cecelia did, too, but it was not that of a majordomo. "Perhaps some other post—" she began.

"He has a great deal of pride, you know. And he is quite capable."

"I have no doubt of that." She did doubt that he understood all of a butler's tasks. "But another position might be better. I was thinking we should talk to the Gardeners about whether they would like to be in town or the country. We will have many positions to fill, since we must assume that Uncle Percival left his properties…unkempt."

James stared at her. "You don't think they're all like…"

She saw visions of endless chaos in his eyes but could only shrug.

James groaned. "I believe I shall go to the club."

Knowing she would accomplish more in his absence, Cecelia encouraged this plan. And by late afternoon, she'd found everyone she required for now and felt smugly efficient. She would have been happy to share her successes, and be praised for them, but there was no sign of James. She was upstairs making ready for bed when she finally heard him call her name.

Footsteps bounded up the stairs, and he appeared in the bedchamber door. "Prince Karl has left England," he said. "Word is buzzing about town."

"Has he?"

"Couldn't tolerate the taste of his own medicine seemingly. You routed him." James's glance was admiring. "Tipped him a leveler, as they say."

She enjoyed his approval, though not the way it was framed.

And she did not, of course, mention the two men's actual fight. That would be folly.

"Also, I found a new valet."

"Did you?" That was one position she had left to him.

"Henry Deeping's man knew of a fellow. Served old Falcourt until he died last month, and as you know Falcourt was always complete to a shade."

She didn't know, but she nodded anyway.

"The valet's not a doddering fossil though. He'd only been with Falcourt two years."

"Oh, good."

"So I went right over and engaged him. I knew you wouldn't want me to delay."

Perhaps this was meant to be an excuse for his lengthy absence. Cecelia didn't require it.

"Bingham, the sneaking cur who stole Hobbs from me, is sorry now. He looked nohow when I told him. Because if he'd left Hobbs alone, he might have had Phipps, you see. A much better choice."

James looked elated. How he liked to win. "So you have paid Bingham off for his sneakiness," she responded.

"And more."

"Well, bravo."

James bowed as if to an appreciative audience. "And then I had to go by Tereford House, as I'd told Nordling I would."

Definitely excuses, Cecelia decided. She was enjoying them a little. She continued brushing her hair. "Have they made a good beginning?"

"It's going much faster with a team of brawny haulers. And Nordling's keeping a close eyes on things."

"Will you tell him to keep an eye out for the family silver? And china? I don't want to purchase things we may find later in one of those piles."

"Umm," said James. He finally had a bit of attention to spare for his surroundings. "There's a fresh scent in here. You've made the bedchambers very pleasant."

"It's potpourri."

"Ah. It's become a very comfortable room."

"I hope to make you comfortable."

"Only that?" He came over and put his hands on her shoulders.

"Well, more than comfortable perhaps," said Cecelia. She turned from the mirror. He bent. Their lips met. The kiss began softly and rapidly rose to incendiary.

They had acquired some skill in removing their clothing by this time. In this at least they moved in perfect unison. And they'd learned the caresses that roused passions to a fever pitch—fingertips on silken skin, flurries of kisses. James made his wife cry out in delight, and his own release was like drowning in pleasure. Sleep overtook them in each other's arms.

But the next morning, the deluge of business descended on their heads once more, so different from the soft and fiery intimacies of the bedroom. James's new valet arrived early, and Ned had to be placated because James had forgotten to tell him that Phipps had been hired. Other new servants were joining them as well, and the house felt nearly as chaotic as great-uncle Percival's for a time.

Then when James went out to discover how one arranged for an apprenticeship with a fashionable tailor, he was nonplussed to discover that the Terefords' positions in the world were now reversed. His minor, personal success in securing a new valet was utterly eclipsed by Cecelia's triumph over Prince Karl. Everyone was talking of her assurance and aplomb, admiring her courage. The tale of her confrontation at the ball was told and retold. James was the nonpareil—or he had been—and yet all anyone thought of now was his wife. On top of that, he was taxed with a day of drudgery. How had this happened? It was hours before it occurred to him that Mr. Dalton was the man to deal with apprenticeships and dispatched a note to the man of business saying as much.

James retreated to Tereford House, fully aware that this was what he had done the last time he felt vexed by society. But the situation was quite different, he told himself. Tereford House had become an active place. Men called back and forth from room to room, vying for Nordling's attention. Mrs. Gardener was kept busy providing refreshments to fuel the search. And one never knew what would turn up. Yes, most of it was detritus. There were long, boring stretches. But once in a while a gem emerged, sometimes, as today, quite literally.

James headed back to the rented house with a velvet case in his pocket containing a diamond necklace. He bore it to Cecelia as a lavish gift, imagining her surprise and praise. When they were apart, he yearned for her. Yet when they were together, outside of the bedroom, they could not seem to avoid friction.

He found her in the small back parlor surrounded by a mass of papers. Before he could bring out the necklace, she said, "I had Mr. Nordling send over the basket of letters from the Tereford House library. Can you imagine, I'd nearly forgotten about them!"

There it was, the basket they'd found that first day, as long as his arm and nearly as deep, mounded with correspondence. "Without asking me?" he said.

"Asking you what?"

She seemed to have no idea of consulting him. "About the letters," he replied, jaw tight.

"We can't neglect them any longer, James."

"They have been neglected for months. More than that perhaps. And nothing dreadful has occurred."

"We don't know that." Cecelia gestured at the papers around her, which he realized now were these letters. "Who knows how many tragedies have befallen the writers in that time?"

"Tragedies! You exaggerate."

"How would you know? You've never even glanced at them."

"They are not addressed to me. They are begging letters to

Uncle Percival. Very likely from people making unwarranted demands. Or even false appeals, fabricated to extract funds."

"People in distress," she began.

"As you imagine," he interrupted.

She frowned at him. "We cannot know until we look. I shall read them and make some response. It is not a task I look forward to, but…"

"Yes indeed, you are the poor martyr who must do everything. Fortunately, you are eminently capable and always right. Don't worry, everyone admires you." James regretted these words, and the cutting tone, as soon as they were uttered. Particularly when Cecelia drew back as if he'd struck her. "I did not mean…"

"That is why you married me," she interrupted. "So that the work would get done. How can you complain now when I do it?"

"That is not why I married you!" James snapped, exasperated by this repeated accusation. She started to speak, and he held up a hand to forestall her. "And do *not* throw my first proposal back in my face again. You know very well that things changed after that."

"Do I?"

"You are a fool if you do not. And everyone knows you are not a fool, Cecelia."

"Everyone but me, perhaps." Her voice had gone softer. "You said that love was a ridiculous illusion and that you would marry as a duty." She recalled his words so clearly. "Add another portrait to the long line of languishing females in the gallery. You called marriage dreary."

"It is inexpressibly annoying to have my foolish opinions thrown back in my face," he said. "*Might* we make a pact never to do that again?"

"Why did you marry me, James?" she asked.

"Because I love you, of course." He knew his first utterance of those words shouldn't have sounded angry. But it did.

"You…"

"These past weeks have made me see how much." That sounded so flat to convey all he meant. "I brought you a diamond necklace." He pulled the case from his pocket and dropped it among the letters. "Nordling's people found it today." This was all going wrong. She was staring at him as if he was mad.

She didn't open it. Instead she said, "I've loved you for years, you know. Even when I was the bane of your existence."

James's heart began to pound. "You never were."

"Are you sure?"

There was a small smile on her face. A vast relief. "Oh yes."

"It took me longer than that to understand love," he said.

"And now you do?"

She was teasing him. Thank God, she was teasing him. James's heart seemed to expand in his chest. "A large claim, I am aware. But I believe it is made up of desire and friendship and respect."

"Like a recipe?"

"More a magical spell. Some mystical power takes those elements and makes them into a greater thing."

"How poetic, James." She looked happy. She truly did.

He opened the jewel case and held up the necklace.

"It's lovely!" she exclaimed.

He stepped over to fasten the glittering stream around her neck. "You outshine them."

The kiss that followed was soul deep. It would no doubt have led to more intimate caresses, but a clatter of footsteps heralded the entrance of Lady Wilton, waving a sheet of paper. Ignoring their embrace, she said, "I have had word from Ferrington Hall."

"Have you?" James was lost in his wife's gorgeous eyes. He refused to let go of her. His grandmother could simply endure the sight.

"I have!" she replied. "Which is more than your useless agent ever managed. There is a group of Travelers camping on the land near there."

"Travelers, like the lost earl's mother?" asked Cecelia.

The old lady scowled at the mention of this supposed disgrace. "Yes," she replied curtly.

"That *is* suggestive," said James.

"Very," answered his entrancing wife.

"Perhaps we should pay them a visit."

"I think we must."

"Well, someone must," said Lady Wilton. "And it seems that all I have are two mooncalves with no more sense that a booby. Nevertheless, you will depart immediately!"

"Yes, Grandmamma," said James.

"You know, I still mean to read these letters," said Cecelia, gesturing at the flood of paper.

"Yes, my darling duchess, I do," said James.

Keep reading for a sneak peek of
Earl on the Run, the next book in
The Duke's Estates,
coming soon!

JONATHAN FREDERICK MERRILL, APPARENTLY THE THRICE-
damned ninth Earl of Ferrington, known to himself and his old
life as Jack, encountered the Travelers on the third day after he
left London. They were ambling along the road he was walking,
and he caught up with their straggle of horse-drawn caravans and
swarm of children when the sun was halfway down the western
sky. The sight of them was the first thing to lift the black mood
that had afflicted him since he'd fled the city. "*Grált'a*," he said to
the man apparently serving as the rear guard.

This produced a ferocious scowl and a spate of words he
didn't understand. "I only know a few words of the Shelta," he
replied, naming the language these traveling people spoke
among themselves. The adult men had begun to gather round
him, looking menacing. "My mother was born to the *an lucht
siúil*, the walking people, over the sea in America," Jack added.
"She left them to marry my father, but many a tale she told me
of life on the road."

The first man surveyed the landscape around them, an empty
stretch of forest. "You have no horse?" he asked contemptuously.

Jack had thought of buying a horse. He had a sizable sum in a
money belt, his passage home and more. But he'd put it off, thinking he would soon be leaving England. "Only my own feet and a
bit of coin in my pocket. I'm happy to work for my keep, however."
Nobody needed to know the extent of his funds.

The group scowled at him. Jack had already noticed that his
accent puzzled the English. They were accustomed to judging
people by the way they spoke, but his mixture of North American

with the intonations of his parents didn't fit their preconceived notions.

"Perhaps we just beat you and take your coins," the man said.

Jack closed his fists. "You could try, I suppose."

A wizened old woman pushed through the circle of men. Leaning on a tall staff, she examined Jack from head to toe.

Jack stiffened. He wouldn't be enduring abuse from another crone. He'd had his fill of that and more from his newfound great grandmother. She'd discovered nothing to like about him. His brown hair, dark eyes, and "undistinguished" face were nothing like her noble English get, apparently. A poor excuse for an earl with the manners of a barbarian, she'd said. Though how she could tell about the manners when she'd hardly let him speak a word, he did not know.

"We are not brigands," said the old Traveler woman to her fellows. "No matter what they may say of us."

"Nay, fine metalworkers and horse breeders, or so my mother told me," Jack replied.

"Did she now?" Jack caught a twinkle of good humor in the old woman's pale eyes. Perhaps she wasn't like the ill-tempered Lady Wilton after all.

"She did," he replied. "And inspired me to be footloose. I've been a frontier explorer, a bodyguard, and a sailor." He'd been told he had charm. He reached for it as he smiled at the small woman before him.

"And now you are here."

Jack nodded. He wasn't going to mention inherited earldoms. That would be stupid. "Seeing the world," he answered. "I don't care for sitting still."

This yielded nods of understanding among his audience.

"Might I walk along with you?" Jack dared. "I'm headed north, as you seem to be." The truth was, Jack was lonely. He was a sociable man. He'd had many friends back home. Why had he left all that at the behest of a stuffy Englishman? He should have known that any legacy from his feckless father would be tainted.

"North to what?" the old Traveler woman asked.

It would be as unwise to mention estates as to reference an earldom, though Jack had decided to take a look at this Ferrington Hall he was supposed to inhabit. "North until I decide to turn in some other direction," he replied jauntily.

One man laughed.

"The road is free to all," said the woman.

"It is that. But companionship is a gift beyond price."

She laughed. "You have a quick tongue. If you wish to walk with us a while, we will not turn you away."

"*Maa'ths*," said Jack, thanking her with another of his small store of Shelta words. He was surprisingly glad of the permission.

The caravans started up again. Jack walked along beside them. But with this matter settled, his thoughts began drifting back to the scene that had driven him from town. Much as he'd like to forget it, he could not.

Until the high-nosed Englishman had shown up in Boston with his astonishing summons, Jack had only half believed his father's stories of a noble lineage. His Irish mother claimed that Papa bragged about being an earl's son before they wed, but once they were, he wouldn't take the least advantage of it. He refused to lift a finger to introduce Jack, his only child, to his rich relatives before he drank himself to death. And so she'd decided it was all a lie. Jack wished she'd lived to see the arrival of that "man of business" who'd lured him back here. He'd come partly because of her. How she would have reveled in the idea of her son as an earl.

His mother would *not* have stood for one single insult from his scold of a great grandmother, however. She'd have scratched the harpy's eyes out.

Jack had been taken before this Lady Wilton as if he was a package to be dropped in her lap. And she'd received him like a delivery of bad meat. Facing her distaste, he'd actually felt as if he smelled. The small, gnarled woman with snow-white hair and a nose seemingly designed for looking down on people had proceeded to deplore his appearance, his lowborn mother, his upbringing, his accent, and the sins of his scapegrace father, whom she'd never expected to hear of again after she packed him off into exile. But there was no help for it, she'd declared at the end of this tirade. Jack was now the earl. She would have to force him onto Society. It might just be possible if he followed her lead in every respect and kept his mouth shut.

Of course Jack had rebelled. No red-blooded man would stomach such words, particularly about his mother. The mixture of motives that had brought him across the sea evaporated in an instant. He had no interest in joining any society that included people like Lady Wilton.

Bruised and resentful, Jack had nearly boarded a ship and returned to Boston right after that meeting. But he hadn't quite. He'd set off north instead. Only when he'd been walking for a full day did his anger cool enough to acknowledge that he was hurt as well as outraged. The truth was, he'd been drawn here by an idea of family, a homely thing he'd never had. He'd read stories about domestic tranquility and seen glimpses of it among his friends, but his childhood had been fragmented and contentious. His parents couldn't seem to agree on anything except their tempestuous reconciliations after a shouted dispute. Jack had been audience or afterthought, often left to fend for himself.

When the summons to England came, he'd actually imagined a welcome by a circle of kin, a place where he belonged. He'd found disdain instead, rejection without any chance to show his worth. It was painful to be the unwanted earl, the bane of his father's kin. The inner bruise had been expanding rather than fading as time and distance separated him from London.

"Are you a dreamer?" said a voice near his knee.

"What?" Jack looked down to find a girl of perhaps six or seven trudging along beside him. Tiny, dark haired, and bright-eyed, she peered up at him.

"You didn't hear what I said three times. That's a dreamer."

"I beg your pardon. I was thinking."

"About what?"

"My great grandmother."

"Do you miss her?" asked the little girl.

"No, she thinks I'm a disgrace."

"What did you do?"

That was the point. He'd done nothing but be born into Lady Wilton's precious bloodline. Half into it. His mother's lineage was not to be mentioned. Jack hadn't *asked* to come here or be an earl. "Not a thing."

The little girl took this in solemnly. She seemed to decide to believe him. "You're too old to be scolded."

"A man might think so."

"How old are you?"

"Twenty-four."

"I'm nearly eight. My name's Samia."

Jack stopped walking, doffed his hat, and gave her the sort of elegant bow he'd learned from his wayward father. He had absorbed a good deal from the man, whatever his great grandmother might think. "Jack…" He hesitated. His last name might be better concealed. Lady Wilton was no doubt furious at his disobedience and perfectly capable of organizing pursuit. "At your service, Miss Samia," he added. "Very pleased to make your acquaintance."

She giggled, then looked around to see if any of her friends had noticed his bow. They had. Samia preened as they walked on, and she assumed a proprietary air as other children joined them and Jack told them tales of another continent.

When the group stopped for the night in a clearing well off the road, Jack helped gather wood for the fires and carry water.

Borrowing some lengths of cord, he set snares that might yield a rabbit or two by morning. He was given terse thanks and a tattered blanket to augment his meager belongings.

Later there was shared stew and music around the central fire. When he rolled up in the blanket and pillowed his head on his arm, Jack felt the first stirrings of contentment. He went to sleep in the pleasure of companionship, wondering only how he might best contribute to the group and earn his meals. His snares gave a partial answer to that question in the morning, yielding several rabbits for the pot. He vowed to discover more.

Jack fell easily into the Travelers' erratic schedule. Some days the caravans moved; others they stayed in a place to sell objects the Travelers crafted or offer repairs to the people of a village or farmstead. The old lady sometimes read fortunes for those who came to inquire. Jack didn't mind the slow pace. There was no particular hurry to see his ancestral acres, and he enjoyed the rhythm of the road. He did have wandering feet. He began to make—not friends for this was a closed group, but cordial acquaintances. Some exhaustive conversations had established that his mother was not directly related to any of these Travelers, so he couldn't claim kin right. But similarity of spirit created bonds. He enjoyed them, along with the certainty that his continuing absence must be infuriating his noble great grandmother. That was a solid satisfaction. He would see what others he could find as time passed.

❦

"Not that you would know anything about that," declared the fat, choleric-looking man taking up the entire front-facing seat in the traveling carriage.

"No, Papa," said Harriet Finch's mother meekly.

Harriet gritted her teeth to keep back a sharp retort. She'd had years of practice swallowing slights and insults, so she wouldn't let anything slip. But hours in a coach with her grandfather had tried her to the limit. From the less comfortable rear-facing seat she looked at her mother's father, Horace Winstead. Winstead the nabob. Winstead the all-knowing, according to him. She'd never spent so much time with him before. They hadn't been thrown together like this during the months of the London season. Now that she'd endured a large dose of his company, she was afraid that their new living arrangements were a mistake. How long would she be able to hold her tongue?

She hadn't met her grandfather until this year because he had so disapproved of her parents' marriage that he disowned his daughter. More than disowned. He'd vengefully pursued the young couple, ruining her new husband's prospects by saying despicable things about him. Horace Winstead had consigned Harriet's family to genteel poverty for her entire life. And then, suddenly, after the death of a cousin she'd never met, he'd turned about and declared he would leave his immense fortune to Harriet, now his only grandchild.

The reversal had been dizzying. New clothes, a lavish house in London for the season, a changed position in society. Young ladies who'd spurned Harriet at school when she paid her way with tutoring pretended to be bosom friends. Young men suddenly found her fascinating. A thin smile curved Harriet's lips. They found her prospective income fascinating. Some hardly bothered to disguise their greed.

Harriet was expected to receive this largess with humble gratitude. She couldn't count the number of people who'd told her how lucky she was. She was not to mind her grandfather's 'abrupt' manners or ever lose her temper in his presence. He was to be catered to like a veritable monarch lest he change his mind and eject them. It was nearly insupportable. And one of the hardest parts of all was, her mother had felt redeemed.

Harriet glanced at her sole remaining parent and received an anxious look in response. Mama knew she was annoyed, and her eyes begged Harriet not to let it show. Years of worry had carved creases around Mama's mouth and added an emotional tremor to her manners. She continually expected disaster, and she'd often been quite right to do so. Brought back into the fold of her youth, she'd been so happy. Had she really thought that Grandfather had changed? He still treated her with something close to contempt, even though she agreed with everything he said.

Harriet gave Mama a nod and a smile, silently promising that she wouldn't add to her burdens. Harriet might sometimes wish that her mother had more fire, but Mama's youthful rebellion had brought her years of scrimping, an early grief, and very little joy. She deserved some ease and comfort now. Harriet could not take it from her.

She sat back and watched the landscape passing the carriage window. She took deep breaths to ease her temper, a method she'd learned at an early age. At least she could revel in the knowledge that she resembled her father, Harriet thought. Her grandfather must notice it every time he looked at her. She'd inherited her red blonde hair, green eyes, and pointed chin beneath a broad forehead from her Papa. He'd been a handsome man, though bitterness had marred his looks as he aged. His fierce drive to support his family, continually thwarted, had broken his health. Harriet could not actually prove that her grandfather's meanness had killed her father, but she thought it. And this made her present life a painful conundrum.

"The countryside here is very fine," said the old man. He pointed out the window. "That is Ferrington Hall, the principle seat of an earl. A neighbor of mine."

Harriet perked up at this name and leaned forward to look. She'd heard of Ferrington Hall while in London. An acquaintance, Lady Wilton, had complained that its new owner, her great grandson, was missing. Peering through a screen of trees, she could just see a sprawling stone manor. "Is the earl in residence?" she asked.

"Not at present," replied her grandfather.

She could tell from his tone that he knew nothing about it. Harriet remembered her friend Charlotte Deeping saying, "We will unravel the mystery of the missing earl." How she missed her friends! She'd been allowed to invite Sarah and Charlotte for a visit later in the summer. She couldn't wait.

Ferrington Hall disappeared from view as they drove on, and in another few miles they came to her grandfather's country house, the spoils of the fortune he'd made in trade. But Harriet was not supposed to think of that, let alone ever mention it. People in society despised business, and those who benefited from commercial success hid it like a disreputable secret. It seemed ridiculous to Harriet. Everyone knew. And how was it any better to have gained lands and estates with a medieval broadsword?

"Here it is—Winstead Hall," said her grandfather. "I changed the name when I bought it, of course."

Of course he had. Horace Winstead put his stamp on anything he touched. Or, if he could not, he demeaned it.

They passed through stone gateposts, traversed a tree-lined avenue, and pulled up before the central block, a red brick building studded with tall chimneys. It was not large, but a sprawling wing constructed of pale gray stone had been added at one end, and another was going up on the opposite side. The sound of hammering rang across the lush summer lawns.

Servants appeared at the front door, hurrying out to receive them. As more and more emerged Harriet realized that she was to meet the entire staff in her first moment here.

"They ought to be ready," grumbled her grandfather. "I suppose the coachman forgot to send word ahead."

She understood then that the servants were required to turn out every time he arrived. Her grandfather probably imagined that was how great noblemen were received at their country homes. She'd noticed that he equated pomp with rank.

Horace Winstead longed to be accepted by the aristocracy. He'd planned to purchase entry into those exalted circles by marrying his daughter to a title. That was one reason he'd been so vindictive when Mama met and married a junior member of his company. Papa's intelligence, diligence, and business acumen hadn't mattered a whit. He'd thwarted Horace Winstead, so he had to be punished. Now Grandfather expected Harriet to fulfill his social ambitions. She'd heard him say that his fortune ought to net him a viscount at least. Harriet's fists clenched in her lap, and she had to wrestle with her temper once again. Her London season had been shadowed by Grandfather's demand for a lord. If she so much as smiled at a commoner or seemed to enjoy dancing with one, he scolded her mother into tears.

They stepped down from the carriage and walked toward the door. The servants bowed and curtsied as they passed along the line. Harriet saw no sign of emotion from any of them—certainly not welcome. Slade, the superior abigail her grandfather had hired to dress her, would not appreciate this ritual. In fact, Harriet couldn't imagine the thin, upright woman participating. She would view it with the sour expression she reserved for cheap jewelry and fussily ornamented gowns. It was fortunate that this display would be over by the time the vehicle carrying Slade, her mother's attendant, and her grandfather's valet arrived.

They entered the house, moving through a cramped entryway into a parlor crammed with costly furnishings, eastern silks, and indifferent paintings. It looked more like a shop offering luxury goods than a cozy sitting room. Harriet felt as if the clutter was closing in on her, strange and oppressive. Her mother wandered about in a seeming daze. She had not grown up here; her father had purchased the house after her marriage.

"You can see we will be quite comfortable here," said her grandfather with his usual complaisance.

Harriet's spirits sank as she thought of the days ahead. There would be long, heavy dinners, tedious evenings, and many difficult conversations. Indeed, all the conversations were likely to be hard. How would they manage, just the three of them? She knew her grandfather had not received invitations to fashionable house parties, and she doubted that his neighbors here included him in their social round. As far as she had seen, he had no friends.

"We will settle in and plan our strategy for next season," the old man said. "You have not made a proper a push to attract a noble husband, Harriet. You must try harder."

Harriet started to reply, saw her mother's worried frown, and bit her lip. She didn't know what she was going to do. She couldn't swallow her anger forever.

About the Author

Jane Ashford discovered Georgette Heyer in junior high school and was captivated by the glittering world and witty language of Regency England. That delight was part of what led her to study English literature and travel widely. Her books have been published all over Europe as well as in the United States. Jane was nominated for a Career Achievement Award by *RT Book Reviews*. Born in Ohio, she is now somewhat nomadic. Find her on the web at janeashford.com and on Facebook at facebook.com/JaneAshfordWriter, where you can sign up for her monthly newsletter.